INTEL SUGGESTED AN UNHOLY ALLIANCE

"A radical Arab group like Hezbollah and mercenaries of the Germanic Freedom Railroad working together? It almost seems absurd, and yet all the evidence so far points to it," Price announced.

Brognola shrugged. "We just got the data from the computers at the OME in St. Louis, and one of the deceased that ran up against Able Team earlier was positively identified as not only Hezbollah, but a known associate of the Kadils Tarif bin Nurraji sect."

"I'd say that's proof positive," Price agreed. "So what do you think it means?"

"Because Burke's operation has always been small, I think he bit off more than he could chew at this time. I think it ended up costing him every dime he had, and he stole the LAMPs either in the hopes of selling them to the highest bidder, or configuring them for use against some target."

"Yes, but *what* target?"

DON PENDLETON'S

STONY

AMERICA'S ULTRA-COVERT INTELLIGENCE AGENCY

MAN

CRITICAL EFFECT

A GOLD EAGLE BOOK FROM

WORLDWIDE

TORONTO • NEW YORK • LONDON
AMSTERDAM • PARIS • SYDNEY • HAMBURG
STOCKHOLM • ATHENS • TOKYO • MILAN
MADRID • WARSAW • BUDAPEST • AUCKLAND

First edition June 2008

ISBN-13: 978-0-373-61979-5
ISBN-10:   0-373-61979-0

CRITICAL EFFECT

Special thanks and acknowledgment to
Jon Guenther for his contribution to this work.

Printed in U.S.A.

CRITICAL EFFECT

PROLOGUE

High above the fertile fields of northeastern France—
altitude approximately 24,223 feet—engines No. 1 and 2
suddenly quit and threatened to send the SOF C-141
Starlifter into a nosedive.

Only the quick thinking of the two British RAF pilots
prevented the giant special-operations cargo plane from
plunging to an unforgiving end. Warning alarms and
Klaxons screamed through the cockpit. Every circuit
board demanded attention. Lights flashed asynchro-
nously as the shimmies nearly shook the crew to death.
The pilot and copilot joined hands on the throttle in an
effort to coax more power from the remaining pair of
engines. The sheer weight of their cargo testified to the
futility of the effort.

Welby Blythe, Group Captain, tuned his radio to the
emergency band and issued a Mayday while his copilot,
Flight Lieutenant Graham Little, made every effort to
control their descent. The joint operations center at

NATO's Northern Command Office had accounted for the possibility of a single engine failure and taken precautions to ensure the plane could still make a "short" hop from Geneva, Switzerland, to Portsmouth. They had never even considered the disastrous consequences of a double-engine burnout.

Blythe received no response to his hails and gave up the radio for the moment. He tried to quell the shock and terror that rode through him with the same intensity and fearsomeness of his charge. Blythe had logged more successful missions than practically any other officer of his rank in the RAF, a record he'd remained quite proud of through his years as an airman. Now, however, it appeared the Devil had stacked the odds against him on this one. Blythe couldn't recall having faced a grimmer situation in all his time behind the stick.

The captain clenched his teeth. "If we get her down in one piece, boys, it'll only be a bloody damn miracle!"

A few alarms continued to chatter incessantly, although the first officer and two navigators had cleared most of them to reduce noise and confusion. After all, they knew they were losing altitude and didn't really need the sensitive instruments to point out the fact.

Both the digital and mechanical altimeters continued to plummet in concert with their descent as the remaining pair of operable Pratt & Whitney turbofan engines groaned in protest. Blythe considered other options. He first thought about ordering the cargo haulers seated in back to dump as much of the payload as necessary to keep the craft airborne, but he knew the risk of such equipment falling into the hands of a potential enemy. Terrorists or other criminal elements might not realize the value of that cargo, but at minimum they could make use of the armament. He also recalled the accompanying detail of Special Air Service operatives assigned to protect that cargo at any cost. Their orders would include immediate termination of even a crazed, military pilot desperate to save his own ship.

With no other real options at their disposal, Blythe and Little continued to guide the C-141 toward its inevitable course.

That course eventually put the belly of the cargo plane just yards above a copse of trees. Blythe engaged the landing lights and then coordinated with his copilot to execute their landing. Above the strain of engines they could feel the vibrations of the nose landing gear as it rolled downward and locked into place. The basso thrumming of engines ceased in favor of the high-pitched whine when they opened the throttle to maximum to raise the nose, followed by immediate dissipation to stall speed. The belly just scraped the tree line but reached a point of long, open field beyond it.

The soft earth proved an almost demonic force, its spongy resilience pronouncing death on the landing gear supporting the heavy aircraft. The tail of the plane performed a violent sashay, uncontrollable from the cockpit with the nose gear still airborne. All four men leaned forward simultaneously in their seats, subconsciously hopeful the additional weight would bring the NLG in contact with the ground. When it finally touched earth, the vibrations became doubly vicious.

Blythe felt as if his teeth might literally dislodge from his gums. A wash of mud, grass and weeds instantly coated the cockpit windows and all but eliminated visibility. The plane continued for about another 150 yards or so, then jolted the crew in their seats with a sickening crack to port that could only have been a tree taking out the wing. The sensation of centrifugal force took over as the plane began an almost lazy spin.

The torque nauseated Blythe, made him dizzy and threatened him with total blackout.

The landing ended suddenly with a bone-crushing stop as the aft section of the plane came into contact with something hard and unyielding. The impact slammed the flight crew against their harnesses and back into their seats. One of the navigators emitted a short yelp, and Blythe saw something sail past his shoulder and strike the main panel. The object performed a flip-flop dance down the front of the instrument panel with wet, smacking sounds, and in the half light of a gauge Blythe could see it was part of a human tongue.

For a minute or two Blythe didn't want to move. He didn't want to deal with the whimpers of a nearly tongue-less navigator, the hushed reassurances of the other men for his friend. Blythe looked slowly to his right and averted his eyes when he saw the gross dangle of Little's head against a restraint. Blythe reached out slowly. Bile rose in his throat when he touched his fingers to the soft cleft of Little's throat where it met with his jawline. No pulse.

Sanity took hold quickly then—almost as if Little's demise had confirmed Blythe's continued existence—and after a wiggle of fingers and toes to verify all his body parts were still attached, Blythe disengaged the restraint harness and squeezed out of his seat. He watched as the navigator held his injured comrade's head against his shoulder. Blood ran freely from the other man's mouth onto the sleeve of his friend, but the navigator didn't seem to notice.

"Get the first-aid kit and see if you can stop that bleeding," Blythe instructed. "I'm going to check on the hold."

The navigator nodded. "Aye, sir. How is Little?"

"Dead," Blythe reported plainly. He could see the pain in the navigator's expression and softened the tone in his voice. "Friend?"

"School chum, sir."

"I'm sorry."

With that, Blythe continued to the rear hold before the navigator could see the tears well in his eyes. He had to use all his body weight to open the door enough that he could squeeze through it. Stacks of boxes, some of them containing survival gear, had dislodged from their bins and wedged open the door. Blythe managed to get to the hold.

At first glance in the damp, red-orange glow of emergency lights, he assessed the special titanium-alloy containers that contained their ultrasecret cargo that appeared intact. Miraculously, they had somehow maintained their position in the center of the hold, held in place by thick canvas moorings, a testament to the skill of the loading crews. Blythe moved around them to the passenger bench on the starboard side of the craft and stopped abruptly.

Bodies were strewed everywhere. It appeared that a

large part of the jump bench had completely dislodged
from its moorings and been tossed every which way.
Acting as a lever, it had obviously tossed around the
SAS team members secured to it like so many rag dolls.
The unforgiving metal edges had dismembered a couple
of the men, the impact had been so great, and something
that flew through the hold had even decapitated one
man. Only two of the nine men who had been seated
there even moved, and on closer inspection Blythe
could tell one man was on his way out just by the way
he breathed.

Blythe stepped past the grisly scene and moved rapidly toward the back, hopeful at least some of his loading crew survived. He found he could not squeeze past
the last container in line. The entire rear of the Starlifter
C-141 had folded into itself, crushed by some unseen
force, the same force that had stopped the cargo ship
cold. Blythe ducked to see if he could detect movement,
cupped his hand to his mouth and called out, but only
the echo of his voice in the cavernous hold returned—
it seemed almost as if the echo answered of its own life
to mock him.

Blythe turned and started toward the fore section
when he heard the clang of metal followed a moment
later by a hissing noise. Blythe turned his eyes for the
ceiling, attempted to determine the source of the noise,
but he couldn't pinpoint it. It grew more pronounced
and familiar, and Blythe stood still for several minutes
as if bound in some sort of suspended animation. He felt
tired, more tired than he ever had before in his life, and

he couldn't imagine how this whole situation could become worse.

Blythe shook off the weariness and marched toward the front of his plane with renewed purpose. As he reached the section beyond the foremost cargo container, he saw the remainder of sparks spitting through the wall of the fuselage just a moment before an entire section of wall fell inward. Men dressed in camouflage, weapons held at the ready, charged through the glowing rim of that gaping hole.

Blythe didn't bother to try reaching for his sidearm. He knew how it would end if he attempted to resist the shadowy figures. They continued to pour through the hole, one upon the other, like locusts invading the harvest.

Somewhere in that outpouring a man stepped through the opening who possessed the regality of a monarch and wore a presence of exclamatory command authority. Blythe guessed the man's height at about six and a half feet. Muscles rippled across his abdomen, for all intents appearing they might tear through his black T-shirt. Equally sculpted pectorals, biceps and triceps formed mountainous lines that reached to a bulging neck and strong, chiseled face. Shoulder-length brown hair and a trimmed beard framed that face. A patrician nose jutted from jade-colored eyes masked behind the yellowish tint of bifocals. The man rested his sledge-hammer-size fists on a narrow waist that veed straight to hips and legs in camouflage fatigue pants. The man wore midcalf paratrooper boots with steel toes polished to a mirrorlike glisten. A military web belt encircled his hips, and he wore a sidearm in quick-draw fashion on his left thigh.

"You are now a prisoner of the Germanic Freedom Railroad," the man announced. "Your life, as your cargo, is now forfeit at my discretion."

Blythe could barely contain a squeal of outrage. "Now look here, I don't give a goddamn who you are! You have seized an aircraft belonging to Her Majesty's Royal Air Force under the command of NATO forces. And I can guarantee they'll come quickly looking for us! You would be best to leave things be!"

The man stepped forward and leaned close to Blythe's ear, his breath hot on the officer's neck as he whispered, "I know *exactly* what I have seized, Group Captain. In fact, we've been expecting you."

CHAPTER ONE

David McCarter sat on a large rock, a Player's cigarette in one hand and a sweating can of Coca-Cola in the other.

The Phoenix Force leader chewed absently at his lower lip while he studied the lush foliage that ran along the base of Monti Sirino, about twenty miles from the Golfo di Policastro, Italy. A mission from Stony Man, the ultracovert operations unit of the United States government, had brought them here less than forty-eight hours earlier. With their mission complete in record time, McCarter and the other members of Phoenix Force could look forward to a long-needed week of R & R.

McCarter glanced over his shoulder as the turbofans on the twin Rolls-Royce engines of the C-20 Gulfstream whined into preflight action. The time had come for them to get the hell out of there. He took a last, long drag before he crushed the cherry against a rock, field stripped the remainder and dropped the butt in his pocket. It wouldn't do to have someone find the thing and extract his DNA.

The fox-faced Briton's boots crunched on the refined gravel of the makeshift airstrip. The running lights glowed faintly in the half light of dawn, most of the sunlight peeking over the horizon still obscured by trees and tall grasses at the base of the mountain. McCarter glanced at his watch before rushing up the narrow steps and into the plane. He looked toward the cockpit, wishing he would see the familiar figure of Jack Grimaldi there, although he knew he wouldn't. Grimaldi, Stony Man's top gun and usual pilot for Phoenix, was back in Washington recovering from a hell-raising mission in Afghanistan.

McCarter downed the last of his Coca-Cola in a few swallows, crushed the can and tossed it into a nearby waste receptacle.

"Oh, baby!" a voice called from the cabin. "You're such a stud. Come over here and give us some love!"

McCarter turned toward the sound of the voice. The fresh and eager visage of T. J. Hawkins gazed at him in mock adoration. Thomas Jackson Hawkins was a straightforward guy with a heart of gold and a Texas accent so smooth it could melt the wills of even the strongest women.

"Don't write checks your body can't cash, youngster," McCarter quipped. "I've been doing this kind of thing since just about before you were born."

"You two settle down or I'll have to separate you," Calvin James said from beneath the skullcap pulled over his eyes.

McCarter didn't doubt the streetwise black man from the south side of Chicago could do it. A former medic, Navy SEAL and member of a San Francisco SWAT team, James had proved his skills as a formidable warrior time and again. When the chips were down, McCarter could think of few men he'd want more by his side.

"Can't we all just get along?" asked Rafael Encizo.

McCarter jammed a finger in Hawkins's direction. "He started it."

"Shut *up!*" James demanded. His lack of sleep was taking a toll.

McCarter took a seat and clammed up. He could see the wisdom in resting. The return flight to the States would be long and tedious. McCarter didn't like being cooped up that long; he enjoyed stretching his legs, which made it difficult to keep still with all that pent-up energy.

Once their plane got airborne, McCarter's eyes drooped and he laid his head back, eager for a one-or-maybe-two-hour snooze....

MCCARTER'S EYES SNAPPED open as he felt his pager vibrate against his thigh. He rose quickly from his seat.

"Get it in gear, mates," McCarter said. "The boss's calling."

Everyone knew what he meant. Stony Man, more specifically Barbara Price or Hal Brognola, was signaling that a secured satellite uplink would connect to the high-tech communications systems aboard the Gulfstream jet. They wouldn't be calling for an idle chat.

McCarter had transmitted his mission report to them more than four hours earlier. They either needed some type of immediate clarification or something had come up.

McCarter and the rest of the Phoenix Force warriors quickly made their way to the lounge at the back of the plane. This area also contained a number of LCD and CRT screens with two-way digital cameras. The sensitive electronics package hardwired into the aircraft's special systems could transmit or receive microwave signals from any location in the world. These high-amplitude transmissions ensured Stony Man could reach Phoenix anywhere and anytime.

T. J. Hawkins fired up the equipment while Encizo put on coffee to brew. They all sat at the table, waiting for the coffee while staring at one another's bleary red eyes. Gary Manning, a Canadian who served as Phoenix Force's chief demolitions expert, seemed to be the only one really awake, but probably his immediate rush to grab some sleep following their mission had a good deal to do with that fact.

Harold Brognola and Barbara Price suddenly appeared on screen. Neither looked happy.

"Morning, boys," Price began. "Sorry about the rude awakening."

McCarter waved it away. "It's our lot in life."

"I know we promised you some R & R as soon as you finished there," Brognola interjected, "but we've got a serious situation on our hands and the Man wants action yesterday. Barbara, why don't you lay it out for them?"

Price cleared her throat, tucked a strand of honey-blond hair behind her ear and said, "Approximately five hours ago one of our NSA SIGINT stations in Luxembourg intercepted a distress call from a NATO special-operations flight out of Geneva, Switzerland. Just minutes after the call came through, all transmissions ceased and the plane dropped off radar.

"The operative immediately reported the signal to his station chief, who in turn contacted the British RAF, since it was their plane. What none of us or them knew at the time was the exact nature of their mission. The aircraft has since been identified as an SOF C-141 placed under the command of NATO eighteen months ago."

"Starlifter," McCarter said. "And that particular nomenclature would indicate it was on special-operations duty."

Brognola grunted. "That may very well be the understatement of the year."

"What was their cargo?" Hawkins asked.

"Top secret," Price replied. "It took officials in the intelligence agencies of nearly ten countries to get that information. Apparently the entire operation had been classified need-to-know. There are apparently some very angry delegates haranguing Britain's PM this morning."

"Any idea where the plane went down?" James asked.

"We have a very good idea," Price replied, "but we're apparently the first, and not ready to share the information. The President's chief concern is to guarantee the cargo doesn't land in the laps of terrorists or other criminal elements. We're sending the coordinates directly to your navigational computers. Your pilots will get orders to change course immediately and head for the approximate target area."

"Which is?" McCarter asked.

"German countryside on the western border shared with France. We estimate it's about forty klicks east of the Rhine River. At best, it's heavily forested and navigation is treacherous."

"Nothing like a brisk walk through the woods to get the blood pumping," Manning quipped.

"You're such a ray of sunshine in the morning, Gary," Hawkins cracked.

"Stow it, mates," McCarter ordered. "Go on, Barb."

"You'll want to look for survivors, of course, but your instructions are to secure the cargo at all costs. All other secondary considerations are rescinded."

"That comes straight from the Oval Office," Brognola interjected, the gravity of the situation evident in his tone.

"This plane was carrying six highly experimental vehicles called LAMPs, or Low Altitude Military Platforms. We don't have all the technical specifications yet, but what we do know is they're apparently remote-controlled dishes, about twenty-five yards in diameter. Preliminary intelligence leads us to conclude these things are weapons-delivery mechanisms."

"What kind of weapons?" Encizo asked.

Price shrugged. "Just about anything, we're supposing. Nuclear, biological or chemical. They might also be used as troop transport. Once Aaron's finished cracking the CERN systems, we'll be able to send you a much better idea of what you're dealing with."

"Is that CERN as in CERN Laboratories?" Hawkins asked.

"Yes," Brognola said with a nod. "Does that ring a bell with you?"

"Well, CERN specializes in particle physics," Hawkins replied. "They're predominantly concerned with scientific research in that arena. There's a good reason they're in Switzerland. They've always chosen to focus their efforts on peaceful pursuits. I'm surprised they would become involved with any type of military weaponry."

"Times change," Brognola countered. "Although I think this development fell more out of some type of research in radio-magnetism. When CERN couldn't make any use of the things, NATO stepped in and agreed to buy the research and prototypes to pursue the military aspects."

"Correct," Price added helpfully. "Originally, we understood the *M* in LAMP stood for *magnetic*."

"Whatever the bloody things are," McCarter said, "it sounds like the Man's right. We can't afford for something like this to come under hostile control. What's the bottom line here?"

"Find the aircraft, rescue any survivors and secure the cargo until we can send in a multinational extraction team for salvage operations. If for any reason you do encounter a threat, you're authorized to use whatever force necessary to neutralize the aggression." Brognola tapped the table. "But don't go overboard, boys. This one's very political."

McCarter waved it off. "Yeah, yeah, isn't it always."

"Excuse me if I sound a bit paranoid here," Calvin James said, "but do we have some reason to think there's the possibility of a terrorist organization at work behind this plane going down?"

"We don't know," Price said. "But we're taking every precaution given the circumstances under which it disappeared, plus the cargo aboard. My contact with the NSA tells me that plane could have maintained altitude even in the event of an engine failure."

"So we're figuring either more than one engine crapped out or someone shot the thing out of the sky," James concluded with a nod. "Gotcha."

Encizo sighed. "We also have to consider the possibility of a midair explosion. Maybe a bomb on board."

"It's another possibility," Price admitted, "but we figure less so because of the value of its cargo. *If* a terrorist organization or other criminal element were involved, one would think they wouldn't expend that much effort to simply destroy the plane. There are plenty of easier, nonmilitary targets that would work just as well in attracting attention *and* result in a higher body count."

McCarter shook his head. "No point in theorizing to death. We'll make contact as soon as we know something. Anything else?"

"Be careful," Price said. "You'll be low-altitude parachuting on this one."

WITHIN THE HOUR, Phoenix Force received a signal from the cockpit they had reached the coordinates sent to their navigation systems by Stony Man's secure satellite downlink. The warriors collected their weapons and equipment, donned their jumpsuits and awaited the all clear to indicate they could proceed with the operation. Hawkins's parachuting experience nominated him for jumpmaster.

The beacon light went from red to amber, the signal for Phoenix Force to test their static lines in prep for the jump while Hawkins opened the door. They'd gone through this same exercise countless times—in training as well as live missions—to the point they could do it in their sleep.

The light went green and Hawkins pointed to James, who was first in line. James stepped up, slid the line to the jumpmaster and went out the plane without a moment's hesitation. Encizo followed behind him, just as planned. As soon as they reached ground zero, the pair would set up a perimeter. Hawkins slapped the buzzer on the wall to signal the pilots they should continue on for a minute and then perform a 180 so the rest of Phoenix Force could jump.

Phoenix Force's commander couldn't have asked for a more perfect timetable. As he neared the ground at a peak speed of thirty-three feet per second, McCarter could see Encizo and James had established their secure perimeter. Both men knelt behind massive trees on opposing sides of the target zone, watchful for any potential threats. McCarter sucked in a breath and let half out as his feet hit the ground, then he rolled, coming to a standing position in time to watch his chute waft lazily to the ground.

The Briton quickly gathered the parachutes. He could hear Manning and Hawkins hit the ground near him, but he didn't bother to check on them. If they had suffered any injuries, he knew he'd have heard about it right there and then.

Less than five minutes later, all five men were reunited near the edge of the clearing.

"Fall in on me, mates," McCarter ordered.

They gathered around him as he knelt and spread a topographical map on the ground. McCarter whipped a compass from a pouch secured to the strap of his equipment harness. He shot a quick azimuth and calculated the approximate distance to the crash site based on the coordinates he'd committed to memory.

"We're about here," he finally said, pointing to a spot on the map. "That puts us a fair distance from the crash site, if there even bloody is one."

"There is," Hawkins said. "I can feel it."

"Over this terrain, I figure it'll take us about an hour to get there," Manning said after an expert look around.

"Agreed," McCarter said as he stowed the map and compass. He checked his watch. "We should be able to reach it before 1200 hours."

"Well, what are we waiting for?" James said. "Let's do it."

CHAPTER TWO

A jangling telephone roused him into semiconsciousness. The second and third rings seemed no less shrill as he turned his face into the mattress and pulled the pillow over his head, intent on ignoring the irritating device. By the sixth ring, he knew whoever had intruded on his slumber didn't plan to give up. He removed the pillow, lifted his head and glared at the clock.

Blurry green numbers stared back at him.

Dr. Simon Delmico, associate professor of microbiology at Washington University St. Louis, grabbed his glasses from the nightstand, sat up and yanked the phone from the receiver. The coiled cord had become entangled with Delmico's ceaseless habit of talking and pacing, and he nearly dumped the base onto the floor. He caught it one-handed and dropped it onto the bed as he barked into the receiver.

"Yeah. What? Who the hell is it?"

"Not a very pleasant way to answer the phone," the caller replied. "Where are your manners?"

Delmico immediately recognized the voice of Choldwig Burke, leader of the Germanic Freedom Railroad. The GFR had a short history, being only a few years old, but it had already built notoriety as one of the finest smuggling operations in all of Europe. Burke didn't discriminate when it came to his clientele, either. He had a reputation as an intelligent and educated man, and possessed a criminal mastery for aiding and abetting the very worst terrorists in the world. Thus far, Burke's unit of highly specialized mercenary commandos had smuggled or hidden more than a hundred terrorist members from al Qaeda to the Qa'idat al Jihad.

"What do you want?"

"I'm simply calling to check on an old friend," Burke replied.

Delmico knew that was crap. "How touching. Now, what do you really want?"

"I thought it might be a good idea to call and advise you of our latest acquisition. We succeeded in liberating the platforms, just as I had hoped. That only leaves me to solicit what you've promised me so I may go forward with my plans."

"That couldn't have waited until a more civilized hour?" Delmico asked, now able to actually see the time on his clock-radio. "I have to get up and teach this morning, you know."

Delmico heard something become dark, even ominous, in Burke's intonation. "Do not presume insolence and belligerence are acceptable to me, Doctor. I would have no qualms about boarding the earliest flight solely for the purpose of coming there and cutting out your tongue. We had an agreement. I've proved I can satisfy my end of the bargain. The time grows short for you to capitulate."

"You don't have to act like a thug and threaten me," Delmico recanted, adjusting his glasses on his nose unnecessarily. "I'm merely trying to say I'm still waiting on the final test results. I want to be absolutely certain you're getting what you've paid for."

Burke sounded more congenial. "Well then, I guess I cannot fault you for a desire to be thorough. Honesty is, after all, the mainstay of our type of work. If we don't have honor, what do we have? A man without honor cannot even call himself a man, can he?"

"If you say so," Delmico replied. "By my estimates, I have seventy-two hours before the deadline. You will have the material by then, if not before, *assuming* the tests are positive. Is that satisfactory?"

"Of course, Doctor. I am a reasonable man."

"Yeah? Well then, try calling me at a more reasonable hour next time." He slammed down the receiver. "Fucking kraut."

Delmico whipped back the sheet covering his nude body and swung his legs to the floor. He stood and then carefully limped his way through the semidarkness to the bathroom. Practically every time he walked, Delmico thought of his impairment. The skin on the nub of his left leg—the only remaining evidence of his foot—had grown callused with use. Delmico had undergone complete amputation after the accident in Washington, D.C.

Yes, once upon a time, he'd been a respected microbiologist with the U.S. Department of Defense, Bio-

Chem Counter Warfare section. A single mistake had cost him a foot as well as his job. That pompous board of safety directors hadn't even bothered to *look* at all the evidence. They only took into account Delmico's decision to disobey the orders of his supervisor, and terminated him for violations of a half dozen safety regulations. While Delmico had been the only one injured, the character references from half a dozen colleagues saved him from permanent exile. Instead those arrogant assholes at the Pentagon, he recalled, decided they would make his infraction part of his sealed file, call the loss of the limb an accident—although he would receive no federal disability for it—and recommend him to a teaching post in some out-of-the-way school.

The salary he received being an associate professor at Washington U had proved little more than a meager stipend for the bare necessities of life. To a man who had made nearly $150,000 a year working for the government, his present rate amounted to a pittance. And then during a guest lecture in Bonn, an impressionable giant of a man approached and offered to buy him a drink. That's when fortune struck him like a blow to the back of the head. What Simon Delmico didn't know at the time was he'd be selling his soul to Satan's archangel.

Delmico agreed to hold up his end of the bargain only after making Burke promise not to use the chemical agent against American targets. Burke agreed, a bit too readily Delmico thought, but the deal got made. Through the course of the past year, Burke had funded Delmico's research and the microbiologist's efforts finally came to fruition. He christened his formula Shangri-La Lady, a mnemonic of sorts for the compound's chemical makeup: solanine-lithium liposome.

Now the only task remaining would be a test on live subjects; Delmico had already chosen them. He'd agreed to let three of his present Chemistry I students—obnoxious jocks who wanted nothing more than a free ride through college simply because of their athletic prowess—improve their failing grades by conducting experiments at the campus after hours. Delmico had given them enough information that they'd actually created the delivery mechanism for Shangri-La Lady. The microbiological spores did the rest.

Already, he'd noticed the youths begin to look increasingly unwell when they arrived at class. Their condition began to worsen on almost a daily basis, and Delmico had even heard talk of one of them collapsed in the locker room after evening practice. A visit to the team nurse left everyone assured their star linebacker had merely suffered from a case of dehydration and exhaustion coupled with a lack of adequate rest. Delmico had lied to Burke. He had more than enough positive results to know the poison would work. At the moment, he simply took satisfaction in making the pedantic bastard wait as long as possible. Wake him up at this fucking time of the morning and expect Delmico to act like Susie Sunshine….

Two of the boys had been taken away by ambulance and admitted to the infectious ward of a local hospital. The third had taken a sudden leave of absence to attend his sister's funeral, so the scientist had no idea of the youth's present condition. Delmico hadn't told anyone about the extra-credit project at their request. After all, such publicity would not only threaten their scholarships but it might make their coaches consider suspension of activities until they got their grades up. Nearly a week had passed since the original experiments and Delmico doubted the boys would draw any connection between the two.

That was, of course, if they lived long enough to tell anyone at all. Delmico took great satisfaction in thinking about the shocking repercussions that would soon come. He chuckled at the thought, in fact, as he relieved himself and then returned to bed. He removed his glasses, fluffed his pillow and lay down. He still had a few hours before having to rise again.

Within minutes the world around him faded to black and he drifted into peaceful slumber.

CHAPTER THREE

Carl Lyons wiped the sweat from his brow with a white towel that encircled his neck and picked up the pace. He turned to check the progress of the two men behind him, surprised to see they had fallen back a bit. Lyons wanted to shout a jibe at them, but he reconsidered. It was better to not pick on the ladies.

The sudden incline of the road signaled the final stretch to Stony Man Farm. Lyons had made this trip more times than he could count. The Farm served as haven and headquarters for the Stony Man operations, but through the years Lyons had also come to call it home. When he or one of his partners said they wanted to go home, the others knew it really meant Stony Man Farm. The farmhouse, Annex and grounds lay deep in the conifer-thick terrain of the Blue Ridge Mountains, approximately eighty miles from Washington, D.C., by chopper. Lyons couldn't think of a nicer place to rest, as little as he got, but he took more stock in the bonds forged with his colleagues. Those relationships built from fighting side by side with others sworn to the same call of duty had grown stronger than most family ties.

Lyons really poured it on at a final bend in the road, which opened onto the Stony Man property. Directly ahead, the two-story farmhouse greeted him. The warm earth tones of its wood-and-brick exterior seemed to reach out to him as if extending arms of welcome. Lyons slowed to a walk when he reached the perimeter of the front lawn, and breathed deeply to slow his heart rate and allow his body to cool down. He walked in circles a bit, hands extended to his sides to permit maximum expansion of his chest. The "Ironman" moniker—earned by not only his record in that event but also his personality—fit him well. He'd proved a formidable ally for Stony Man through the years, and a capable leader in spite of his flammable temperament and sarcastic humor.

Neither of the men who had lagged behind and now joined him would have traded Lyons for the ten best commandos in the world, primarily because that wouldn't have been enough.

"Looks like Ironman has been eating his Wheaties," Hermann "Gadgets" Schwarz remarked.

Droplets of sweat rolled from his hairline, traveling down Schwarz's swarthy face and glistening like rain dew on his mustache. He broke into a grin when Lyons flipped him the bird, but he didn't take a bit of the ribbing personally. He'd come to know his teammate too well.

"I would just like to die," said the other man, hardly able to respond through all of his heavy breathing.

Rosario Blancanales had always carried a slight paunch—many a foe had underestimated him for that, much to their dismay. Not that it mattered. They called him "Politician" due to his gregarious mannerism and ability to charm his way out of just about any confrontation. Only hostilities against the enemies of America were nonnegotiable, and Blancanales minded his business well.

The men of Able Team turned toward a voice calling them from the farmhouse. Sun rays danced off the golden highlights of Barbara Price's hair. She beckoned to them with a wave, and the three men immediately double-timed it to where she stood on the front porch.

"Sorry," she said, smiling as they filtered past her and through the open doorway. "We've got a situation and Hal needs you guys to hoof it over to the Annex ASAP."

"We got time to clean up?" Blancanales asked.

"After."

"Okay," Lyons said, "but I don't want to hear any complaints about how we left the place smelling like a used gym sock."

"I've been told you do that without P.T.," Schwarz cracked.

"Up yours," Lyons grumbled.

The three men made their way through the farmhouse to the elevator, then stood and waited expectantly for Price to join them.

Price flashed a wicked grin as the door began to close. "Um, I'll wait for the next one."

They rode the elevator to the basement in silence, crossed through the War Room to the hallway, and continued on to the end until they reached a wide corridor perpendicular to it. A walkway ran parallel to an electric rail car that could take them the 250 yards to the Annex, but Able Team opted to walk. They reached the end of the tunnel in no time flat and gained entry to the Annex via a coded access panel. Built beneath a wood-chipping facility, the Annex had become Stony Man's operational nexus. It warehoused the most advanced cybernetic and communications systems available—under constant monitor and upgrade by Aaron Kurtzman's unit—as well as an operations center for Stony Man Farm security.

Able Team took concrete stairs to the Computer Center, where they found Brognola and Kurtzman staring at a screen. The Stony Man chief turned at their arrival, greeted them with a nod and a grunt, and then returned to perusing the data on the screen.

"What's up?" Lyons asked.

"Whew!" Brognola said, whipping an unlit cigar from his mouth and wrinkling his nose. "Couldn't you guys have showered first?"

Lyons tossed a bland look at his cohorts, who shrugged, and then returned his attention to Brognola.

"Never mind," the big Fed stated, directing their attention to a large screen that spanned an entire wall of the center. "Bring it up there for them, will you, Bear?"

Kurtzman nodded and punched a couple of keys.

As the three Able Team warriors turned, a man's face filled the screen. He had pale skin and wide blue eyes that looked magnified behind his large glasses. A hawk's-beak nose protruded from between puffy red cheeks. Lettering below his named read: U.S. Department of Defense, CL: Q, DoDID#: 176243-SD.

Lyons emitted a low whistle and remarked, "Geek city, gents."

"Maybe," Brognola replied, "but I wouldn't underestimate him for a moment. His name is Simon Delmico. Age, forty-three. He was one of the youngest and brightest in his graduating class from Stanford. He holds a doctorate in medicine with a specialty in microbiology. Up until five years ago, he'd served with the DOD as a specialist in countering biochemical warfare agents. Since then, he's worked as an associate professor with Washington University in St. Louis."

"He left voluntarily?" Blancanales asked.

Brognola snorted. "Hardly. Against orders from a superior, he violated experimental protocols and damn near blew up part of ST-2 at the Pentagon. As it was, he lost a foot. To keep things quiet, the government decided not to charge him criminally. They set him up at WU and that was that."

Schwarz raised his eyebrows. "Until now?"

"Precisely," Brognola said. "A few hours ago we had to divert Phoenix Force to search for a plane that went down somewhere over the Federal Republic of Germany. We're still waiting for them to report back. But before that, there were some interesting outbreaks of a mysterious illness in St. Louis, which has local physicians puzzled enough to call the CDC. That sent off all kinds of alarms for us, given Delmico's background in microbiology."

Schwarz chuckled and looked at Kurtzman. "Why, I'd say your new program's doing a heck of a job, Bear."

"I can't take all the credit for it," Kurtzman replied in his deep, booming voice. "My crew certainly did their part. It's amazing what they've accomplished in these few short years."

Lyons knew the men were referring to Kurtzman's new cyberscanning application, codenamed Postulate. The Able Team leader didn't even begin to pretend he understood it all, but he did have some idea of how it worked. Rather than query specific data sets through the use of keywords, Postulate would search for situations based on an incalculable number of different scenarios, partly through the use of key phrases, partly through mathematical theorems and hypotheses. In short, Kurtzman and his team had spent years programming different scenarios based on everything from mission reports and briefs to the core intelligence of foreign nations. Then, Postulate had begun to rework the scenarios on its own and built a dictionary database with millions of terabytes of information.

During a briefing of the entire Stony Man group, Kurtzman had explained it this way: "For the most part, the data remains static until Postulate acts on it. Then it becomes dynamic, the computers start to hum and it starts to search around the world for incidents that could fit that scenario. This information might be anything from newswires and insurance claims up to police reports and military statistics. Whatever the information, Postulate will use it if she can, and over a period of time she grows smarter by dismissing what seems irrelevant in place of facts that fit the highest degrees of probability."

The door opened and Price strode into the room.

Lyons shook his head. "Okay, I'm still not following. What the hell do sick students and one-footed scientists have to do with Phoenix Force?"

"Less than an hour ago, we logged a call placed to Delmico's home from a public phone in Wiesbaden. The call was too long to be a wrong number. And twelve months ago, Delmico was in Germany as a guest lecturer on microbiology."

"Too much to be coincidence, maybe," Blancanales admitted. "But it's hardly enough proof of collusion with terrorists by Delmico."

"I'm with Pol on this one, guys," Lyons said. "It sounds like you're grasping at straws."

"Are we, now?" Brognola asked. "You may not think so when you hear what was on that plane."

"The information just came through," Kurtzman said. "The plane that went down was a special operations cargo plane carrying six large dishes with magnets attached to them."

Lyons made a show of yawning. "Magnets, eh? That's what has our panties in a bunch? Magnets?"

Kurtzman shook his head. "I know magnets don't sound like any great threats to you, Ironman, but given they're attached to what the British are calling Low

Altitude Military Platforms, you might want to reconsider. These dishes were being shipped from the CERN Particle Physics Laboratory in Switzerland. The magnets were remnants of pieces being assembled for their flagship project, the Large Hadron Collider.

"You see, elementary particles of matter are typically studied through the use of magnetism. The larger the magnet, the deeper the matter and energy can be probed. These magnets are particularly important because they operate under the magnetism between Earth's polar opposites."

"Basically," Brognola cut in, "it means they can operate under self-propulsion for the most part. We now have evidence the plane that went down with these things aboard might have been sabotaged. Moreover, we think it wouldn't be unlikely for a terrorist organization or other element to use these platforms to deliver chemical or biological contaminants to a large populace."

"Or at least *threaten* to do so if their obligatory list of demands isn't met," Price said.

Schwarz looked at Blancanales and Lyons. His furrowed eyebrows chiseled lines of seriousness across his face. "What they're proposing sounds damn plausible, guys. I think we ought to check it out."

"All right, all right," Lyons said, visibly irritated. "But if this turns out to be some wild-goose chase—"

"Then we bought you a wonderful two days of fun and sun in scenic St. Louis," Price finished for him. "Jack's on his way here, so you've got about an hour to clean up and gear up."

"Jack's feeling up to getting back into the game already?" Blancanales asked in a surprised tone.

Price smiled. "You're kidding, right? Wild horses couldn't hold him back."

"I think he's been chomping at the bit to get back into action," Brognola added. "And since the doctors have cleared him for flight duty, I see no reason why this wouldn't be the perfect job."

"So what exactly do you want us to do out there, boss?" Lyons asked.

"Get to those kids and see if you can find any commonality between their illnesses outside the fact they go to the same school," Brognola said. "I don't think the doctors are looking hard enough for it. That's part of your mission. The more important part will be to get close to Delmico and stay close."

"You'll be operating as FBI agents," Price said. "You're just there to look things over and ensure this isn't an anthrax-related issue or something else that could evolve into a pandemic."

"How clever," Lyons grumbled.

"Aw, cheer up, Ironman," Blancanales said, punching his friend in the shoulder. "It's St. Louis, home of the Gateway Arch and Anheuser-Busch. You'll have a great time!"

"Yeah," Schwarz added. "What could possibly go wrong?"

CHAPTER FOUR

David McCarter knelt in a large, mushy patch of moss that had started life on a nearby large rock and spread beneath the shade of a massive pine. Dry breezes rustled the leaves in the upper branches of the tallest trees, causing sun spots to reform and reshape themselves.

Phoenix Force had come to a stop on a precipice that overlooked the crash site. The plane lay about fifty yards below them in a massive clearing with its port side visible; its jagged, broken hull jutted silent and still from the ground. The entire T-shaped tailfin had been smashed inward against one of the largest trees McCarter had ever seen. The port wing had been snapped from the plane, probably on impact. The deep gouges in the soft terrain of the clearing bore evidence of exactly where the plane had come down and how it had ended up in such an odd position.

McCarter brought a pair of binoculars to his eyes, although he didn't really need to see it up close to know they had found the missing bird. Markings all along the plane clearly identified it as a NATO aircraft. McCarter squinted to make out the large, white writing just below the cockpit windows obscured by mud and grass: GpCpt W. M. Blythe, RAF.

"W. M. W—" McCarter lowered the binoculars. "Welby Blythe? Aw, bloody hell."

Encizo immediately noticed the faraway look in the Briton's eyes. "What is it, David? Look like you've just seen a ghost."

"Nothing," McCarter said, shaking himself back to the present. "It may be nothing."

"It doesn't sound like nothing, Chief," Hawkins pressed.

"Let's just drop it for now, okay, mates?" McCarter snapped.

Manning broke the uncomfortable silence that followed McCarter's uncharacteristic reaction and nodded toward the plane. "I'd say the fastest way to get there would be to rappel straight off this overlook."

"Agreed," McCarter said. "Set it up."

The five men shrugged out of their day packs and immediately began to prepare for a rappelling operation. Manning and McCarter had the most experience with it, so they would take belay man and safety positions, respectively. Manning quickly retrieved two ropes and tied them to the base of a thick trunk nearest the knoll in a double figure-eight knot. McCarter and Hawkins nailed in pitons while Encizo and James cinched themselves into rappelling harnesses.

When they were ready, Manning donned his own

harness and went down the side of the treacherous rocky outcroppings. Despite the danger of sharp and jagged rock protrusions, Manning made his controlled descent in as carefree a fashion as if he'd been sipping cocktails beneath a poolside cabana. The Canadian was about as rugged as they came.

McCarter assisted James as he straddled the ropes and prepared to go down next. The fox-faced Briton put his hand to his mouth. "On belay!"

"Belay on!" Manning echoed.

"On rope!" James shouted.

"Rappel on!" Manning replied.

"Rappelling!" James called, and he pushed away from the cliff.

The Phoenix Force warriors continued in this way: next came Encizo, then Hawkins and finally McCarter. One by one they went down the ropes, and soon all were reunited at the bottom. The Phoenix Force commander ordered the team to fan out as they approached the plane. While he couldn't exactly have called their rappelling operation stealthy, he didn't think it safe to assume the plane crash had been the product of an accident. Given its cargo, McCarter could understand Stony Man's reservations in leaving this to outside agencies. It would either turn out to be something or it wouldn't, and if they relied on foreign powers to deal with the situation, it could turn out to be a huge public embarrassment.

Encizo and Hawkins approached on the starboard flank, Manning and James on port and McCarter up the center. They emerged from the brush after a low-pitched whistle from the Phoenix Force leader, and converged rapidly on the plane. McCarter reached it first. He knelt just aft of where the shattered wing had broken away, and swept the area with the muzzle of his MP-5 SD-6. Nobody rose to challenge him.

McCarter watched with interest as Manning and James approached the plane roughly parallel to its nose cone. They moved silently, dwarfed by the hulking shell of the Starlifter's fuselage. McCarter signaled them to skirt the nose of the plane while he moved in a crouch beneath it and came up on the side of the Encizo-Hawkins team a moment later. What he saw at that moment caused his jaw to drop. A better portion of the plane's body had been completely cut away by torches. The charred remains of humans were scattered throughout the plane. Some of them were unrecognizable, but McCarter quickly spotted one body attired in clothing that had partially survived the scorching. The sleeve of the corpse's shirt bore the patch of the Special Air Service.

The remainder of the carnage sickened the Phoenix Force warriors. They had seen such things many times, but none of them could ever say they had grown accustomed to it. Flies and other insects buzzed lazily around the bloated bodies. They could see dried patches of blood on the interior of the port-side fuselage. The back end had been mangled, twisted and mashed into an unrecognizable collage of metal and fiberglass. The cargo, if there had been any, was long gone.

James whistled softly. "Looks like something out of *Hotel Rwanda*."

"I'd say this was no accident," Hawkins said.

"Yeah, but what the hell *did* happen?" Manning wondered.

"Whatever's happened here, it was no bloody accident," McCarter replied. "And whoever's behind it is damn sure not friendly."

Enzico walked away for a minute as James and Hawkins climbed up and into the fuselage to make a more thorough inspection. Hawkins brought out his digital camera and took shots of the most important elements. Stony Man would need that as proof positive for the President and his advisers. Kurtzman would also be able to use it as evidence in detecting who had committed such an atrocity.

Enzico returned a minute later. "I looked at the other side of the plane, and also went to study that broken wing. It's clear they went down due to a double-engine failure, but there's little doubt as to why. There are unoxidized cordite burns on both the port engines."

McCarter looked straight to Manning. "Explosives?"

The Canadian nodded and in a matter-of-fact tone replied, "Probably."

"Plus, let's consider the fact the other side of this plane is intact," Enzico continued. He stepped up to the edge of the massive opening and ran the edges carefully between his fingers. "This puppy was cut, probably with an acetylene torch. There's no way this happened as the result of the crash."

"David," James called from the plane. McCarter looked up and the medic jerked his head in the direction of the cockpit. "I think you're going to want to see this."

McCarter hoisted his body up and into the plane, moving past James in the direction of the cockpit. He stuck his torso through the cockpit door and studied the interior. The copilot's head dangled awkwardly from his neck, and a safety harness suspended his slumped body. Both men in the navigator's chairs were dead, one with a considerable amount of dry blood on and around him, which made it damn difficult to determine cause of death. A quick inspection of the other man revealed a bullet hole between the eyes. The whole enclosure smelled of death. McCarter turned and walked back to where his comrades stood and waited for him.

McCarter jumped to the ground and said, "Captain's missing."

James nodded. "That's what I thought."

"You're sure?" Hawkins asked.

"I was serving as crew and mission specialist aboard these puppies while still working with the SAS, T.J.," McCarter said. "Crew complement for these birds is four. There are three bodies in that cockpit, and none of them is wearing the rank of a group captain."

"I saw one had been shot execution-style," James noted. "You think the pilot might have been in on this?"

McCarter shook his head. "No bloody way, mate. He's either among the burned bodies there, or whoever took the cargo took him, as well."

"Well, one thing's for sure," Encizo said. "We'd better get Hal up to speed on this pronto."

The air suddenly filled with the whip-crack reports of automatic weapons fire, and the Phoenix Force warriors wasted no time getting bellies to the ground. Bullets buzzed over their heads, a few burning the air with a whine as others ricocheted off the broken skin of the aircraft. McCarter and Manning crawled beneath the plane for cover while Encizo, James and Hawkins rose and sprinted for the shelter of the wood line. A fresh salvo of rounds took out tree limbs and zinged overhead, raining leaves on the warriors.

Hawkins happened to grab the cover of the same giant fallen log as Encizo. "Guess this removes any doubt about hostiles involved."

"I'd say so," Encizo retorted as he unslung his MP-5 and put the weapon in battery with a quick jerk of the charging handle. "Well, we can't afford to sit here and wait. They still have David and Gary pinned down."

"Agreed. I'm open to suggestions," Hawkins replied.

"We should head along the tree line, see if we can outflank them."

"Roger that."

Encizo looked a few lengths over and spotted James, his back to a tree trunk, readying his own weapons for action. He managed to get the warrior's attention and, using a series of hand signals, communicated the plan. James returned it with the okay signal and indicated he'd provide covering fire. It would require time to get into a flanking position, and James couldn't afford to expend all of his ammo, even if Manning and McCarter could provide additional support. Still, he only had to keep them occupied a few minutes.

Encizo and Hawkins got to their feet, moved deeper into the darkness of the woods, then set off at a furious pace. James watched them go, counted to three and dashed from the cover of the tree to the back of the plane. He happened to be carrying Phoenix Force's squad weapon, the Colt M-16 A-2. While it used the gas-driven, rotating Stoner bolt, it had a loaded weight nearly three pounds lighter than an empty M-60 E-3 machine gun. Its high-capacity box magazine, wrapped beneath the magazine well just aft of the heavier barrel and thicker hand guards, held a hundred rounds of 5.56 mm NATO ammunition.

James dropped to his stomach, flipped down the bipod and steadied the weapon by locking the butt against his shoulder and pressing his cheek to the stock. He set his sight post on the general area where he spied an occasional muzzle-flash and returned fire. The reports hammered in his ears as the weapon dispensed a cyclic fusillade of 700 rounds per minute at a muzzle of velocity of 900 meters per second.

The intensity of fire decreased with James's assault, and during two sustained bursts he called for Manning and McCarter to get out of there. The pair didn't have to be told a second time. James continued to lay down covering fire while his comrades jumped to their feet and rocketed for the edge of the woods.

McCarter crawled up on James's six and slapped him on the back. "Thanks for that, mate."

James stopped long enough to say, "Don't mention it."

"What's the sitrep on T.J. and Rafe?" Gary Manning asked.

"They split off, headed out to greet our new friends from the back end."

McCarter nodded. "Nice thinking. But I wish to hell they would have checked with me first."

James cast a sideways glance at McCarter. "You were a little busy right then."

"Excuses, excuses," McCarter said, but the grin told the real story.

The Briton turned to Manning. "Let's spread out along this perimeter to see if we can keep them occupied long enough to buy our boys the time they need."

Manning nodded as he produced his Galil 7.62 mm sniping rifle. Through the years, Manning had come to appreciate the IMI-made weapon for its versatility. It chambered the 51 mm NATO round, but the four-groove rifling provided optimum stability and made it one of the most accurate sniping rifles of its kind. Manning had found this a chief advantage since the weapon could double as a standard assault rifle, formidable at 650 rounds per minute.

Manning sprinted through the woods until he was about a hundred yards from his friends. He crouched and reached the wood line, settled in and set up the rifle on a bipod. Manning removed the covers protecting the Nimrod 60-power scope and brought his eye within inches of it. He watched carefully, pushing the sounds of autofire from his mind. Manning scanned the trees, high at first and then low to the ground.

The first target came into view.

The big Canadian put the green crosshairs of the reticule on his target's skull. He could almost make out the color of the man's eyes through the powerful scope. The guy kept ducking his head, moving it up and down in an attempt to find a target. He appeared to be fixated on McCarter's and James's positions. Manning figured he'd get maybe three or four of them before they'd pinpoint his position. He took a deep breath, counted to four, let out half and squeezed the trigger. The enemy gunman's head exploded in a crimson cloud that seemed to erupt from his neck as the guy's skull caved under the impact.

Manning swung the muzzle to the right and left in search of his next target.

RAFAEL ENCIZO AND T.J. Hawkins made excellent time.

In just eight minutes, the Phoenix Force commandos had managed to flank their enemy. Eight minutes could turn into what seemed like hours under heavy fire, but Encizo could only hope his friends had maintained a foothold on their area. In another moment or two, they would hopefully turn the tables on their attackers. The ever-increasing sounds of autofire signaled they drew nearer to the enemy's position. Encizo called a halt and the two came together to confer.

"I'd say maybe twenty meters ahead?" the little Cuban said.

Hawkins nodded. "Sounds about right. It's your show. How do you want to do this?"

"I'll go right and you go left. About a hundred meters. If you catch them bunched up, use grenades. Otherwise, we'll have to pick them off one at a time."

"Cool," Hawkins said.

Encizo flashed him a grin. "Good luck, amigo."

"Same to ya'll," Hawkins said, and he whirled and disappeared into the deep brush.

Encizo made distance to the agreed point and then swung around at the sounds of weapons fire, carefully estimating approximate positions. He could really hear the shooting now, and the woods had started to thin, growing lighter as he drew near the wood line. The smell of gunpowder tickled his nostrils, and a moment later Encizo stopped dead in his tracks. Directly ahead lay the first target, planted on his belly behind a bipod-mounted machine gun. The Cuban grimaced, cursing himself for not being more alert.

He'd been closer to the wood line than he originally thought.

Encizo reached to his equipment harness and withdrew a Cold Steel Tanto combat knife as he quietly slung his weapon on his left shoulder, barrel down. He crouched, looked around one more time, then charged his opponent and threw himself prone. The enemy gunner detected something was wrong, but he did so a moment too late. Encizo was on him. The man tried to resist, but his attempts died with him as Encizo plunged the combat knife deep into the side of the man's neck, slicing through tendons and arteries.

Encizo waited until the man stopped struggling beneath him and then removed the knife and wiped it clean. He stowed it back in its sheath and rose just a moment before he heard the slap of footfalls crunching leaves and sticks. Encizo whirled and whipped up his MP-5, bringing the weapon to bear just in time to prevent his opponent from cutting him in two.

The machete glanced off the barrel of the SMG with a loud metallic clang that seemed to reverberate through the woods. Encizo whipped the stock around and caught his opponent with a blow to the temple. He followed up with a front kick to the knee. The man's leg gave only partially and yet the distraction proved enough to grant Encizo the advantage. The MP-5 would not be viable in such close-quarter combat, but that didn't stop Encizo from reaching to his thigh and unleathering his Glock 21.

Encizo squeezed the trigger at point-blank range and put a bullet through the man's upper lip. The impact ripped away a good part of his jaw and punched him backward to the ground.

THE SINGLE PISTOL SHOT from the enemy's area of operation seemed out of place enough to draw their attention in the direction Encizo had gone.

Hawkins knew he couldn't worry about that, however—he had his own battle to fight. That battle started off all wrong as he somehow managed to get bushwhacked by a treetop observer. He hadn't thought to look for such a trap, and the force with which he'd been knocked to the ground and set upon clearly demonstrated his mistake.

Still, Hawkins had survived worse experiences.

The Phoenix Force warrior seemed to have two things his opponent did not: speed and experience. Hawkins quickly recovered the initial blow by bringing his head back and catching his adversary square on the nose. Hawkins felt the warm blood pepper his head and ears as he came away, and the arm wrapped around his throat loosened its hold considerably. Rising to one knee, Hawkins bucked his lower back and sent his opponent sailing over him. He immediately executed a somersault and came down on the man's chest with the heel of his boot. All remaining fight in his opponent dissipated.

Two men who had been up on the wood line firing toward his friends left their positions and swung their weapons toward him. Hawkins responded with catlike reflexes, rolling to his left in time to avoid a hail of gunfire. He came out of the roll on one knee. The muzzle of his Colt Model 635 flashed as 9 mm Parabellum rounds punched holes through the pair of enemy gunners. One took a full burst to the belly, which ripped out his guts. The second gunner caught two rounds to the head, which nearly decapitated him.

A sudden, violent explosion erupted nearby, and Hawkins hit the ground in anticipation the next one would be closer. All at once, it seemed as if all sound ceased—as though someone had stopped the world via remote—and Hawkins didn't move for a full minute. He waited and listened, watched for additional enemy, but there were no further outbreaks of autofire.

It looked like the battle had ended.

Hawkins rose and went to the side of the man who'd jumped him. He felt for a pulse at the man's neck and quickly determined he'd live. Hawkins raised his rifle at the crunching approach of feet but Encizo quickly came into view.

"It's me, Rafe," he said loudly and clearly. "Don't get itchy."

Hawkins pointed downward at the unconscious form.

"Looks like you managed to take one alive," Encizo said. "That'll make the other boys real happy."

"If he talks," Hawkins said.

Encizo's smile lacked any warmth. "Oh, he'll talk. Cal will see to that."

"How many did you get?"

"Two under small-arms, three more by grenade."

"I took out those two over there," Hawkins replied, gesturing in the direction of the deceased. "Including this one, that puts the count at eight. That's not many."

"Enough for an ambush. Any ID on them?"

Hawkins shook his head. "Haven't had the chance to check yet."

"Well, I'll go gather up the rest of the boys while you do that."

As Encizo turned to leave, Hawkins called, "Hey, Rafe?"

"Yeah?"

"Hell of a good call you made here."

The Cuban warrior just grinned, nodded, then headed off to give his teammates the all-clear signal.

CHAPTER FIVE

Calvin James studied the prisoner intently as Phoenix Force trudged through the woods in the direction of civilization. They had bound the man's hands behind his back with plastic riot cuffs, then attached those to a thin rope. Manning agreed to take the first watch duty and tied the rope securely to his harness. They now strode side by side, with James, McCarter and Encizo to the rear.

The prisoner had stared defiantly at them for a while, but once they set off on their hike across the German countryside, he'd dropped his gaze and held his tongue. James had tried more civilized methods to get the man to speak but he adamantly refused, apparently convinced it was better to remain utterly silent. In most other scenarios his actions would have been impressive, even commendable, but in this case it would only prove to make things more difficult for him.

David McCarter fell into step beside James and

scratched his sandpaper chin while looking at their prisoner. He needed a shave—no opportunity had presented itself aboard the plane—which also reminded him his crew could all use a clean-up and a few hours' rest. Hungry, weary and unkempt warriors weren't exactly a team morale booster, and the fact they had just come off one difficult mission without a respite didn't make it easier. As it was, they still had a ways to go before they reached the village town of Rodenbach.

"Has he said anything else?" McCarter asked.

James shook his head. "Not a peep. What outfit you think he's with?"

"No telling," McCarter replied with a quick shake of his head. "Could be any one of a dozen organizations I can think of, and we've tangled with just about all of them."

Hawkins had been eavesdropping on their conversation and interjected, "Just as long as it's not another one of those resurrected neo-Nazi groups. I'm getting plum tuckered out shooting at skinheads and anti-Semites."

"Ditto," James replied.

"You guys get a first-class ticket to Germany, a tour through some of the greatest woodlands in all of Europe, *free* of charge, mind you, and lodgings in a first-rate *gasthaus*," Manning taunted. "And what do you do? Bitch, bitch, bitch."

James saw an opportunity and decided to exploit it. "Well, I'd say we shouldn't let this prisoner slow us down. He isn't going to tell us anything, so why not just do him right here and get it over with?"

James looked back at Encizo on rear guard, ensuring

the prisoner couldn't see his face, and winked. The Cuban nodded almost imperceptibly to indicate he understood where James was headed. The badass warrior from Chicago figured if he could turn the conversation into an issue of racism, maybe it would prompt their German friend to start talking.

"Ease up there, soldier," McCarter said, also alert to James's plan. "We need him for interrogation, and we're going to stick with that."

James came to an immediate halt and the others followed suit. Everyone knew their part and they would just follow James's lead. It wasn't the first time they had pulled a stunt like this, and given its past effectiveness it wouldn't hurt to try it again. McCarter had agreed to defer to James's approach beforehand but kept it from the others so things would unfold in a more spontaneous way. The only thing that would make the whole thing pointless would be if their captive didn't speak English. James had decided to play those odds.

"What difference does it make?" James demanded of McCarter.

"What?" the Phoenix Force leader asked, putting some edge in his voice.

"I asked you what differences it makes." James gestured at the prisoner with the muzzle of his M-16 A-2. "He doesn't look to be in real good shape, which means he probably won't survive the effects of the drugs I gave him during the interrogation. Since it could be a while before we get to where we're going, why not just take the time now to question him?"

James turned and looked straight at the prisoner now.

"We could just beat it out of him, you know. I think that would be faster. He doesn't like my kind, anyway. And since there isn't a soul in sight, we could do it all right here and nobody would ever be the wiser."

Hawkins emitted a laugh. "You know something, he's right. Why not just get what we need and then move on? Leave his corpse here for the bears to pick clean. He's just slowing us down, anyway."

"Look, both of you," McCarter said. "I'm in charge of the squad, and I'm telling you we'll do this the right way. And that's all the discussion it needs. Get me?"

"I'm with them," Manning said. He looked at the prisoner and then got up close, towering a few inches over him. He pulled the rope taut and added, "He's probably just another German warmonger, hates anything or anyone that's not part of his alleged superior race. He's not going to talk, especially not to a black man."

Encizo stepped up to join the production. "He probably hates Spanish people, too!"

James looked McCarter in the eyes and shrugged, then broke into a broad smile. "Looks like maybe you're outnumbered on this one, pal. Nobody likes this guy and nobody wants him around."

McCarter exchanged glances with each of his comrades and then made a dramatic show of reaching to his holster, thumbing away the safety strap and drawing his 9 mm Browning Hi-Power. A wicked glint flared in his eyes as he held the pistol high for all to see, then pulled back the slide. McCarter paused a moment for effect, then chambered a round. He extended his arm and aimed the pistol straight at the prisoner's head.

"You guys are bloody well nuts if you think I'm going to let you beat this guy to death," McCarter said. "I'll just blow his brains out before that."

"No!" the man cried. "Please don't kill me. I will talk. I will talk to you! See…see how good English I speak?"

"I don't believe him," McCarter said.

"Yeah, maybe you're right," James said, and he raised his M-16 A-2. "Maybe we should just get this done and over with. Not risk it."

"No!" The man began to plead with them.

"Now wait a minute," Manning said, raising his hands. "Let's be reasonable, gentleman. If the guy's willing to talk, maybe we should hear what he has to say."

"Yeah?" Hawkins queried. "Well, how in the world can ya'll be sure he'll tell the truth?"

"Aw, I don't think he'd lie to us," James said, lowering his rifle. McCarter had holstered his pistol, as well. James turned to their prisoner and smiled. "Now, would you?"

THE MEN OF ABLE TEAM touched down in St. Louis, Missouri, just after noon, and took the Ford Expedition arranged by Stony Man straight to Our Lady of the Resurrection Hospital near the Washington University campus. The OLR physicians who'd been caring for the two ill college youths had immediately consulted the Centers for Disease Control and Prevention when they determined no potential causes for the illness, and the fact that both patients had come from the same school.

"It's going to be hard to keep this under wraps for long," Schwarz said from behind the wheel.

"Yeah, well, we'd best act fast, then," Lyons replied.

The three men arrived forty minutes later and headed right to the second floor. Their credentials as agents with the FBI would only buy them so much latitude, but that didn't bother Able Team. They were really there on more of a fact-finding mission than anything else. The place and time to be tough wasn't the hospital; they had planned to save that for Delmico if their investigation revealed any foul play.

Able Team reached the third floor of the MedSurg ward, infectious diseases section. A pert young woman with dark hair pulled back in a ponytail buzzed them through the access doors. A large red strip with a sign warned all unauthorized personnel not to advance past the desk without being fully protected by isolation equipment.

"Agent Irons with the Federal Bureau of Investigation," Lyons said, flashing his credentials at the dark-haired woman whose tag identified her as the charge nurse. He whipped out his mini notebook, made a show of flipping through it and said, "Um, we're looking for… Just one moment, got it here somewhere… Uh, hmm. Ah! Here it is, yes. We'd like to speak with Dr. Kingsley or Dr. Corvasce. Is either of them available?"

The charge nurse eyed the three men warily. "Dr. Kingsley's off today and Dr. Corvasce is in with a patient right now. Is there some way I can help you?"

"Nope," Lyons said shortly. "I doubt it."

Blancanales smiled and immediately wedged himself between Lyons and the counter. Clearly this would take something with less frostiness and a bit more tact, the former of which his good friend possessed plenty and the latter almost none at all.

"Good day, Nurse…Bluesilk." Blancanales smiled. "That's a very nice name."

The nurse's demeanor changed almost immediately. In fact, she appeared to melt under the twinkling dark eyes of the Politician. "Thanks. It's Native American, actually."

"Interesting," Blancanales replied. "Actually, it's very important we speak to Dr. Corvasce as soon as possible."

"I can certainly see if he has a moment. Would you be able to maybe tell me what it's regarding?"

"I'm sorry, but that's confidential." Blancanales looked around and then leaned over the counter and gestured with his head for her to come a bit closer. "Although I *can* tell you it's about the college boys who came in here ill. You see, Atlanta contacted us and we're just making sure this isn't related to any, well, you know… We don't want some major scare on our hands. We'd prefer someone not go off the deep end and start guessing wildly about how this might be anthrax or some other terrible thing. Since Katrina, we've uh, well, we've had to change the way we do things."

The nurse looked for any sign of tomfoolery in Blancanales's expression, but obviously she could only detect altruism in those legitimate lines.

"Why don't you gentlemen have a seat in the lobby, and I'll see if I can get Dr. Corvasce to come talk with you."

"That would be great," Blancanales said. As his cohorts turned and headed for the door, Blancanales ges-

tured toward Lyons's retreating form and added quietly,
"Don't mind Irons there. They don't let him out much."

She smiled, giggled and quietly replied, "I can see
why."

Blancanales winked and then retreated to join his
friends.

ALMOST AN HOUR HAD PASSED before a tall, distin-
guished man exited through the double set of hermeti-
cally sealed doors leading from the infectious disease
ward. His lanky form strode toward Able Team in confidence, the gray eyes studying them resolutely on approach. The three men got to their feet as the man
reached them. After handshakes and introductions all
around, Dr. Michael Corvasce led the trio to a nearby
coffee bar with an outdoor veranda.

Gray afternoon clouds had rolled in and brought the
smell of rain with them. It felt as if the humidity levels
had doubled in just the few short hours since they had
arrived, and it had only served to sour Lyons's mood.
He'd decided to let Blancanales and Schwarz do most
of the talking, content to just sit back and listen.

"I'm a little surprised to see the CDC got you boys
involved," Corvasce said pleasantly as they sat at an
umbrella-covered table.

"It's not really such a big surprise," Schwarz said.
"We understand they didn't seem too interested."

"You can say that again," Corvasce replied with a
frown. "Hence why I can't understand your interest in
the case."

Blancanales cleared his throat. "Listen, Doctor, we

realize you're probably not at liberty to tell us a whole lot about the condition of either of these patients. But we would appreciate any latitude you could show us."

"Well, between us, I'll save the politics for Dr. Kingsley. We've been trying to contact my patient's parents since he arrived, but apparently they're on vacation somewhere in South America and their house-keeper barely speaks English. I've had to pull in the hos-pital administration and work through an interpreter, who is now calling all over the Western Hemisphere trying to locate these people. So, I'm not going to worry about patient confidentiality at this point *if* you can assure me you're here strictly in the best interests of the public health."

"I can promise you that is definitely one certainty," Blancanales said.

Corvasce nodded. "That's good enough for me. Basi-cally, Willis Mallow is a twenty-year-old male who came into the emergency room night before last almost unconscious after complaining of a stomach ache and then collapsing. At first we thought your standard, run-of-the-mill frat party, but we quickly realized some-thing else was going on when his tox screen came back negative. Not that that means anything. These days, kids are into all kinds of stuff, including a combination of legitimate pharmacological agents that produce a short and intense euphoria just before they kill you.

"Dr. Kingsley was actually on call that night, but I got involved because it was right during shift change re-port and I was the oncoming attending. We went down to the ER and I agreed to examine Willis because a second emergency had been brought in and they were immediately calling for Kingsley, stating the patient was exhibiting many of the same signs and symptoms as Mallow. By the time we got done stabilizing both boys, we'd come to the conclusion they were suffering from the same problem. What we *didn't* know was exactly what the hell that problem was."

"Are you any closer to a diagnosis?" Schwarz asked.

Corvasce shook his head and took a sip of coffee before continuing. "Frankly, both of us are completely stumped. Once we'd ruled out drugs or alcohol, we obtained thorough histories. Both kids were athletes in good health, and neither had traveled recently to any foreign countries. They're regularly screened for steroid use, so coupled with their negative drug testing, we were able to rule that out immediately. Tell me, are you guys at all familiar with cholinesterase poisoning?"

All three nodded. They had once faced a terrorist group bent on launching poisonous chemicals against targets all over the world simultaneously using stolen missiles. They had nearly failed in that mission, and none of them had ever forgotten the effects that would have impacted millions of people if they hadn't stopped the terrorists in time.

"Ah." Corvasce shook his head. "Acetylcholine is produced from nerve endings to stimulate smooth muscle and parasympathetic nervous response. In cholinesterase poisoning, the patient suffers from excessive vomiting, diarrhea and profuse sweating. Body temperature and blood pressure fall rapidly, heart rate increases. If the condition goes untreated, the patient will suffer a condition known as disseminated intravascular coagulation. Third-stage shock in simplest terms. Multiple organ failure usually follows shortly thereafter.

"In both of these cases, that's the way they acted, except there were some opposite signs I'd never seen before. Urticaria, high fever and *polycythemia vera,* which is typically an idiopathic condition only seen in patients suffering from congenital heart disease. Neither youth has such a disease, and right now they're both at very high risk for clots or severe hemorrhaging. That's why we've had to admit them to the ICU wing."

"If you could put your finger on this at all," Blancanales interjected, "would you say these kids were poisoned?"

Corvasce shrugged. "Possibly, but if so, it's unlike any poison I've ever seen. It's almost as if they're suffering from part cardiac disease, part allergic reaction. But the sudden onset and other environmental factors, coupled with their age and unremarkable past medical histories, *does* certainly suggest exposure to some type of pathogen."

"Would somebody with experience in microbiology have the expertise to concoct a pathogen of this nature?" Lyons queried.

"Oh, most certainly," Corvasce replied immediately. "Why? Do you think this was purposeful?"

"I never said that."

"But we have to consider it a possibility," Blancanales added quickly, throwing his blond friend a furious look. "For the good of the public health, you understand."

Corvasce rendered a thin smile. "Yes. I understand."

Something in the physician's eyes told Able Team he understood all too well. While Lyons had played a good game with the nurse—passing himself as more of a fumbling bureaucrat than a highly trained antiterrorist—he'd studied the files of both doctors thoroughly during the trip to St. Louis. All of Able Team admitted they would have expected more cooperation from Corvasce than Kingsley. Of the two doctors, Corvasce had attended medical school at a university of significantly lesser prestige, and had not nearly as many awards and credentials. It was always easier to get the down-to-earth folks to spill their guts than some stuffy, highbrow type who wore monogrammed shirts and drove a BMW with vanity plates. For now, they had enough information to go on. The four men made a little small talk before thanking Corvasce and leaving the hospital. As they drove toward the college, they talked over what he'd told them.

"Sounds like this would be right up the alley of a schizoid like Simon Delmico," Lyons began.

"Now, Ironman," Blancanales chided him, "you know better than to believe everything you read in a person's psych profile. I mean, we never believed any of the stuff the shrinks at Stony Man Farm have said about you."

"Ah, yes, that *did* make for some fun reading, didn't it?" Schwarz quipped. "Besides the fact, they said they thought Delmico was more of a paranoid-delusional."

Lyons threw up his hands with a scoffing laugh. "Now you'd think the guys in the government who know this kind of stuff would lock up somebody like that instead of letting him run around on the streets. And with college students, no less."

"They probably didn't think a guy with one foot could be much of a threat," Schwarz said.

"There are a lot of dead terrorists I know who thought the same thing about a sixty-something Israeli with one arm," Lyons countered.

The other men fell silent for a time, more out of respect than anything else. The Ironman's reference to the former leader of Phoenix Force had hit close to the mark. Katz had lost his life battling the heinous Abu Nidal Organization. Although he'd gone like a true warrior, the loss of such a man was still felt.

"Whatever's going on here," Blancanales said after a time of silence, "I'd have to agree with Carl. It seems highly probable Simon Delmico's involved in this somehow. It begs the question of why, though. What's the motive?"

"Maybe Phoenix Force's mission into Germany will uncover some answers," Schwarz replied.

He brought the vehicle to a halt in the parking lot adjacent to the Natural Sciences building on the campus of Washington U. It had started to sprinkle minutes before they arrived, which would make it more difficult to spot Delmico when he came out of the building. Lyons checked his watch as he removed a piece of paper from his pocket. He unfolded it and spread it across his left leg with a noisy crinkle.

Schwarz looked at it. "What's that?"

"Class schedule. I had Bear hack it out of the

school's computer mainframe. Looks like there's still about ten minutes to go in Delmico's last class."

"Hey, um, fellas?" Blancanales said from the back seat.

The pair turned to see their friend staring through the right rear window. "I make about six guys in a Lincoln SUV parked over there near the fire lane. You see them?"

Lyons turned and cracked his window enough to see over the top. "I got them, too. What do you make of it?"

"They're a bit old to be local fraternity just looking for a place to happen on Friday afternoon."

"Yeah," Schwarz agreed. "Something about the headpiece that driver's wearing just doesn't add up."

Lyons reached beneath his windbreaker and withdrew a stainless-steel .44 Magnum Colt Anaconda. He flipped out the cylinder and checked the action, then locked it in place and holstered the weapon. Blancanales and Schwarz performed similar action checks on their SIG P-239 and Beretta 92-F semiautomatic pistols. And they waited.

CHAPTER SIX

They didn't have to wait long. Fifteen minutes later Simon Delmico emerged from the building, and the SUV left the curb at a crawl.

"It's going down," Schwarz said slowly and evenly.

"Stay sharp!" Lyons told him. "Pol, with me!"

Lyons and Blancanales bailed from their vehicle and sprinted toward Delmico. At the same moment, the Lincoln increased speed and reached the scientist first. Students were crossing the walkway, chatting and laughing, or hanging around shelters to avoid the risk of getting drenched in another sudden torrent of showers. Lyons shouted for everyone to find cover as he withdrew his Colt Anaconda on the run.

Blancanales saw the barrel of an SMG protrude abruptly from a slit in the rear passenger window, Lyons apparently oblivious in his focus on Delmico. Blancanales shouted a warning and pushed his friend out of the line of fire as flame spit from the muzzle. A Kalashnikov cut loose, one of the rounds intended for Lyons ripping through Blancanales's forearm.

The former Black Beret went low and rolled to avoid certain death. Lyons staggered but kept his feet, then raised the Anaconda. He snap-aimed just above the muzzle of the barking assault rifle and squeezed the trigger twice. A pair of 300-grain slugs punched through the glass of the window. A head exploded as the slug rounds punched through the gunner's skull in a spray of blood and brain matter.

The tail door swung upward and two men in turbans, blue jeans and black leather jackets jumped from the back. They swung their vehicles toward Lyons and Blancanales, but then something roared between them in a blur of smoking rubber and dust. The front of Able Team's Ford SUV T-boned the Lincoln, effectively pinning it to the curb. Autofire resounded through the air as the driver's door shot open and appeared to vomit Hermann Schwarz. The lithe warrior landed on his hands and knees as glass shards, vinyl and cushion filling sliced through the air like ticker tape at a Macy's parade.

"Perhaps we were a bit rash," Blancanales noted.

Schwarz looked at his friend in amazement. "Ya think?"

"Split up!" Lyons commanded.

The trio did as ordered. It would be difficult for their opponents to take all of them at once if they headed in different directions. The time it took the pair of gunners to clear the Ford bought Able Team what they needed to find adequate cover. Lyons secured safety behind a purple PT Cruiser, while Schwarz charged in the direction of a metal bus shelter.

Blancanales opted to skirt the front of the Lincoln, keeping below the driver's line of sight until he reached the curbside fender. He arrived in time to see another pair of gunners trying to hustle Delmico through the rear passenger door. Blancanales stood, raised his SIG P-239, aimed directly at the driver and squeezed the trigger three times. The man's eyes widened as a trio of .40 S&W hardball rounds first made short work of the windshield and then his face. The impact slammed what was left of the man's skull backward and the reciprocal force drove it forward to rest on the steering wheel.

Blancanales turned the pistol on the pair just as they got Delmico inside the SUV in time to realize their enemy had them dead to rights. The pair foolishly pawed for their weapons, but they were too late. At that range, the Able Team warrior couldn't miss. Blancanales dispatched the closer man with a single round through the chest. It perforated his heart and exited his left shoulder blade. Blancanales swung into acquisition on the second gunner as the man brought his weapon to bear, and ended the face-off with a double-tap center mass and number three to the head. The impact lifted him from his feet and slammed him against the open passenger door.

The door swung backward as Delmico burst from the rear seat. The scientist's suit snagged on the catch and the door pinned it there. He slid from the jacket and started to run. Blancanales started after him but suddenly went prone when a second Lincoln crew wagon pulled up.

Blancanales rolled as their weapons opened up.

HERMANN SCHWARZ REACHED the bus shelter, got behind the corrugated metal and crouched. A screech caused him to turn and he found himself staring at a pair of wide-eyed college girls.

He gestured in the opposite direction with his pistol. "Get out of here! *Run!*"

He didn't have to tell them twice. They burst from the shelter like a pair of spooked gazelles.

Schwarz returned his attention to the matters at hand. Two gunners appeared at the rear of the Expedition and swept the area with their weapons. The Able Team commando braced his right wrist against the shelter post, steadied his Beretta 92-F in a Weaver's grip and squeezed the trigger twice. Twin 9 mm Parabellum rounds struck one of the gunners' weapons and knocked it from his grasp. A lucky ricochet grazed the man's neck, and his hand slapped at the spurting blood as if he'd killed a mosquito. Schwarz swore under his breath as he reacquired and sent a third round booming from the pistol. This one drilled through the terrorist's chest and drove his back against the Ford. The man slid to the ground as the light left his open eyes.

The other terrorist never stood a chance under the crack marksmanship of Carl Lyons. The Able Team leader got it done with a single squeeze of the Anaconda's trigger. The .44 Magnum weapon reported thunderously, even from that distance, its message to the hardman plain and simple: game over. Lyons's round caught the guy square in the chest and dumped him on the pavement next to his deceased partner.

Schwarz turned in time to see Blancanales had bought himself some fresh trouble. He broke cover and beelined to help his friend, signaling Lyons with a loud whistle between thumb and forefinger on the move. Lyons waved and burst from behind the PT Cruiser. Schwarz came up the sidewalk on the passenger side of the smashed Lincoln in time to see Blancanales find sanctuary behind a small brick alcove near the building entrance.

The electronics expert reached the rear bumper, dropped and squeezed off a volley of rounds in the direction of the new arrivals. He didn't have anywhere near the firepower of the enemy, but what he lacked in quantity Schwarz made up in quality. The combat veteran put two rounds in the chest of the closest gunner. The 9 mm slugs ripped through the tender flesh of lungs and pink, frothy sputum erupted from the man's mouth. The impact spun him into a second gunner who had been a bit too close. The falling corpse tied up the second man long enough for Schwarz to draw a bead. He finished their dance with a single skull-buster to the forehead.

Lyons got one at the front left fender with a single shot to the hip. The bullet shattered the man's thigh and his weapon fell from number fingers. The guy fell. Schwarz got to his feet and rushed for Blancanales, sending a few more rounds at his enemies for the sole purpose of keeping heads down.

It did little good. The next ten seconds seemed to run through Schwarz's head like a slow-motion replay.

Two other gunners got Delmico into the SUV.

The Lincoln's driver leaned out the window and pumped a volley of rounds into the man Lyons had wounded.

The Lincoln jumped into Reverse with a roar, churning up a cloud of smoke, dust and bits of gravel.

Schwarz reached Blancanales just as Lyons pumped out his last two rounds at the retreating SUV.

Everything after seemed to return to normal time.

Lyons trotted over to his friends. He crouched, nodded at Schwarz, then looked at Blancanales with mild concern. "You okay?"

"Got winged," Blancanales said, breathing a bit heavily as he gripped his arm to stanch the flow of blood.

Schwarz jerked his head toward the Ford. "There's a med kit in my satchel. Why don't you grab it."

Lyons rose and trotted for the bag.

"Hang tough, partner," Schwarz said. He showed Blancanales a reassuring grin. "You're going to pull through just fine."

'Thanks, amigo," he replied. "But I sort of already figured that. Really, there's no reason to get all mushy on me. People will talk."

IN THE WAR ROOM of Stony Man Farm, Brognola and Price sat and listened as Carl Lyons relayed his report of the past few hours.

"So Rosario's going to be okay?" Price asked when Lyons finished.

"Fine," Lyons replied.

"We thought there might be a connection between yours and Phoenix Force's mission," Brognola said. "But we sure as hell didn't expect you to walk into a firestorm like that."

"Don't sweat it," Lyons said. "That's why you pay us the big bucks."

"The only question now is how this relates to what went down in Germany," Price said. She directed her voice toward the speakerphone receiver in the center of the conference table. "Carl, we have a theory based on some leads we've been pursuing here. It's still a bit thin, but it may be enough for you to move forward. And we can always fill it out once David checks in."

"We'll take anything you've got," Lyons replied.

"Well, we started looking into Delmico's recent activities," Price said. "We have it on reliable word that while he was in Germany giving that lecture, he became acquainted with a man named Choldwig Burke. Other than a sheet of misdemeanors, Burke seems clean. However, about seven years ago he did an eighteen-month stint in jail. He didn't have any more run-ins with the authorities, successfully completed his six months of parole as required by German law, so he fell off the radar."

"I've heard this story," Lyons cut in. "Suddenly he shows up at a seminar and befriends a microbiologist formally employed by the DOD."

"Right," Brognola said. "We think he was working with inside information. Somebody told Burke who Delmico was and how to contact him."

A low buzz sounded for attention from an overhead speaker, followed by Kurtzman's voice. "I've got David McCarter on our secured satellite line."

"Conference him in, won't you, Aaron?" Price asked.

"Your wish is my command," Kurtzman replied.

A moment later McCarter joined them.

"David, we have Carl on with us," Brognola said. "What do you have to report?"

"We found the plane," McCarter replied. "Cargo was gone, and the entire crew dead except for the captain. We also ran into some friends."

"Terrorists?" Price inquired.

McCarter snorted. "Hardly, although they'd probably like to think they are. We took a prisoner and he did some talking. We got all we could from him, so now we'll probably need a way to unload him on local authorities."

"We'll make the arrangements," Brognola said. "I'll have someone get with Interpol and take him off your hands."

"Thanks," McCarter said. "He's starting to get on our nerves."

"What did he tell you?" Price asked, steering the conversation back to topic.

"He said he's a member of some bloody outfit calling themselves the Germanic Freedom Railroad. He alleges to know nothing about any operations there in the States. Apparently he's just a grunt and has only been with this group for about six weeks."

"Aaron, are you still on?" Brognola asked.

"You bet, and I'm looking it up now," Kurtzman replied.

"Go ahead, David," Price urged the Phoenix Force leader.

"There were eight men in the squad behind to see who came to find the plane. They were apparently expecting military or police agencies, but when the leader of the squad saw us he panicked. From what we can gather, they thought we were competitors instead of a legitimate agency. That's when this brilliant lieutenant of theirs gave the order to open up on us."

"Big mistake," Lyons cut in.

"You said it, mate," McCarter replied.

"What's your current status?" Brognola asked.

"We're holed up in Rodenbach. Our ammunition and weapons situation is fine. I've got the team cleaning up now, but we could use some food and duds that are a wee bit less, say...conspicuous."

"I'll make it happen," Price assured him, and she immediately excused herself from the room.

"Barb's going to see you get everything you need," Brognola said. "What about the leadership of this Germanic Freedom Railroad? Did he give any names?"

"He claims he doesn't know any, and Calvin's said he thinks the bloke's telling the truth about that."

"You concur?" Lyons asked.

"I'd say so," McCarter replied quickly. "I trust his judgment, and it doesn't seem like the guy would benefit from telling us lies at this point. I figure with at least the name of this group you can get more information."

"What do you guess is their main angle?" Brognola asked.

"Supposedly they're smugglers for VIPs in the terrorist network. Mostly, they handle al Qaeda and other affiliates with strong ties throughout most of the ECU."

"Well, it's no secret Germany's always been somewhat of a terrorist sanctuary," Brognola said.

"Right."

"That would also fit the guys we tangled with," Lyons added. He quickly brought McCarter up to speed on Able Team's activities.

"Does anybody have a plausible theory on what this all means?" McCarter asked.

"I'm wary about speculating on this thing," Brognola said. "The situation has obviously grown more complex. And you guys need hard intelligence. Facts. It's up to us to get them to you in the best and most efficient way possible. I don't want either of your teams acting on conjecture. Give us a little time to put together some reasonable data and we'll get back to you within… I don't know. Aaron?"

"Two hours should be more than enough time," Kurtzman said. "We'll definitely have something solid by then."

"Fine," Brognola said. "In the meantime, both of you sit tight and try not to get your asses shot off until I can get back to you."

"Don't have to tell me twice, Hal," McCarter replied.

"Ditto," Lyons said.

Brognola sat back with a deep sigh once his men disconnected. The information about the Germanic Freedom Railroad had proved interesting. The big Fed searched his memory and couldn't recall hearing of them before now. Apparently they had been operating in relative secrecy. Had he been a betting man, Brognola would have let it all ride on the odds Choldwig Burke was the number one guy in the GFR.

The man from Justice got to his feet and headed for the Annex. He didn't plan to breathe down Kurtzman's neck—or maybe he would and just wouldn't make it seem like that—but he wanted to be involved with the process.

He reached the Computer Center and found Kurtzman hunkered in his chair and focused on a wide, flat-panel computer screen.

"What do you know?"

Kurtzman looked at Brognola with a cocksure grin. "You mean, since ten minutes ago? What makes you think I'd have something that fast?"

Brognola grinned as he dropped into a nearby chair. "Come on, Aaron. We're talking about *you* here."

"Yes, we are, aren't we?" he replied, his normally booming voice rising in tone. Somehow the higher pitch sounded funny on him. Kurtzman made a production of looking at his nails, exhaling on them and then rubbing them against his shirt. "But as it just so happens, I do have something for you."

"Shoot," Brognola said, settling back in his chair.

"The GFR apparently has a reputation in certain circles. We haven't picked up on it until now because they've made a point of never referring to the organization by name."

"Any idea on the hierarchy?"

"Pretty much what you'd expect from your run-of-the-mill smuggling operation," Kurtzman replied. "It's been proposed by the international law enforcement community that the secret of their ability to remain virtually nonexistent is because they operate in teams of no more than three to four on any given job. Additionally, they deal strictly in cash and all up front."

"Makes for a good way to keep your clients silent," Brognola said.

"Sure. Collect the entire advance and your customers will do just about anything to make sure they get their money's worth."

"What else?"

"Well, I'm just spit-balling here, but it seems a little interesting that a group like this would risk blowing it for these LAMPs. The technology hasn't been completely researched and is relatively untested in any kind of legitimate trials. They haven't even been retrofitted with delivery systems. And insofar as I can tell, the GFR's never been into actual commission of terrorist acts. It seems they've stuck to smuggling, hiding and criminal acts that meet those ends."

Brognola nodded. "I agree. They make their money by optimal discretion, not drawing any attention to themselves. Why risk that on a major operation like bringing down a military plane so close to their home turf and stealing untried technology?"

"Maybe it's a special job," Kurtzman proposed. "Maybe, just maybe, the hostiles Able Team encountered are part of the deal, and that's why they grabbed Delmico."

"It fits. The GFR gets approached about this job. It's so big, bigger than anything they've ever done before, they spend nearly a year planning it. Then they make their play, but things don't go quite right."

"Then their clients get nervous when Phoenix Force shows up at the plane, and Able Team lands in St. Louis and starts asking a whole lot of uncomfortable questions."

"So they decide to take over the operation before it gets out of control," Brognola finished. "It all seems plausible."

"Well, as it stands now, that's about the extent of our facts. Other than the fact it's become plainly obvious these are some tough customers we're up against."

"A band of overachievers," Brognola mused. "Marvelous."

"Where do you want to go from here?"

"Keep plugging away at it, Aaron. We'll need a bit more to give Phoenix Force and Able Team something to act on."

"Oh, you'll get it," Kurtzman said as Brognola rose. "Or your money back."

Brognola chuckled. "Aren't you the same Aaron Kurtzman who's always complaining I don't pay you enough?"

"Why, Hal, don't you get it? That's just my little way of endearing myself to you."

Brognola shook his head and quipped, "Glory."

CHAPTER SEVEN

Choldwig Burke quietly placed the cordless telephone handset on his makeshift metal desk and swiveled in his chair to look upon the dusk cityscape of Wiesbaden. He had a perfect view of it from the abandoned automobile factory on the south side of the city, and it calmed him. He had purchased the factory a mere six months earlier for a song under a deal he'd worked out anonymously through a third-party agent.

Burke considered the recent news. He opened and closed his hands, clenching his jaw in tandem with the movements, as if keeping time with an orchestral piece. The detachment he left behind to observe the plane failed to check in at either of their scheduled times, and then he received the message that most if not all were probably dead. The informant didn't have much more information than that, but she had noticed one of his men in the custody of five strangers of various ethnicities. He'd instructed her to call back as soon as she had more information on their current whereabouts.

The other issue weighing on Burke's mind was the unsteady alliance he'd formed with the Palestinians. Mukhtar Tarif, leader of the Hezbollah unit under sanctuary provided by the GFR, had proved himself totally unpredictable. Such men were not trustworthy to Burke's way of thinking, and he didn't know how much longer they could maintain a credible alliance. Burke hadn't wanted this whole thing to begin with, but the people he employed expected payment for their services, and being they were very good at what they did, they didn't come cheap, either.

When Burke's operation had still been small—with just a couple dozen men able to handle the business in the way it needed handling—these kinds of troubles hadn't been an issue. But with growth came greater risks, and greater risks demanded upping the ante for certain types of services. Tarif had stepped forward and made an offer Burke resisted at first. But Burke's second in command, a brilliant ex-military strategist named Helmut Stuhl, convinced him to accept the deal. He regretted every minute of it. It had turned out to be very risky and expensive for the GFR, which meant it hadn't resulted in as much profit.

Burke planned to change all that with their successful theft of the LAMPs. He had supreme confidence in them to do the job necessary, and once he sold them out to the highest bidder, Burke could rid himself of Tarif and his band of fanatics forever. First, however, he needed to deal with the incident in St. Louis.

A knock sounded at the door of his makeshift office. "Come in."

The door swung open to admit Mukhtar Tarif and his pair of bodyguards. He never seemed to go anywhere without them. The bodyguards tried to look imposing, menacing, but to a man of Burke's size and physical prowess they were a joke. Burke possessed the physique of his father, but he'd inherited his brains from his late mother. Liesl Burke had served as a nuclear power engineer and consultant to the government of Luxembourg. She'd held a degree in nuclear physics, and many colleagues had considered her one of the most innovative and brilliant scientists in her field. Then cancer took hold and ravaged her body, eventually overtaking not only her life but her beloved career.

Liesl Burke also left behind a saddened ten-year-old boy.

Sworn to model his life after that of his mother's, Burke excelled in his studies. By sixteen he'd been wooed by the finest universities in Germany but eventually he set his heart on the study of particle physics. He spent several years at the CERN Laboratory in Geneva. That later proved extremely valuable in gaining knowledge of the Hadron magnets used in the LHC project, and ultimately proved instrumental in understanding the Low Altitude Military Platform brainchild of the British RAF.

Mukhtar Tarif dropped into the straight-backed metal chair in front of Burke and propped his feet on the desk. Young and impetuous, the terrorist leader had treated Burke with impunity and disrespect nearly from the

beginning of their relationship. Burke had only tolerated it because of his belief in the GFR and his stead-
fast ideology that the needs of his organization far
exceeded those of any individual, including its founder.
Such idealism had earned him the respect of every
member in the organization, and he didn't intend to
sacrifice their loyalty on what amounted to little more
than ego.

"I'm told you needed to speak to me," Tarif
announced in flawless German. He'd mastered the language in one of the terrorist training camps sponsored
by al Qaeda deep in the mountains of Afghanistan.
"What do you want?"

"I want to know exactly what kind of a fool you think
I am," Burke replied in a no-nonsense tone. "You didn't
actually think I wouldn't find out about Delmico?"

"On the contrary, I knew you would find out. He is
no longer of any concern to you."

"I will judge what's of concern to me and what isn't."

The effect of the implicit warning in Burke's voice
became evident with the dangerous hue visible in
Tarif's expression. "That sounded much to me like a
threat, Mr. Burke."

"Take it as you like," Burke replied with a smile.
"But Dr. Delmico is *my* contact, and I want him released
unharmed. Immediately."

"Correct me if I'm mistaken, but I understood our
positions to be on equal ground. I don't recall answering
to you."

Burke shrugged, never dropping the smile. "You
don't. But you have altered the bargain by taking what

doesn't belong to you. I bought Delmico, and I assume all the risks in that investment. You're forgetting this is *my* money, not yours."

Tarif waved the point away. "Money we paid you. Money you wouldn't have right now had my people not chosen to contract your services. And all at my recommendation."

"That money was simply the agreed-upon fee," Burke reminded him. "You didn't have to work with my organization. But since you have, you also must know there are bounds, certain lines that I must draw, and your actions have grossly crossed them. I would like an explanation."

"It became apparent to me you'd let the situation get out of hand," Tarif replied evenly.

"Out of hand in what way?"

"Clearly, you haven't put Delmico on a short leash," he said.

"Short enough."

"Really?" Tarif said, smiling and pausing as if savoring the confrontation. "Then perhaps you can explain to me why three men from America's FBI were in the hospital asking questions about Delmico's test subjects."

This revelation surprised Burke, but he feigned nonchalance with a shrug. "It's of no concern. They won't learn anything because the doctors don't know any more than they do."

"Is that why they nearly got to Delmico before my men did? If anything, I've saved you money and aggravation by taking some additional risks I didn't have to take. You should be thanking me."

"That's exactly right," Burke said. "You didn't have to take those risks, and shouldn't have taken those risks. Now, I want you to tell me where Dr. Delmico is, and I want you to tell me now."

"Be careful of your tone with me, Mr. Burke. I don't answer to you. We are your clients and you have an obligation to meet."

"I've met the obligation. I've provided sanctuary for more than fifty of your men, along with the means to carry each of them along in complete anonymity and safety for the next six months. I would say I've honored my end of the agreement."

"So, it would seem we are at an impasse," Tarif said, and he threw up his hands and rose. "I will take your *request* to release Delmico under advisement with my superiors. In the meantime, he remains alive and well in our custody."

"I'll give you twenty-four hours to effect his release," Burke said, standing also to impose his point. "After that, you and your men will no longer be welcome here."

"That is not part of our agreement!"

"You should have thought of that before taking what does not belong to you," Burke replied.

Tarif spit on the floor. "You won't do this. You would not sacrifice your reputation."

"My reputation stands more to be impugned by allowing you to continue operating as you are and letting you violate our agreement than it does by cutting you loose. And I will do it because I have the numbers and firepower to do it. Think about that before making your decision. If anyone here cannot afford a war right now, I would say it's you."

"We shall see," Tarif said in a menacing tone. He turned on his heel and marched smartly out of the room.

Burke sat and mumbled an old Hessian curse. He returned to his previous position, looked out over the city again, then rose and left his office.

Burke shoved his hands in the pockets of his fatigue pants. His combat boots tapped the cheap linoleum flooring of the hallway and echoed back at him, almost as if mocking his train of thought. In some ways he felt a bit helpless, and he didn't like feeling that way. He wasn't accustomed to answering to other men, particularly not the likes of Mukhtar Tarif, and he wondered how much longer he could endure the Arab's presence. He'd meant what he said about having the guns to back up any dispute. Tarif's rather young age and lack of experience remained the terrorist's two main problems; they had probably also posed problems to the Hezbollah leadership, hence their reasoning to make Tarif keep his head down.

The entire third floor of the factory had served as business offices for the administrative side of the auto manufacturer, and the GFR had converted them to makeshift billets. One room had been reserved as a combined office and tactical operations center for Burke, and he now stopped before the door of the other: a cell.

Burke knocked twice and the heavy metal door with bars, with which they had replaced the standard door, swung open to admit him. He stepped inside and acknowledged the pair of guards on duty with a nod. He then gave his full attention to a lone man seated in a plain metal chair bolted to the outer brick wall. The man looked haggard and tired, predominantly because Burke had ordered sleep deprivation. He walked over to the prisoner and came to a standstill before him.

Burke scratched his chin and eyed the man with interest. "You do not look well, Captain Blythe. I would have expected a military man to possess a bit stronger constitution."

Blythe's head dropped at moments but he kept his bloodshot, narrowed eyes on Burke's face. "If I get out of these bonds, I'll bloody well show you constitution, you German bastard."

"I believed a man of your experience would have passed beyond mere vulgarities," Burke replied. "Completely childish, in my humble opinion. I am sorry for the treatment you have received thus far, but you must understand that I cannot risk any further leaks or delays. I need to know what your people would most likely do if they discovered my group had seized the LAMP systems, and I think you can tell me that."

"How should I know? I'm just a pilot."

"Ah, yes, there is that. But a highly decorated pilot with an impeccable record. I know you were at least aware of the sensitive nature of your cargo, even if you didn't know exactly what it was. But I don't need any of that information. I simply need to know how your government will respond."

The change in Blythe's complexion betrayed his apoplexy. "I've already told you, I don't know how they're going to respond! But you can be sure they *will* respond."

Burke reached out and cuffed Blythe. It came so smooth and easy it seemed like he'd barely touched the pilot, as if they were simply a pair of vaudevillians walking through a slapstick routine. But Blythe didn't see anything comedic about it as the blow seemed to nearly render him unconscious. It caused him to bite his lip, and his eyes rolled upward while a steady stream of blood began to run from the fresh wound. Burke dispassionately studied Blythe for another moment, then turned and signaled the guard who had admitted him. The guard immediately left the room and returned less than a minute later with two large pails; both sloshed over with a clear liquid.

Burke fixed his gaze on Blythe as the guard set the pails next to him. "You may be wondering what I intend to do with these pails of warm saltwater. That is a very good question. You see, the large majority of those in my trade believe the best way to deprive a man of sleep is by shocking his system. For example, they would probably advise me to use cold water because that would cause a specific set of responses designed to keep you awake. The trouble is, they are only useful in short-term instances."

Burke, arms folded casually, began to circle Blythe's chair at a deliberate pace. "Cold water causes the body's reflex systems to slow and the vasculature of the skin to narrow, hence drawing blood away from the surface. This, in turn, lowers body temperature and in effect allows you to enter a state of hibernation that it takes rapid rewarming to bring you out of. Hypothermia is a fantastic protective mechanism when one is overly tired." He stopped, bent and looked Blythe square in the face. "Wouldn't you agree?"

The RAF pilot glowered at Burke but remained silent.

Burke continued circling like a buzzard around a feast of fresh desert carrion. "However, warm water is much more effective for what I have in mind. Warm water causes a relaxation of the muscles, but it enhances blood flow and expands the vasculature. That brings blood to the skin, causes a rise in pulse, but a decrease in blood pressure."

Burke stopped in front of Blyth once more and performed a perfunctory about-face similar to that performed by the goose-steppers of the SS, although Burke held nothing but contempt for that group. He didn't hold with their ideals of book burning and the pursuit of baser, carnal instincts. He considered them nothing more than bloodthirsty fanatics with no respect for human life or the sciences. From the beginning, Burke had made it clear to his members the goals of the Germanic Freedom Railroad were much higher.

"The salt, of course, is to improve electrical conductivity," Burke concluded with a death's-head smile. "Just like any mineral in the body, such as magnesium and potassium, sodium greatly enhances the ability to move electrical impulses through the body."

Burke nodded at the guard, who picked up one of the pails and immediately doused Blythe with the warm water. His expression told Burke he wanted to scream, to lash out in anger, but his dignity and training wouldn't permit it. That was good—that was very good, in fact, because Burke planned to enjoy this. Neither he nor his men considered themselves barbarians, in fact quite the opposite. Most of them saw themselves as gentlemen, aristocrats in an army of problem solvers. So what if some of them happened to be skilled in the arts of warfare; some were scientists and others business people. The culmination of their skills made the GFR stronger as a whole. That was the whole idea.

The guard put Blythe's manacled feet in the other pail, then stood back with a smile of satisfaction while Burke produced a long, slender cylinder with a pair of rectangular contacts at one end and an insulated handle at the other.

"And now, good Group Captain Blythe," Burke began. "Where shall we begin?"

A SOFT RAP SOUNDED at the door of McCarter's room in the guest house just as he zipped into the jeans provided by Stony Man.

The Phoenix Force warrior tucked his 9 mm Browning Hi-Power pistol into his waistband where it met the small of his back, shrugged into a flannel shirt, then padded barefoot to the door. He slid aside the old-fashioned, oval-shaped metal piece that covered the monstrous viewing hole and muttered a greeting loud enough to be heard but quiet enough not to betray his accent.

A round-headed face with a square jaw filled the view. The man grunted as a reply and held up credentials identifying him as Otto Volkner, an officer with

Interpol. McCarter demanded to see the identification of the man who accompanied Volkner before allowing both to enter the room. He closed and bolted the door behind them, then waved toward the adjoining bedroom as he dropped into the wing-backed chair and quickly donned socks and shoes.

McCarter immediately followed them into the room where they were keeping the prisoner, buttoning his shirt on the go. "There he is, and he's all yours."

Volkner looked at the snoring form of a man stretched across the bed, then looked at McCarter. His voice had a heavy Bavarian accent. "This man has been drugged."

"Only a tranquilizer to keep him still until you could take him off our hands, mate," McCarter said. "My guy says he's fine. That drug should wear off in another hour or two."

"It will not be easy for us to take him out of here without drawing a significant amount of attention. Our orders were to remain as inconspicuous as possible."

"We can give you a hand," McCarter assured him. "Is there a back way out of here?"

Volkner frowned but turned and nodded to his partner, who silently left the room, probably to bring their car around back. McCarter gestured for Volkner to wait, then went into the other room and called the adjoining suite where Encizo and James waited. He'd sent Manning, who spoke German, to acquire some food and other sundries they might need—especially in light of the fact they had no idea how long they would have to spend here. Hawkins had decided to go with him.

James picked up on the first ring. *"Ja?"*

"If you're trying to sound like a native, I'd tell you to keep practicing," McCarter quipped.

"Sorry, don't seem to have my Jive-to-German dictionary handy," James countered.

"Need you two to hop over here and give the blokes from IHOP a hand with our friend."

James immediately picked up McCarter's American code word for Interpol. They were being especially careful in their unsecured communications, since they had no idea who might be watching or listening.

"We'll be over in a sec," James replied. He hung up.

The pair showed up two minutes later and yanked their sleeping prisoner from the bed. The guy didn't so much as stir. James got under one arm, Encizo under the other, and Volkner led them out the door. McCarter decided to tag along, just in case they had problems or needed a substitute. He took up the rear position, watchful for anyone who inadvertently observed their movements. As it was going on evening, he didn't expect to see anybody. McCarter could hardly have called Rodenbach small, but they had wound up in an older section of the town, and it seemed they rolled up the sidewalks by 1700 hours.

They took the elevator to the ground floor. Fortunately the doors opened onto a hallway not viewable from the front desk, so the men were able to get their prisoner out the back entrance unobserved. A Citroën idled at the back, Volkner's partner waiting behind the wheel. Volkner opened the door so Encizo and James could get their burden into the back, then closed the door and climbed into the front with his partner.

As the vehicle pulled away, McCarter reached under his shirt for the Hi-Power. "Stop them!"

All three men whipped their sidearms into play and aimed at the retreating sedan.

CHAPTER EIGHT

Hermann Schwarz used his foot to edge open the hotel room door enough to slip inside with an armload of Chinese takeout.

Blancanales sat on a love seat in the main living area, his bandaged arm propped on a pillow and both feet on an ottoman, engrossed in some history program on the Vietnam war. Lyons sat at a nearby table, going through files on his personal digital assistant.

Schwarz placed the containers on a nearby kitchen bar. "Having a little trouble, Ironman?"

"Stupid machine," Lyons rumbled. He dropped the PDA on the table in resignation and launched from the chair on a straight-line course for the food.

"Yeah, get a little food in your stomach," Schwarz said. "I'll work it out later for you."

"What were you doing, anyway?" Blancanales asked, only now seeming to take interest in Lyons's plight, although he'd probably been half listening to Lyons gripe the entire time.

The big ex-cop ignored the question in favor of pawing through the thick-paper containers. He opened each one unceremoniously, couldn't appear to make up his mind and finally settled on one helping of each. He dumped more than half the contents on the set of plastic plates Schwarz had acquired with the food, doused all with soy sauce, then returned to the table.

Schwarz started to make a quick plate of fried rice and sweet-and-sour pork for Blancanales, but the man climbed from his roost and raised his good arm. "Thanks but no thanks, Gadgets. I'm not crippled. I'll do for me."

Schwarz shrugged, piled on some more fried pork and sauce, grabbed three egg rolls and dashed from the serving area. "Suit yourself."

Blancanales and Schwarz soon were sprawled across the couch. They'd killed the television and discussed their options. So far, Lyons hadn't made much of the information Stony Man had relayed to them. While it had proved useful to know about Delmico's connections to Burke and the Germanic Freedom Railroad, it still didn't explain the Arab gunmen, or why they had wanted to spirit away Delmico.

"I think their theory's pretty plausible," Blancanales said.

"Which part?" Schwarz asked.

"About the GFR's relationship with al Qaeda terrorist sects. Think about it. They hire Delmico to produce some type of chemical pathogen they plan to distribute with the LAMPs."

"Yeah, but why snatch Delmico?" Lyons asked. "Obviously his pathogen works. What else do they need him for? Why not just snuff him out?"

"Who knows? Maybe they didn't know he'd perfected the formula yet. Maybe the terrorists got a whiff of us and tried to protect Delmico. Maybe that isn't the way the GFR operates."

"Yeah, maybe they feel bad because Delmico's got a mother," Schwarz offered.

Lyons chuckled sardonically. "Everyone's got a mother, Gadgets."

"Yeah, everyone except you," Schwarz quipped while jerking his head in Lyons's direction.

"Stop it," Blancanales cautioned. "You'll hurt his feelings."

"Why don't both of you knock it off?" Lyons snapped.

Schwarz batted his eyelashes at the Able Team leader.

"Anyway," Lyons continued, "good theory or not, it doesn't put us closer to finding Delmico."

"Maybe it does," Blancanales said.

"Uh-oh," Schwarz said, eyeing his friend with a suspicious glance. "I see those wheels turning."

Blancanales smiled. "Whatever happened, if our Arab friends are connected with the GFR in any way, they had to have known we were onto them."

"You **think** something spooked them?" Lyons asked.

Blancanales nodded. "Think about it, boys. Those guys sent not one, but two separate details to pull off the job. That says they knew someone was onto Delmico, and that someone was us. They probably had his test subjects watched, also."

"Makes sense," Schwarz agreed. He looked at Lyons.

"If they saw us show up at the hospital asking questions, it might have made them nervous enough to snatch Delmico right out from under the GFR's nose."

"So let's say you're right," Lyons said. "What next? I suppose you have a plan?"

"Yep!" Blancanales beamed triumphantly. "It seems we're not finished here. If there's any chance of us finding Delmico alive, we're going to have to rattle enough cages so they're forced to come after us."

Schwarz lifted his eyebrows. "And just how do you propose to do that?"

"Well, it won't be easy to locate the terrorists, but we can sure as hell start a manhunt for the chemicals he was using. Somehow he managed to expose those two kids to this pathogen. In all likelihood, he'll have to go back to the school or to his house."

"Or at least he'll have to send his people to get it," Lyons said.

"Exactly. And when they do, we'll be ready for them."

"Searching the campus area could take some time."

"Not really," Schwarz countered. "In fact, there are only a limited number of places he could do that kind of work. Think about the lab equipment he'd need, not to mention a place to grow a bacterial pathogen, space and materials to construct the delivery mechanism, yada, yada, yada."

"That's a good point," Blancanales added.

"Okay, but where——" Lyons began, but the ringing phone on his belt cut him off.

"Yeah," he said into the mouthpiece of the cellular phone with secured satellite communications capability direct to Stony Man Farm. After a minute of listening, he nodded and said, "Got it. And thanks, Barb. Out, here."

"What's up?" Schwarz inquired.

"It looks like we aren't going to have to go far to find that stuff after all," Lyons said. "There were just seven more reported outbreaks from students at Washington U."

"Damn," Blancanales said through clenched teeth. "The stuff is a contagion?"

"Looks like," Lyons said. "The Farm wants us to get to the campus and find this pathogen, and real quick."

ONE SECOND.

That's how long it took for Calvin James and Rafael Encizo to respond to McCarter's command to open fire on the retreating Citroën. The men of Phoenix Force had learned never to question an order in the heat of battle, no matter how absurd it might seem. The pair reacted with admirable speed and opened up judiciously but responsibly with their pistols. Three neatly placed rounds entered each rear tire and brought the vehicle to a skidding halt.

Volkner and his partner burst from the sedan but neither had to contend with the trio pointing pistols at them. The squad of five armed men who jumped from various points of cover scattered throughout the courtyard rear of the guest house demanded more immediate attention. The Phoenix Force trio obliged them with a response equal to the task.

Calvin James tracked on the closest gunner, who had burst from the door of an exterior storage unit bearing an SKS, and squeezed off a double-tap from his Glock

Model 26. One of the 9 mm hardball slugs blew out the guy's left lung while the second punched through his upper lip and crushed bone against the back of his head. The impact spun him into the door he'd used for partial cover and he bounced off and hit the ground flat on his back.

Encizo got the next gunner spraying their area wildly with 9 mm rounds from an Uzi. The Cuban warrior delivered a single shot from his own Glock. The .45-caliber round struck the man's chest. Under high pressure from the cavitation of the bullet, blood spewed from the enemy gunman's mouth and he pitched forward, landing face-first, his lifeless corpse unable to react to the fall.

McCarter ordered his teammates to grab cover as three more of the gunners opened up with a variety of SMGs. The Phoenix Force leader could see Volkner and his partner trying to get their prisoner out of the car, but he could do little about it at that point. Self-preservation had to be the priority. Toward that end, McCarter found cover behind a nearby trash bin and grabbed his first target. The Briton snap-aimed at a terrorist who had broken cover for better position, led him by no more than an inch with the muzzle of the Browning Hi-Power and squeezed the trigger. Modified by John "Cowboy" Kissinger—Stony Man's chief armorer and gunsmith extraordinaire—the semiautomatic pistol had long been a favorite of McCarter's. It proved rather effective here as all three 9 mm semijacketed hollow point rounds caught the guy in the stomach. The gunman performed an awkward tumble and then lay still.

Welcome relief came through the entrance at the opposite end of the courtyard in the forms of Manning and Hawkins. The big Canadian drew a bead on one of the gunners McCarter couldn't see from his position, and popped off two shots. Manning's Walther P-5, a weapon McCarter knew the Canadian trusted implicitly, did the job nicely. Manning didn't slow a step as he continued toward the vehicle.

McCarter, James and Encizo left cover and approached the Citroën from their end, intent on boxing Volkner and his partner before they could escape with their human prize. Hawkins covered their movements against the remaining gunner by pumping out a series of successive shots from his Beretta. Smoke flashed from the barrel with each whip-crack report as Hawkins dispatched the man with 9 mm rounds to the chest and head. The gunman staggered under the shots and then fell into a nearby flower bed.

All pistols now trained on the Volkner and company.

"Stand down!" McCarter ordered them.

Volkner and his partner dropped their weapons and raised their hands. The Phoenix Force warriors converged on the vehicle. McCarter and Hawkins kept their pistols pointed at the phony Interpol officers while Manning disarmed them and then patted them down for additional arms. Encizo and James hurried to the prisoner—James quickly checking him over for any serious injuries—then placed the unconscious man on the back seat with his legs protruding from the open back door.

Encizo turned to McCarter. "How the hell did you—"

"Two things, mate," the Briton cut in with a wry

grin. "Interpol SOP says at least one escort in back. Considering our friend there wasn't even handcuffed, it seemed strange they'd throw him into the back of their car and both jump up front."

"And the other?" James asked, obviously as amazed as Encizo at McCarter's remarkable perceptions.

McCarter went to the vehicle and slapped the trunk a few times. "This is a brand-new Citroën. Interpol's central European vehicle contractor is VW, and has been for years."

"How in tarnation would you know that?" Hawkins asked.

"They don't let him out much," Manning quipped.

McCarter flashed his friends a brief smile, then walked purposefully to Volkner, grabbed the man by the collar, and pulled him up to his height so they were nose to nose and Volkner had to stand on his toes.

"Who sent you?" McCarter asked.

Volkner's eyes revealed his fear, but he kept silent. McCarter looked at him another moment, then released the man. They didn't have time to conduct an interrogation here. At best, the real Interpol agents would arrive soon to take the prisoner off their hands, and the Phoenix Force leader knew they wouldn't have time to question them then.

"Get these clowns into the car," McCarter ordered Encizo and James. "Get them away from here for the time being. We'll take sleeping beauty here back to the room until the real Interpol agents come for him."

"So much for keeping out of sight and out of trouble," James told Encizo as he waved their two impostors into the Citroën. "Now we've got twice as much to worry about."

"We'll get it figured out," Encizo replied.

"Maybe next time, we should give the Interpol guys the password," Manning said as he and Hawkins each got under one arm of their prisoner and started dragging him toward the rear entrance.

"*And* teach them the secret handshake," Hawkins added.

ABLE TEAM ARRIVED at Washington University within a half hour of the call from Stony Man. They proceeded straight to the administrative offices to consult with the dean and president of the college, along with a number of the advisers. Dr. Corvasce also happened to be present to advise, along with members of the CDC, a representative from FEMA and a pair of investigators with the St. Louis PD.

The president of the college, a tall and distinguished-looking black man named Wilford Johnson, opened the meeting. "I'd like to thank each of you for taking time to be here. While I'm sure we all have questions about what's happening, I would ask that we keep those questions to a minimum until the end of this meeting. I would like to turn the chair over to Dr. Michael Corvasce to get us started."

Corvasce nodded, stood and cleared his throat. "Approximately forty-eight hours ago, two students from this campus were admitted to our hospital under the care of myself and a colleague. We've been carefully monitoring their respective conditions, which I can assure you grow worse by the hour."

A middle-aged, red-haired woman from the CDC raised her hand. "I apologize for interrupting, but I was wondering if you could be a little more specific about what you mean by 'worse.'"

Corvasce sighed, looked at the table and replied, "In short, they're dying. Neither I nor the consulting specialists think these boys will survive the night."

Blancanales saw silent expressions of mixed emotion in the faces ranged around the conference table. These things were never easy, especially when they involved young people. For a moment Blancanales began to wonder if his idea of waiting for the terrorists to come to them had any true merit. In the past, they had always been able to locate the targets, isolate them and do whatever needed to be done to neutralize the threat. This particular situation had him and his teammates a little worried since they didn't really have anything to go on. And biological weapons didn't make it easy to isolate and minimize danger to the innocent bystanders.

"Well, we don't exactly know yet what to tell the parents of the additional students who have now been exposed," said Lieutenant Maebrook of the SLPD's Special Crimes squad. "And they're getting testy without answers."

Bruce Stratton of FEMA spoke up. "I would like to know how this could even happen. And why it's happening."

"And I'd like to know why the local CDC office wasn't informed sooner about this," the red-haired woman said.

Blancanales squinted to see her name tag read Erma Something-or-Other.

"Hold on, folks," Johnson finally interjected, waving his arms. "Now, we're going to have an orderly meeting if nothing else. Why don't we give Dr. Corvasce a chance to finish?"

"That's about all I really have," Corvasce said. He looked in Able Team's direction for help. "I've already explained more of the medical details to these three gentlemen from the FBI. Perhaps they could expand on what I've said in a more practical way. A lot of medical jargon won't buy us the answers we need unless there's something there we've missed, and I doubt that."

This almost caused Blancanales to smile as Corvasce took his seat, but the opportunity was immediately lost to Maebrook. The big, lanky cop had struck all three of Able Team's members as kind of a jerk, especially after encountering him earlier in the day.

"Yeah, I for one would like to hear if you fellas have any insight myself," Maebrook said with a cocky look. He dropped his notebook and pen on the table, sat back and interlocked his hands behind his head. "Do we have another government foul-up on our hands?"

"Knock it off," Lyons said before Blancanales could open his mouth. "You don't know any more than we do, pal, so don't pretend like you've got all the answers."

Blancanales figured it better to move in before the two men started tossing hooks. Guys like Maebrook had a tendency to rub him and Schwarz the wrong way, but they made Lyons absolutely livid. The Able Team leader didn't like bureaucrats, and he couldn't tolerate mouthy cops. He'd spent many years as a disciplined LAPD detective; he expected the same level of professionalism from any other law-enforcement professional.

"All right, why don't we all just relax," Blancanales said. "I'll be happy to tell you what we know within the boundaries allowed us. We suspect that all of the students who are sick have been exposed to a pathogen of some kind, and that pathogen may have been created by Simon Delmico."

"God help us all," Wilford Johnson murmured.

Arthur Higbee, Dean of Students, shook his head. "No. I refuse to believe that. I've known Simon since he started here. He's a fine man and an outstanding teacher."

"He was also the subject of ridicule by many of your students, sir," Blancanales countered. "No disrespect to your friendship is intended when I say that, but the profile we have on him says he's quite capable of doing something like this. Do you know the circumstances surrounding his dismissal from the Department of Defense?"

It was Johnson who spoke up. "We thoroughly investigated that. It was ruled an accident. And the injuries Dr. Delmico suffered did not permit him to return to work."

Blancanales lent them a half smile. "If that's what you've been told, then I guess that will have to be good enough for me. But what I can tell you is that Simon Delmico not only possesses the expertise to do this, but he also has a strong motive."

"And recently we've gathered intelligence that ties him to members of a criminal organization in Europe," Lyons added.

Murmurs ran through the room at his announcement. Blancanales held up a hand for quiet. "This may all sound far-fetched to you, perhaps even preposterous, but we're telling you the truth."

"Those men outside your science building this morning, the ones who attacked us and took Dr. Delmico," Lyons said. "Well, they were the real deal, folks."

"Some of these European criminals?" asked Maebrook's partner.

Lyons shook his head. "We think they're members of Hezbollah."

"There are two theories we have right now," Blancanales continued. "One, the terrorists are blackmailing Delmico to make this pathogen, or two, they're paying him to make it. Either way, everything leads back to him right now. He's the best lead we have."

"So what are you proposing we do about this?" Higbee asked.

"Shut down that science building," Lyons said. "In fact, seal it off. We can't afford any more exposures."

"We've already canceled classes," Johnson replied.

He turned to Erma. "What kind of support can we expect from your people as far as containment procedures, decontamination, that sort of thing? I don't want or need a panicked student body."

"You may already have that, once word spreads," she replied. "We can do a lot to protect anyone from further exposure, but rumor control is hardly something in our domain."

"We're not interested in negating culpability," Higbee said. "We just want to prevent the spread of this thing."

Before anyone else could speak, the door burst open and Johnson's secretary rushed in. A sweaty sheen covered her face, and she looked as if she'd seen a ghost. "I'm very sorry to interrupt, sir, but we have another situation at the science building."

Most everyone at the table came immediately to their feet.

"What kind of situation?" Johnson asked. "More exposures? I ordered that area of the campus sealed off."

"No, sir!" she replied. "There are men with guns...not the like the men from earlier. They're...they're not Arabs, I mean!"

Lyons looked straight at Maebrook as Able Team stood. "Call for backup! Now!"

CHAPTER NINE

Barbara Price poured a cup of coffee, then sat in front of the computer terminal in her office.

Her contacts at the National Security Agency had completed forwarding additional information to her less than an hour earlier, but the recent events in St. Louis had prevented her from reading it until now. Price took a sip of her coffee, made a face, then set the cup on her desk and began to review the transmitted data.

She first began to study the schematics of the LAMP. An impressive feat of engineering, to be sure, and the discovery of its capabilities as a hovercraft had been quite accidental. They worked on a principle of magnetic opposites. The Large Hadron Collector project devised by particle physicists at CERN—combined with the sheer size of the magnets—had triggered an unstable reaction causing metal objects to be repelled from the collector at tremendous velocity. Unlike a magnetic resonance image scanner in a hospital, which actually caused metal objects to be drawn to it, the LAMP magnets operated with certain metal alloys in such a way that it provided midair flotation between ten and three hundred yards from the ground. The altitude of the object could be controlled, some of the CERN students discovered, through the use of harmonic pulses transmitted at a very specific frequency combined with the speed of those pulses. The shorter the span between pulses, measurable in terahertz, the higher the LAMP would go. Only limitations in pulse transmission technology prevented the object from achieving higher altitudes.

Price found the speed of the LAMP even more impressive, nearly 200 mph under a miniaturized jet engine. Of course, a jet engine as primary means of propulsion proved impractical due to weight and distance limitations; hence, CERN's decision to turn the project over to scientists of the RAF. Unfortunately the LAMP systems hadn't made their intended destination, and Phoenix Force happened to be literally the closest in terms of a team that could reliably get inside German territory relatively unmolested and locate the downed SOF C-141 Starlifter.

Price looked up at a rap on the door frame, and Hal Brognola waved as he walked into the room. "How's it going?"

"I just started to look over the material from my NSA contacts," she said. "This stuff is pretty fascinating, although some of it goes right over my head. I'm sure Aaron would be better able to decipher it."

Brognola shrugged as he dropped into a chair in front of her desk. "He might be better able to understand the technical angles, but *you're* the one I trust to find that one breakthrough that'll get things moving."

"Well, I have pulled one gem from it already."

"That's my Barb," Brognola said. "What do you have?"

"A few years ago, CERN picked up a boatload of summer interns. It's a pretty standard pattern, really. They're always trying to find the best and the brightest, the next Fermi or Einstein. You'll never believe who one of those students happened to be."

"Oh, let me guess," Brognola interjected. "Choldwig Burke?"

"Give the man a cigar."

Brognola pulled the sopped, unlit one from his mouth and said, "Already got one."

"Anyway, Burke was apparently involved in some of the initial experiments with the LHC project. But then he dropped out, citing a desire to pursue other interests in particle physics."

"But obviously he never forgot about the LAMPs."

"That, and the fact he just happens to surface in Wiesbaden last year and contacts Simon Delmico, makes him suspect numero uno, in my book."

"Mine, too," Brognola replied. "What else?"

"Well, the LAMPs were more or less transferred in serviceable condition."

"Meaning?"

Price sat back, touched her index fingers to her lip and replied in a deliberate fashion, "Meaning they could very well be configured as fully operational without much effort. The biggest problem seems to be a practical means of propulsion."

"In what way?"

"Well, most conventional avenues of thrust haven't proved successful. The weight required by a jet system, for example, is much too heavy to afford any additions to the platform, not to mention difficult to control. Lighter methods like a combustion engine or air jets are either not powerful enough, not fast enough or too costly from a maintenance perspective."

"That doesn't leave many options."

"Nope," Price agreed. "My contacts in the technical center are all stumped. But I did get a report from an old college friend at MIT who happens to specialize in aerodynamic engineering. He said the most efficient way to power a vehicle like this would be with a helicopter turbine. Something equipped with a miniature Pratt & Whitney power plant, for example, could easily be retrofitted to the thing. You see, he reminded me we could negate power requirements for gaining altitude. When you remove that factor, and consider the tail rotors of most conventional choppers today utilize only seven to eight percent of total power requirements, that leaves you with only needing enough power to control pitch, yaw and hover."

"This friend of yours has you talking like a Navy aviator," Brognola cracked.

"Maybe, but he knows his stuff. Moreover, he reminded me that simple turning of the turbines could also be used to provide secondary electrical power sources for additional instrumentation or even a subsidy magnetic field."

"Which could increase the overall effectiveness of

the LAMP," Brognola concluded. "And you think it wouldn't take anything for our friends in the GFR to modify these things such that they could actually become operational?"

"No doubts at all. Especially if a guy with Burke's credentials is behind it. He could certainly summon the right talent for the right price."

"I think there's little doubt about Burke and the GFR's involvement."

Price raised an eyebrow. "I take it Aaron found you some juicy tidbits, then."

"More than that," Brognola said. "Good, hard intelligence. Some time ago, not long after Israel began its attacks on Lebanon, the Hezbollah leadership apparently approached parties unknown for the purpose of providing sanctuary to a number of their cell leaders. This leads me to believe one of those men was Mukhtar Tarif."

"Of the Kadils Tarif bin Nurraji sect?" Price asked.

"One and the same."

Price leaned back and tried to rub away some of the sudden ache in her temples. She could already feel a migraine coming on. She knew that crowd all too well, and now she wished Brognola hadn't told her. The Tarif clan had passed its terrorist activities from generation to generation, with a visible start in the early seventies and into the official paramilitary wing formed in 1982 to fight Israeli Defense Forces occupation. Tarif's family had poured its earnings of blood-money into publication of the *Qubth Ut Alla*—a monthly magazine literally translated as "The Fist of God"—and their television and radio propaganda in at least a half dozen nations supporting the radical implementation of Shia Islam ideologies.

"Nearly every American intelligence agency has tied the Tarif family to one or more terrorist acts committed directly against the United States," Price finally said.

"Mukhtar Tarif's father also has enough clout and funds to solicit the help of an organization like the GFR," Brognola replied.

"I know, but it just doesn't make a lot of sense. Radical Arab groups like Hezbollah and mercenaries of the Germanic Freedom Railroad working together? It almost seems absurd, and yet all the evidence so far points to it."

Brognola shrugged. "Maybe Burke didn't have any choice. Maybe he needed the money. Whatever the reason, there's one of two possibilities—either Tarif hired him to steal the LAMPs, or he did it on his own and he's got some other plan up his sleeve. Either way, we've confirmed Hezbollah involvement. We just got the data from the computers at the OME in St. Louis, and one of the deceased that ran up against Able Team earlier was positively identified as not only Hezbollah but a known associate of the Kadils Tarif bin Nurraji sect."

"I'd say that's proof positive," Price agreed. "So what do you think it means?"

"Well, Aaron and I had actually worked through a scenario I think hits pretty close to the mark. There's every indicator the Tarif family hired the GFR to keep young Mukhtar out of trouble. Because Burke's operation has always been small, I think he bit off more than he could chew this time. I think it ended up costing him every dime he had, and he stole the LAMPs either in the hope of selling to the highest bidder or configuring them for use against some target."

"Yes, but *what* target?"

"That's what we need to find out," Brognola said, getting to his feet. "As soon as you've finished here, I want you to contact David and—"

The ringing extension cut him off and Price immediately grabbed it. "Yes? Put him through." She covered the phone and mouthed "David" at Brognola, who immediately took his seat again. She then placed the phone on speaker and replaced the handset. "David, it's Barbara and Hal here. What do you have?"

"You're not going to like it," McCarter replied. "Another group of GFR goons just ambushed us. This time, they were posing as Interpol."

"Not good," she said. "That means they're onto you."

"It would seem so. What do you want us to do?"

"Hal and I were just here talking," she said. "We're pretty sure that Choldwig Burke's your man. We also think you might have more trouble than you'd bargained for. I won't beat around the bush. The crew Able Team ran into in St. Louis has been positively identified as belonging to Hezbollah."

"Marvelous."

"We think things will get worse before they get better," she added.

"Which is your polite way of saying these may not be our only visitors," McCarter said.

"Right."

"Got a couple of their boys here," McCarter said.

"We *had* thought about turning them over to Interpol, but now maybe we should let them fly and see where it takes us."

"That's probably the best course of action, since now we can't be sure what you're up against. Obviously, you've been compromised."

Brognola interjected, "David, I think it's time to take the fight straight to the source. Effective immediately, I'm authorizing you to use whatever means at your disposal. Figure out what the GFR is up to, where they're at and neutralize them. Permanently. Ditto for any Hezbollah you may and most probably will encounter. If you can recover the LAMPs intact, that's a bonus, but termination of either or both of these groups and their activities is your first and only mission objective."

"Right," McCarter replied. "We wouldn't have it any other way."

MUKHTAR TARIF HAD murder in his heart.

He clapped the receiver of his cellular phone to the closed position and cursed under his breath. His father had ordered him to remain out of sight and not cause any trouble. While he believed his father's promise to take care of Choldwig Burke in a due and convenient season, Tarif's other plans were taking a back seat. He possessed neither the patience nor tolerance for this sort of thing. Only a short time remained before the genesis of their mission. With each passing hour his family remained undecided on the most obvious course of action, he became more impatient to act. Soon, he would lose complete control of Burke and only empty vanity would remain.

Tarif stood in front of a window that overlooked the forest bordering Wiesbaden. According to the latest reports, his men had managed to steal out of St. Louis and stow the captive in Hillsboro, a small town about forty miles south of the American metropolis. Tarif's father had assured him the microbiologist would be isolated and the Americans wouldn't think to look for him there. Tarif didn't doubt it, but he couldn't say he felt the same about Burke. He'd judged their German benefactor as an egotist and bigot whose alleged higher education had somehow managed to get the better of him. The fact Tarif had to wait in such proximity to a man he found distasteful didn't make things easier.

Tarif's life hadn't been easy. His father insisted he attend some of the finest schools throughout Germany and Italy so that he could interact intelligently in various European circles of influence, particularly in the area of academics. Once Tarif developed a reputation as a peace-loving and educated man, his father then sent him to secret training camps nestled in rugged wilderness outside of Kabul and other such areas of strife and constant conflict. The completion of those eighteen months taught him to survive in the harshest environments, the arts of guerrilla warfare and how to outthink the enemy.

This combination made him as deadly as someone coming from Choldwig Burke's background, and probably more so. All of that training had also caused him to devise one of the cleverest plots schemed by Hezbollah. For a number of years now, Burke had made quite a name in his smuggling operations and served as confidant to some the finest of the jihad's warriors. Unfortunately, Burke had also let that fact go to his head.

"It will be too bad for him." Tarif spoke to his adviser and bodyguard, Harb, in their own language. It wouldn't do to have one of Burke's cronies overhear any conversations. Not that he might not have an interpreter listening, although Tarif doubted he'd be that bright.

"Who? Choldwig Burke?"

Tarif spun on his heel and pinned Harb with a flat look. "Of course Burke. Who else?"

Tarif shoved his hands in the pockets of his tailored slacks and paced in front of the large window overlooking the darkened industrial complex of Wiesbaden. "He's too stupid and arrogant to know what we have in store for him."

"There's been talk," Harb said. "Several of the men have overheard Burke's people talking of moving from here and heading to an alternate location."

"Did they say where?"

"I cannot be certain, but from what I've been told it sounds like Munich."

Tarif shook his head with disgust. Movement by a group that size would only complicate matters and draw unnecessary attention to their operations. No, it would actually draw unnecessary attention to *his* operations. It didn't seem Burke had any more of a solid plan now than when they had first approached him for assistance. Nothing ate at Tarif more than indecision. His training had taught him indecision cost money and lives, and time came as a valuable commodity in his line of work.

"I think we're going to have to move on our own."

"That would be unwise," Harb replied. "You would be acting in direct contradiction to your father's orders. He does not tolerate disobedience. I worked many years for him before you grew up and he assigned me to protect you. You should trust my counsel on this matter."

Tarif turned and studied his bodyguard and friend. It was true. He had known Harb since childhood. The man had started as a rather low-ranking soldier in his father's house, but quickly moved up the ranks until appointed head of the younger Tarif's security contingent. He had also served as a loyal adviser and was a friend.

"You know I trust you implicitly," Tarif said. "But the longer we wait, the more we risk our position here. We should prepare ourselves for moving to my backup plan."

"You know I am here to serve you," Harb said. "But I am telling you I think you're making a mistake. And your father is not a forgiving man."

Tarif felt his face flush, but he kept his anger in check. Firmly he replied, "Your first loyalty and obedience is to me, not my father. Are we clear?"

"Of course."

"Excellent. With that understood, I want you to collaborate with our people. Contact all of the men here, as well as those that Burke has hiding in the alternate locations. Tell them only what they need to know. I don't want this getting back into Burke's ears."

"It shall be done, Mukhtar."

"So it shall, my friend." Tarif couldn't suppress a grin. "So it shall."

WELBY BLYTHE'S HEAD LOLLED forward and his eyes rolled back into his head.

Choldwig Burke stepped forward and felt for a pulse at the carotid artery. He found it, albeit thready and weak. Burke whirled to the guards and ordered them to take Blythe to the nearby infirmary for nutritional supplements and fluids. A day or two of rest, and Blythe would be stable enough to start the interrogation again. For the last time, anyway. If he didn't get the information he needed by then, he'd take it as far as he had to. Even if it killed Blythe.

While Burke didn't consider himself a brutal man, he couldn't say he'd come this far by sole reliance on leniency, either. To lead the kind of men he did—mercenaries who weren't fighting for ideology but rather were motivated solely by profit—Burke had to be tough. He had to maintain as much of a corrupted view as his men if he expected to earn their respect and survive, despite any of his personal feelings. His mother had always been a gentle and merciful woman, and part of Burke held on to that precept. Not that he dared to disclose such a thing to anyone else. These cutthroats would have used that knowledge to walk over him a long time ago for the purposes of making everything they could out of the deal.

Burke maintained his realist nature. He wasn't puffed up with ideals of grandeur or how he planned to invent the next world Reich. No, it seemed better to maintain good working relationships with those who had the talents he required, and watch his back for any that might try taking advantage of him.

Right now, Burke knew Mukhtar Tarif stood at the head of that line. He didn't trust the man—never really could find a way to trust him—and now he had even more of a reason to distrust the man. Word had reached him that Tarif knew of his plans to move their operations to the headquarters in Munich. His informants had advised of the capture of his men who had gone to rescue their people from the five foreign specialists who had shown up to claim the booty aboard the plane.

"Burke, I wish to speak with you."

Burke turned at the voice and saw Tarif and his bodyguards approach.

"I've heard you're moving us," Tarif said.

"That's correct," Burke replied, clasping his hand behind his back in an attempt to appear as nonthreatening as possible.

"And when did you plan to inform my people of this?"

"As soon as I knew when we were going to do it," Burke said. "You see, because of the little stunt you ordered your men to pull in America, you have now exposed not only yourselves but me, as well. Therefore, I think you should show me some latitude in these types of decisions."

"Why? We don't owe you anything. You've been well compensated."

"That's true," Burke acknowledged. "But perhaps what you didn't know is that very soon there is a specialized unit of men who will trace us here. And when they come, they will come with the purpose of destroying us. I intend to make sure we're not here, because it is my job to protect you."

Tarif's reply sounded like the hiss of a snake. "We can protect ourselves."

"Your father seems to feel otherwise," Burke replied, raising his eyebrows.

Tarif cocked his head. "You've talked to my father?"

Burke smiled. "Yes. And he's most displeased with the fact you keep circumventing my activities with plans of your own. But that's between you and him. For now, prepare your men to move."

As Burke turned and started to leave, Tarif asked, "And where is it we're going?"

"Munich," Burke replied, without bothering to stop walking.

"One day, Burke, my father will not be here to come between us," Tarif called.

"I look forward to that day," Burke replied.

And he meant it.

CHAPTER TEN

Able Team arrived at the Natural Sciences building on foot.

They could hear the shouts and screams of students still trying to get out of harm's way. It didn't look to Lyons as if anyone had tried to arrange an orderly evacuation.

The trio burst through the front doors with weapons in hand. They waved toward the teenagers who had their hands over their ears, hugging the walls, to move past and to the relative safety of the outdoors. As the hallways cleared, Able Team proceeded in the direction of the shouts and autofire. It didn't take them long to track the noises to their source. Lyons slid up to a closed lab door, risked a glance through the small, frame window of wire-mesh glass and spotted the bloody, bullet-riddled bodies of several students spread across desks or in the rows between them. He quickly assessed the enemy numbers.

He looked to his teammates. "I count five, two with SMGs, the rest with semiautos."

Schwarz nodded. "Let's take it to them."

Lyons looked at Blancanales, who nodded in agreement. He reached down to try the door handle, which turned smoothly and noiselessly. He ripped it open and burst inside the massive lab room.

The pair with the SMGs was positioned immediately in front of a long, wide counter with a black top. The other three riffled through secured metal cabinets and refrigerated safes. They shot off locks on any that were secured. All five wore street clothes. Not even the swarthiest of the bunch looked Middle Eastern—they were Caucasians all the way, probably European.

Lyons took the first man with a well-placed shot from his Anaconda. The big .44 Magnum pistol echoed a thunderous report as it delivered a slug through the man's forehead. The heavy-caliber load did its job, splitting the man's cranium wide open and taking a good part of his brain as it passed through. The gunman left his feet and slammed into the countertop before he landed violently on his stomach.

Blancanales got the other SMG-toting hardman. He snap-aimed the SIG P-239 and triggered a double-tap that connected with the man's sternum and throat. A wash of bubbly blood doused the front of the man's shirt. He was dead before he hit his knees and fell awkwardly onto his back.

Schwarz moved ahead of his partners as they put out covering fire. He triggered the Beretta 92-F on the run in an attempt to neutralize the remaining three aggressors. While their enemy moved like trained combatants, they obviously hadn't counted on going up against skilled men like Able Team. Schwarz got one of them with his first series of shots. Twin 9 mm Parabellum rounds drilled through one gunman's chest. The man pitched forward as his weapon flew from numb fingers.

The other pair split in opposite directions for cover, but the brittle wood-panel cabinetry wouldn't cut it. As Schwarz rounded the corner of the main counter, glass shattered around his head and at his feet. The Able Team warrior hadn't noticed the score of glass vials and beakers sitting along the stretch of shelf above his head, as well as resting on a ledge just below the level of the countertop. A pungent odor—like ammonia mixed with bleach—stung his nostrils. He began to cough and hack as the room immediately filled with a green-white haze. Within a moment or two, the cloud began to spread through the room and it obviously contained large enough particulates to set off the fire-suppression systems. Water immediately began to pour from the ceiling as fire alarms and warning Klaxons echoed through the room and down the halls.

Schwarz managed to get past the initial shock of the gases pretty quickly, but his eyes itched and he rubbed at them. The entire ordeal disoriented him for a moment or two. Then he felt a strong grip on his arm, and he turned to see Lyons's profile. The Able Team leader assisted Schwarz out the door. He could barely see but he heard the frenetic urgings of Blancanales counseling them to get the hell away from the place as quickly as they could.

They got into the hallway and bumped square into Maebrook with a unit of a half dozen heavily armed SWAT officers in full body armor. The detective wore a fully visible bulletproof vest and a glittering gold shield dangled from his neck. He studied the Able Team trio a moment, then ordered his men to fan out.

"We need to get out of here." Schwarz managed to get the words out between gasps.

"What's up?"

"There's a chemical spill in that room," Lyons said. "And it's not pretty. Get the building evacuated."

Maebrook's expression soured. "I don't remember your name on my paycheck."

"Let's leave all the posturing and territorialism for another time, gentlemen," Blancanales said. "Let's get out of here before we wind up in a hospital."

"I'll order my men to don their PPE before proceeding further," Maebrook replied. "But we're mandated to make sure this building is clear of civilians before we leave."

Blancanales understood. "Just don't dawdle."

In moments Lyons and Blancanales were on the move again with Schwarz between them, and they reached the exit in less than a minute. From that distance the men could no longer detect the horrific odor of mixed chemicals. Just outside the building the police had cordoned off the entire area. The total pandemonium of the past ten minutes had settled into an organized emergency response. Fire trucks, HAZMAT units and police cruisers had semicircled the campus at a distance of one hundred yards in every direction. Barricades and caution tape were up, and men were suited into protective gear. Sirens of additional responding personnel wailed in the distance.

"Looks like Maebrook pulled out all the stops," Lyons noted.

Schwarz smiled weakly. "Got to hand it to the guy for being prepared."

"This place'll be a media circus in a few minutes," Blancanales observed.

"Well, let's just see to it we keep our mugs off the TV cameras, boys," Lyons muttered.

They got Schwarz into the back of the nearest ambulance, and in no time they were cruising out of the area and headed toward the hospital. Schwarz pulled an oxygen mask from his face and tried to get Lyons and Blancanales to reconsider, but they refused to budge on the subject. There had already been enough injuries shared among them for that week, and Lyons made the command decision that they would all need to be checked out since they had evidence there was a possible biological pathogen at the center of this terrorist plot.

When they arrived at the hospital, Dr. Corvasce stood ready to meet them in the emergency room. He ordered immediate isolation procedures and instructed all three men be shuttled upstairs to the isolation ward. For the next few hours the various hospital staff poked and prodded the trio, collected blood and urine samples, and ran them through all of the standard biological decontamination procedures.

Corvasce finally entered their room nearly four hours later as the Able Team warriors had finished dressing.

They noted a firm set to the physician's mouth and immediately knew he didn't bring good news.

"What's the verdict?" Lyons asked.

Corvasce removed his reading glasses, dropped their files on a nearby suture tray and rubbed his tired eyes. "I'm afraid it isn't what we'd hoped for. You two—" he gestured at Lyons and Blancanales "—come back negative." His face became a grim mask as he looked at Schwarz. "But you, unfortunately, have been exposed to the same pathogen as the sick students."

Blancanales shook his head. "Wait a minute, this doesn't make any sense. How could he have been exposed but we weren't? We were all in the same room."

"It doesn't appear this pathogen can be spread in an aerosol form," Corvasce replied. "I can only conclude that it requires some other delivery mechanism."

Schwarz nodded. "I do remember getting sprayed with something when those bottles and vials got shot all to hell. If I had to hazard a guess, I'd say this particular pathogen works via absorption through direct contact with the skin."

"Doesn't seem very appropriate for its intended use," Blancanales remarked.

"Right," Lyons said. He looked at Corvasce. "According to the information we have so far, we think a group of terrorists planned to use this stuff by aerial spraying from some type of low-altitude hovercraft. Are you certain direct exposure is the only route of administration?"

Corvasce shrugged. "I'm not sure of anything anymore. But eliminating all other possibilities, I'd say there's a pretty good chance of it. I can't really say for sure since I wasn't there. What I *can* tell you is what you already know. You two aren't infected and he is, but as to how that happened, I have no explanation."

"So, if we dismiss intrinsic factors of susceptibility such as age or ethnicity…" Schwarz began.

"Which we can, since none of the infected kids are your age or Hispanic," Blancanales interjected.

Schwarz nodded. "Then the only difference was I actually got sprayed with some of those liquids and you guys didn't."

Lyons said, "And we *all* inhaled the vapors, so we know this thing isn't transmitted through airborne contact." He looked at Corvasce. "Any evidence this can spread from human contact?"

"Not so far."

"Then that leaves a strong argument for direct contact," Blancanales concluded. "It's only by direct absorption of the skin the pathogen is contracted."

"At least that will make it a hell of a lot easier to protect everyone else. And prevent a worse epidemic."

"It still doesn't give us a cure for those who are infected, though."

Schwarz snorted. "That depends on whether Delmico had time to produce an antidote. How long before I start experiencing the debilitating symptoms, Doc?"

"Well, we don't really have a timeline on that yet, since we don't exactly know when our sickest ones were first exposed. But I would estimate no more than forty-eight to seventy-two hours. A lot of it will have to do with your general physical condition."

The doors to the ward suddenly burst open and the

eyes of a nurse in full isolation equipment fell directly on Corvasce. "Doctor, we need you, stat! Mallow just crashed!"

"WELL, WE SURE AS HELL can't sit here on our asses and do nothing," Carl Lyons announced. He headed for the exit doors.

"Where you going, Ironman?" Blancanales inquired.

"To get some answers."

Lyons left the isolation ward and headed downstairs where he'd heard they'd brought in one of the enemy terrorists, apparently still alive after the encounter with Able Team. He found the gunman quickly enough, conscious, and under the general care of a male nurse. Lyons looked up both sides of the hallway to ensure he could get inside the room unobserved, then pushed through the doors and got up close and personal with the nurse.

"Beat it," Lyons said with a jerk of his thumb.

The nurse, who stood nearly half a head shorter, puffed out his chest and pushed his bifocals up on his nose. "You're not allowed in here."

Lyons flashed his credentials. "Actually, I am. And I have some questions for the prisoner."

"Oh." The nurse lost his composure for a moment, but quickly regained confidence. Obviously he'd convinced himself his medical authority would outweigh the needs of justice. "Nonetheless, you're going to have to wait until he's stable enough to question."

"Don't get tough with me, Junior," Lyons said. He gestured to the door again. "Now walk out of here for a few minutes while you still can under your own power."

The nurse tried to look more imposing, but he knew the attempt to intimidate his visitor failed miserably, as did Lyons. He appeared to give it another thought, then shrugged and placed his clipboard on a nearby tray table. "Well, I suppose it'll be okay for a minute or two," he said before walking out.

Lyons waited until the guy disappeared and then turned toward his prisoner. The man was groggy, but a quick and hard grip on his bandaged shoulder brought him wide-awake, and with it a yelp of pain.

"Now that I have your attention, you're going to answer some questions," Lyons said. He yanked the Anaconda from beneath his jacket and pressed it against the man's good shoulder. "Otherwise, I'm going to give you a matching set."

"I have more reason to fear my superiors than I do you, American," the man said. He had a strong German accent but spoke flawless English.

"That right?" Lyons put the .44 Magnum pistol against the terrorist's shoulder and thumbed back the hammer. "Don't think for a second I won't do it, pal. There are a whole bunch of people upstairs who've been infected with your little virus, one of them a close friend. Now either you talk to me or you experience a whole lot of pain in a very short period of time."

The man looked at the shoulder and his defeatist expression told Lyons he'd balked. "What do you want to know?"

Lyons nodded and withdrew the weapon. "Let's start with who you are and why you're here."

"I am a member of the Germanic Freedom Railroad, an expert in explosives."

"You speak mighty good English for being German," Lyons remarked.

"I was educated in this country," he said. "My father was an American serviceman."

"And after all that you're still out here to terrorize the United States. Great."

"Don't be so quick to judge me, American. I am still devoted to this country. We have no desire to battle the United States. We're simply trying to make our way in Germany. I chose to join the GFR because of the money, and nothing more. I could not get a job here in the States. I had to do something."

"So you join a terrorist organization?"

"We are not terrorists, we are liberators. We hide and protect others from persecution."

"Fine, so you're not a terrorist but you hide them. There's little difference between the two. If you help the terrorists in any way, then you're as guilty as they are of all the murder and mayhem they spread."

"Do not presume I am anything like them."

"If you're not a terrorist, then why not help me catch them?"

"That is what we were trying to do, until you and your friends meddled in the affair. You should have left this to us."

"Left what to you?"

"We were trying to find the Shangri-La Lady when you showed up and started shooting up the place."

"Find who?"

"This is the code name of the biological agent. That is the only thing I can tell you about it."

"Either way, it doesn't matter," Lyons replied. "Your men slaughtered innocent college kids and then fired on us. We're going to defend them and ourselves."

"Well, I guess congratulations are in order then," the man replied.

"And why's that?"

"Because you managed to destroy the chemical, and our only possible lead to finding Dr. Delmico."

"We don't need any of your help finding him," Lyons snapped. "We'll find him soon enough. What I want to know is what you planned to do with the chemical agent."

"I cannot tell you this."

Lyons returned the muzzle of the pistol to the terrorist's good shoulder. "You can and you will. I promise you that."

"You are going to shoot me after what you know about me?"

"Listen, I'll shoot you because I don't like your kind. You're a menace that needs to be eradicated from existence. Now, this is the last opportunity you'll get to quit playing dodge-and-parry with me and start talking up a storm. Get it?"

The man nodded slowly, fear evident in his expression.

Lyons removed the gun barrel again. "You said you're with the GFR. Is Choldwig Burke connected with your outfit?"

"He's in charge."

"And once more, why did your people have Simon Delmico make this bioweapon?"

"It was an insurance policy," the terrorist replied.

"Against what?"

"We recently took a job to protect a high-ranking member of Hezbollah."

Lyons nodded, confident he could now believe what this man told him. Stony Man had advised them of the possible connection between the GFR and Hezbollah. Hearing this now from a member inside the organization only confirmed the intelligence and their worst fears. The idea two completely disparate groups could actually operate together had seemed preposterous to them, even unthinkable. Yet for all practical purposes, it seemed there was some truth to it.

Lyons locked eyes with the terrorist. "Let me guess— this isn't turning out like Burke and the rest of you had planned."

The man nodded. "We don't trust them anymore. They've been planning something from the very beginning. We were only going to use the chemical as a way of defending ourselves. We didn't think Hezbollah would find out."

"No," Lyons replied. "You didn't think, period."

Lyons turned on his heel and headed for the door.

"You're not going to kill me?"

As he opened the door to leave, the warrior replied, "Death would be too good for you."

"SHANGRI-LA LADY?" Hal's voice repeated over the speakerphone of Able Team's replacement SUV. "What the hell kind of name is that?"

"Don't know," Lyons said with a shrug. "But whatever it is, it's nasty stuff."

"How's Gadgets feeling?"

"He seems okay," Blancanales replied. "We left him at the hospital under the insistence of the doctor. He wanted to come with us, but since we're not one hundred percent sure about the actual contagion, we realized there wasn't any point in risking anyone else to exposure."

"Good thinking," Barbara Price said.

"Well, we have a lead from local police in a town not too far from you," Brognola said. "It's possible this is where our Hezbollah friends have taken Delmico. It's not much, but it's all we've got."

"I'll take anything at this point," Lyons replied. "So far, we've come up with nothing."

"There's a town about forty miles southwest of you called Hillsboro," Price said. "Law enforcement agencies there hit on a national-alert Be On the LookOut for the vehicle that you reported they shoved Delmico into. The cops are watching the place now, but they're under orders not to approach until someone with federal jurisdiction arrives. That's you two."

"We'll head there now," Lyons said.

"Although going in without Gadgets will make us as busy as a one-legged man in a snake pit," Blancanales added.

"Do the best you can," Brognola advised. "You made the right decision where he's concerned."

"We'll keep you updated once we get there and get Delmico back," Lyons replied. "Out, here."

For a time the pair rode in silence, each lost in his

own thoughts. Finally, Blancanales spoke up. "You know, it isn't going to be easy taking Delmico alive. If he winds up dead in this, we may not find a cure for Gadgets and the others."

"I'd rather not think about that, if you don't mind."

"Okay," Blancanales said with a shrug. "I just wanted you to know the possibilities."

"I've already considered them," Lyons said. "And we don't have any choice. We need to take Delmico out of the hands of Hezbollah, and we need to keep him alive doing it. Anything less is unacceptable."

"Agreed."

Neither of them really said what they were thinking. They couldn't have imagined their team without Hermann Schwarz. Even now it seemed quiet and out of place, not having him around to crack jokes and liven things up a bit. For that to become a more permanent arrangement made Lyons's blood run cold. And he couldn't even imagine how Blancanales felt right then.

CHAPTER ELEVEN

Calvin James lifted the binoculars to his eyes and studied the automotive plant exterior once more from behind the wheel of the compact car. He panned back and forth across the property to gain a thorough view of the layout. They couldn't afford to make a mistake. They had a tiger to tame; if they made the wrong move at the wrong time, then Burke and his GFR stood a good chance of escape.

"Dambalam," James said around a wad of bubble gum, lowering the binocs. "Place sure is big enough."

"It figures," Gary Manning replied from the passenger seat. "Gives us much more to watch when we go in."

"Right."

Manning pulled away the cuff of the neoprene glove he wore and checked the luminous dial of his watch. "I've got two minutes until H-hour."

James checked his own chronometer and said, "Confirmed."

"Send the signal."

James looked through his open window at the second vehicle parked about ninety yards from their position, this one a small VW bus occupied by the remaining members of Phoenix Force. A full moon dangled in the sky and bathed the vehicle's high-gloss paint job in a shimmering, soft glow. James extracted a laser pointer from the breast pocket of his black combat fatigues and depressed the button twice to signal readiness to his comrades.

The pair then inspected the actions of their weapons and secured their equipment. They had their orders, and they had a plan of action. Manning and James would act as point. They were to move in a minute before McCarter, Encizo and Hawkins, and neutralize any sentries or other opposition. From there, they would focus their main attack on the plant.

As expected, Choldwig Burke's cronies had led Phoenix Force right to their area of operations in Wiesbaden. On initial arrival, McCarter had voiced his concerns that it seemed too easy and there was a strong possibility they'd be walking into a trap. The rest of the team agreed to a point, but trap or no trap they had orders to wipe out the GFR and Hezbollah terrorists they were protecting, no questions asked. That simple call to action was all Phoenix Force needed.

On schedule, Manning and James left their car and sprinted toward the automotive plant grounds. They had previously inspected the place and found their best approach would be the northeast corner of a ten-foot-high, chain-link fence that ran the perimeter of the plant. Questioning of Stony Man contacts revealed the place had been abandoned until recently purchased by a third party for conversion purposes. A quick check by Aaron Kurtzman at the Farm revealed both the alleged purchaser and his company were fake. All the more reason for Phoenix Force to accept they had the right place.

Manning and James cut through the perimeter fence in less than fifteen seconds and gained entry to the plant grounds. They split off in a different direction so they could sweep and clear any guards before the rest of the team made entry.

James ran the perimeter of the fence until he reached about the center of the plant building, then cut in and sprinted across the open grounds. He reached the employee entrance unmolested. James crouched, keeping his back to the wall, and scanned his surroundings. His eyes had adjusted to the darkness some time ago, and with the moon helping to illuminate the night, he had a clear view at least twenty-five yards in every direction. Then again, so would an observant sentry, who'd be able to see him.

What the GFR wouldn't have was the element of surprise, and the main thrust of Phoenix Force's plan counted on that tiny fact.

James continued to watch the building, and after sixty seconds had elapsed, he keyed his throat microphone. "Point one's clear."

He expected to hear Manning's immediate reply but it never came.

Something had gone wrong.

GARY MANNING GOT within a few yards of the south side of the plant building when a door suddenly opened and spilled bright light onto the gravel lot. Two men emerged and stopped short when they spotted the Phoenix Force warrior. They stood stock-still and made eye contact with Manning, who immediately recognized them as the pair they had battled in Rodenbach.

Manning took advantage of the enemy's surprise and sprang into action. He launched a jumping front kick that caught the first man under the chin. An audible crack sounded in the crisp night air as the steel toe of Manning's combat boot fractured his adversary's jawbone and crushed cartilage. Blood sprayed from the man's mouth and his head snapped backward. The kick took the man off his feet and tossed him onto his back.

The man's six-foot-four partner rushed Manning and body-checked him at the waist. Sheer size and weight took the big Canadian down, and he hit the ground with enough force to knock the wind from his lungs. With his enemy still unbalanced from the tackle, Manning twisted sideways and drove an elbow into his opponent's forehead. The skin split and blood spewed from the jagged gash. Manning then rolled away from the attack and tried to get to his feet while simultaneously catching his breath. His first blow didn't seem to have slowed the man much. He also got to his feet and swung a meaty fist at Manning, who barely ducked the wild punch, came in low and stomped his boot heel on the man's instep. The man emitted a roar of pain. Manning followed mercilessly with a knee to groin, which caused his opponent to double up. The Phoenix Force warrior finished the job with a rock-solid punch behind the ear that drove the man face-first to the ground and rendered him unconscious.

Manning bent over, hands on knees, and took a moment to catch his breath. He hadn't quite expected that kind of surprise. Was he losing his edge? Either way, he'd been skilled enough—or just lucky—to neutralize his opponents before they were able to sound a general alarm. Once he'd caught his breath, the big Canadian moved to the partially open door and closed it so that just a sliver of light emanated from within.

A voice in his ear demanded that he respond. Manning keyed up his microphone. "I'm okay. Just ran into a little trouble."

"Sitrep," McCarter growled.

"Encountered the two subjects from our previous nest," Manning said. "Mere coincidence. This side's clear. I have entry."

"Acknowledged," McCarter said. "We're coming to you. Wait there. Out."

Manning kept a vigil at the plant entrance until joined by McCarter and the rest of Phoenix Force a few minutes later. The fox-faced Briton looked at the unconscious pair on the ground and shook his head. Manning could see something like disgust mixed with amusement in the team leader's expression. Like Manning, the Briton had figured the next time they would encounter this pair they would be on the business side of their SMGs.

"All right, mates," McCarter said. "We have no idea what kind of force we'll be up against, but I'm sure the odds won't favor us."

"Do they ever?" Hawkins cracked.

"Listen up. We'll do this by the numbers. We have to assume everyone inside is a terrorist unless we have strong evidence to contradict that. So we move in fast and hard, take out any opposition. Clear?"

The men nodded, then took up positions with their backs to the walls. James would go in first, followed by McCarter, Hawkins, Encizo and Manning. James opened the door and moved inside quickly, his Colt M-16 A-2 up and ready for action. James didn't dawdle at the door; instead he pressed inside the semidark plant and kept to the outside wall. Each man who followed took a different direction. They moved throughout the plant with precision, tracking the area ahead of them with the muzzles of their weapons.

Manning moved in a crouch, the neoprene soles of his boots soundless on the plant floor. Just enough lights were on to cast shadows everywhere. The big Canadian focused every sense on the area ahead, keeping his body and mind alert so he could react to any situation. He had no intention of being caught by surprise again.

Manning reached a set of wide metal steps and began to ascend them two at a time. As he lighted on the second-floor landing, he crouched and checked the hall in both directions. Nothing moved from the shadows. The only sounds were his heart beating in his ears and the deafening silence of his surroundings. Manning pressed onward, moving along the hallway until he reached an open door. He peered inside and saw nothing but a little glass from a broken window glittering in the moonlight. Manning went on to the next room and found it empty, as well.

However, door number three concealed a ghastly sight.

A man was tied to a chair, his feet in some type of tub. Manning let his eyes adjust to the gloom, looking for a hint of movement from the man or some other sign of life. His gut told him he wouldn't find it. He keyed the VOX unit long enough to tell McCarter of his findings. He continued on through the upper levels and eventually met up with Hawkins.

"Find anything?" he whispered.

Hawkins shook his head. "Place seems deserted."

"Could be."

Less than five minutes passed before the rest of Phoenix Force joined them. They all reported finding nothing. Manning led them back to the room with the body. McCarter stepped inside first, his pistol out and pointed at the corpse. Manning followed and as they moved closer he remained watchful of tripwires, sensors or anything else the terrorists might have left as a surprise.

He heard McCarter suck in a sharp breath when they were within a couple of yards of the body. The Phoenix Force leader froze in his tracks. Manning could see the Briton had lost a bit of his color, even in the semidarkness of the room.

"David, what is it?" Manning asked.

"Damn it…" McCarter replied in a hoarse whisper. "Bloody damn them to hell."

Encizo entered the room and stopped to stand next

to McCarter. "You recognize him, don't you? Something's been going on from the very beginning of this mission. I think it's time you told us what it is."

McCarter looked Encizo in the eyes for a moment, opening his mouth as if to chastise the guy, but then he seemed to give it some thought. He looked back at the corpse and said, "His name was Welby Blythe. He was an officer with the RAF and one of the best damn pilots I ever knew."

"You knew him from your days with the SAS?"

"Yeah." McCarter holstered his pistol. "We were friends."

Manning stepped forward and put a hand on McCarter's shoulder. "Sorry about this, David."

McCarter turned and looked at each of his men in turn. "We're going to find these bastards one way or another. And when we do, we're going to make every last one of them answer for this."

"We're with you, boss," Hawkins replied.

Every man in the group nodded in agreement.

IT TOOK ONLY A FEW MINUTES of questioning the prisoners for Phoenix Force to determine what had happened to Burke and his crew. McCarter now relayed that information to Stony Man via their secure satellite phone. Symmetric encryption algorithms consisting of a Blowfish 64-bit cipher were applied to the voice and data transmissions, which created a 448-bit variable-length key virtually impossible to crack.

"Our friends weren't at the automotive plant," McCarter announced.

"You think someone tipped them off?" Barbara Price asked.

"Couldn't say for sure," McCarter replied. "But it's a good bet they know we're onto them."

"Pursue every lead you get," Hal Brognola said. "We can't be certain what the GFR is up to, or how Hezbollah will react if you encounter them."

"In other words, it's business as usual," McCarter replied. "Acknowledged."

"And, David, I'm sorry about Blythe. We'll take any necessary steps on our end to ensure his body gets back to his family for proper burial."

"Thanks, Hal," McCarter said. "He lost his lady a few years ago to cancer, but I know his three daughters are alive and well. They will be devastated."

"Understood. You guys take care."

"Out, here."

McCarter broke the connection. James and Manning had abandoned their compact sedan, and now all five were cruising in the VW bus and headed for the Rhine River. According to the informants, Burke and his group had abandoned the auto plant mere hours before Phoenix Force's arrival. They accompanied Mukhtar Tarif and his people, as well as arranged transportation for the LAMPs.

"I've got a question," Hawkins said from the hindmost seat of the Volkswagen bus. "We know Burke and his people are headed for Frankfurt. Why not just get there ahead of them and wait?"

McCarter replied, "First, because we don't know with certainty that's where they're headed. We're relying on the word of terrorists regarding the movement of terrorists. Second, it will be much easier to identify them traveling along the river than if we had to search for them throughout a city the size of Frankfurt."

"And if they manage to get to Frankfurt before we can get to them," Encizo added, "they could move that stuff out of the country to any secret location they wanted, and it would be damn near impossible to locate them."

They rode the remaining five minutes in silence and soon reached the docks of the Rhine. A short, stout man with graying hair and a full beard greeted them. He wore a pair of traditional knee-length coveralls over a sweater, and a thick wool cap and matching boots. He spoke in a heavy German accent, and his eyes twinkled with curiosity as the warriors disembarked from the microbus. The man they knew only as Menschmidt extended a hand to McCarter, who returned the gesture with a firm shake.

"Guten abend," the man said.

Manning returned the greeting in flawless German. Menschmidt studied each man in turn, then led them to a large river raft. The rest boarded immediately while Manning translated and McCarter made payment from the cash supplied by Stony Man's contact in Rodenbach. The Farm had connections like these all over the world, and it made things much easier for the field crews when they could utilize personnel under hire rather than local resources who usually asked too many questions.

"You were able to acquire the additional gear we requested?" Manning asked.

"Ja," Menschmidt replied with a curt nod. "It is

aboard. And your party of interest left less than a half hour ago. You should have no trouble catching them."

Menschmidt then described the boat Burke and his crew were traveling in. Manning thanked the man before he and McCarter joined the rest of their crew. Encizo had the boat started and engine warmed by the time they finished the transaction, and he immediately powered away from the dock and headed east by southeast along the waterway. The Main branched off from the Rhine about three nautical miles from that point, and another forty minutes or so from that juncture would put them in the heart of Frankfurt.

McCarter spoke close to Encizo's ear so he could hear over the engine. "Our contact says we should be able to catch Burke and his crew before they get to Frankfurt. Apparently they're traveling by a much slower boat."

"What kind?" Encizo asked.

"Not sure of that, mate," McCarter replied. "I'd say probably a small trawler of some kind."

Encizo nodded and McCarter went about making preparations for battle. The remainder of Phoenix Force was already well under way in that activity. Metal clinked and Velcro cracked as the actions on assorted pistols, SMGs and automatic rifles were checked and double-checked before being secured in holsters and bags. They field-stripped pistols for a quick cleaning and stuffed satchels with grenades and other field equipment.

"From this point forward we don't let off the heat," McCarter said as they worked. "Whatever happens, we have to stop this crew. We'll be pushing the wire as it is, and without much time to take a breather. I'd suggest you all grab something to eat from the MREs we brought along, because you won't likely get another chance to eat for a bit."

The men acknowledged him and did as suggested.

Twenty minutes passed before Encizo shouted in the group's direction and twirled a finger in the air.

McCarter leaped from his seat in the boat and ascended the three narrow steps to the bridge. He unclipped a miniature NVD from his web belt, engaged the power and put the lenses to his eyes. Directly ahead, at maybe twenty yards, McCarter could discern the outlines of the larger boat and the heat of human bodies in motion.

"That's got to be them, Rafe," he said. "Good eye."

McCarter turned and whistled his team to ready positions, then he descended to the cockpit to join them after issuing brief instructions to Encizo. James and Hawkins stood on the starboard side, feet on the edge of the hull. Shiny four-pronged grappling hooks dangled from climbing ropes. Encizo poured on the power steadily so as not to knock the rest of the group off balance. He pulled up on the port side of the boat and slowed the engines enough to match speed.

James and Hawkins already had the ropes in motion. McCarter counted off and ordered them to execute. The grappling hooks sailed through the air like a pair of graceful, silver-winged hawks and attached to the thick railings of the larger boat with ease. Encizo then cut the engines to low power and as the ropes became taut he throttled up, this time putting full power into reverse.

Manning and McCarter climbed up the ropes like skilled acrobats and alighted on the deck of the enemy's boat a few heartbeats later.

And the night came alive with the sounds of battle.

CHAPTER TWELVE

Carl Lyons and Rosario Blancanales arrived at Hillsboro in less than hour.

Blancanales noted the population sign indicated there were less than two thousand people. He winced when he thought that in the next few minutes this small, quiet piece of rural Missouri might be turned upside down by violence and bloodshed. Well, there wasn't much he could do about that. The alternative wasn't one he or Lyons could live with, and it would make things a whole lot worse if Stony Man stood by and did nothing.

They found several police squads had cordoned off the area occupied by Hezbollah terrorists.

Lyons emitted a groan. "So much for staying inconspicuous."

"They're just looking out for their own, Ironman," Blancanales replied in an almost chiding tone. "Give 'em a break. They probably haven't had this much excitement since they were founded."

"Fine," Lyons growled. "I just don't need Deputy Droopalong getting his ass shot off, *and* mine, for being stupid."

Blancanales skipped any further comment. Instead he nosed their SUV behind a Jefferson County Sheriff's cruiser. The Able Team pair went EVA and extracted weapons from the back of their vehicle. In addition to the pistols they wore in shoulder holsters, Lyons had procured an S&W assault shotgun and loaded a handful of the three-inch Magnum 12-gauge shells of No. 2 shot. Lyons had affectionately dubbed the shotgun a "room broom" for its ability to pump shells in single 3-shot or full-auto bursts at a cyclic rate of 375 rpm.

Blancanales remained more of the traditionalist. The H&K MP-5 A-3 had served him well through the years, and he didn't think this one time would prove an exception. They were up against a force of unknown numbers, and in all likelihood they were bound to engage the enemy in close quarters combat. The MP-5 was a logical choice.

Rigged for war, the two men made their way to the most likely individual in charge of the operation, based on the fact his vehicle was parked farthest away from the scene and parallel to a SWAT operations van. The man's name tag read Sheriff D. Bowker. Blancanales extended a hand when they arrived.

"Sheriff? I'm Rose and this—" he gestured to Lyons "—is Irons. We're with Homeland Security."

Bowker's large, sweaty palm practically engulfed the warrior's own hand, but Blancanales resisted the urge to wipe it on his pants. Bowker was tall and lean, with closely cropped red hair and a face full of freckles that had long since lost their boyish charm among the pockmarks and wrinkles. Blancanales could only mark him somewhere between twenty and sixty.

"What's the story?" Lyons asked, dispensing with pleasantries.

Bowker yanked a soggy, wooden matchstick from his mouth and gestured toward a two-story apartment building. It sat on the other side of a parking lot adjoining the road they had blockaded for a quarter mile in either direction.

"Seems one of the local boys caught sight of a vehicle matching the BOLO you boys put out."

"Did he get a good look at the occupants?"

"No, apparently the windows were tinted and he couldn't see the occupants or how many. But he followed them until they pulled into here and then alerted his chief."

"How did you get called in?" Lyons asked.

"On account of the fact we have the only fully staffed SWAT team in all of Jefferson County, son," the sheriff replied. He stuck the match back in his mouth, clamped down and nodded with finality.

Blancanales looked at Lyons, who rolled his eyes and quickly interjected, "That's excellent work, Sheriff. But if you don't mind, we'll take it from here. It would be just as well to get as many of your men back as possible—"

"Well, I'm afraid I can't do that, boys."

"Why?"

"Because we're just about ready to storm that building and take these punks into custody."

"You what?" Lyons retorted in a harsh, barking tone. "These aren't punks you're going up against. They're well-trained, highly motivated terrorist fanatics! What the hell are you thinking?"

"Listen, Sheriff, you were instructed to observe and assist *only,*" Blancanales said.

"Son, there're people's lives at stake here."

"Yeah," Lyons said. "Yours included. Now call this off."

"I'm sorry, gentlemen," the sheriff replied. "If I lose my job over this, so be it. But we don't have time to stand by and—"

A young, fresh-faced recruit seemed to appear from nowhere and said, "Sheriff, they're in position and ready."

Bowker looked at the young man and said, "Give 'em the green light, Piper."

Lyons whirled and launched into a sprint across the street, under the barricade and directly toward the apartment complex. Blancanales had seen it coming, but he fell a few strides behind. Lyons's well-trained muscles were still nearly as rock hard and efficient as the day he'd participated in the Ironman contest, and lesser men—which didn't include Blancanales or Schwarz— would probably never have caught up to them.

"Steady, Ironman!" Blancanales said. "We don't know the numbers."

"We have to get in front of this now or the numbers won't mean a damn thing!"

Lyons reached the concrete and metal steps and bounded up them to the second floor. They had no idea if the terrorists were on the first or second floor, but Lyons figured the higher ground gave them some advantage. Blancanales elected to stay on the first floor. He could hear a number of the approaching SWAT team members yelling at him to get down, and it was in that one horrific moment he realized they thought *he* was one of the terrorists.

Blancanales went prone hard, and just in time to avoid being ventilated by the short burst of rounds spit from a trio of M-15 Armalite rifles. He could hear the firing cease a moment later followed by profuse and violent shouts, mixed with a passel of expletives erupting from Carl Lyons. A heartbeat passed before one of the SWAT members fell dead, the result of a bullet striking him in the head.

Blancanales rolled onto his back and looked in the probable direction of the sniper fire. He spotted the flash suppressor of a weapon protruding ever slightly from the crack in an open door. It looked like the door led to a facilities room. He jumped to one knee, sighted on the door itself and triggered a sustained burst from his MP-5 A-3. A volley of 9 mm Parabellum stingers chewed up the door, producing a dangerous flurry of shards. The door slammed outward as the body of the gunman fell to the concrete walkway. His weapon skittered away and ground to a stop a few feet from his twitching hands. Blancanales jumped to his feet, rushed forward and pumped a second, shorter burst into the gunner for good measure.

He looked upward at the sound of footfalls on the second-story esplanade. Only a few seconds elapsed before he determined it was Lyons moving to a position where he could provide support and cover fire. Blancanales put his back flat to the wall to make a narrower profile as two terrorists emerged from a room at the end of the walkway. He raised his MP-5 in one hand and triggered a burst to keep their heads down while he angled for better cover. The remaining SWAT team members, who, while well-trained, were obviously unaccustomed to combat situations of this magnitude, finally realized the Able Team commando was on their side and scattered for their own cover.

The terrorists were barely able to get off a few shots before they fell victim to Lyons's steely resolve. The Able Team leader had apparently taken the back-end stairwell and emerged from the cover of the building closest to the street. He took the first shooter with a 3-round burst that cut through his enemy's legs and spine. The deadly buckshot punctured organs, shattered bones and tore flesh from the body. The terrorist's weapon went skyward, a finger spasm sending half a dozen rounds traveling harmlessly into the eaves of the building. Then he collapsed to the pavement.

The second terrorist wheeled to confront the new threat. Blancanales had no clear shot without a wild round hitting his teammate. The SWAT members, however, had no such restriction. A pair of officers opened up on the terrorist simultaneously at about the same moment Lyons opened up with the AS-3. The terrorist's body did an odd pirouette before hitting the ground, blood pumping from the various holes in his torso.

The scent of cordite pricked the edges of Blancanales's nostrils. He watched the surrounding area, eyes roving and ears pricked like a hunting dog, searching for any sound or movement to betray the arrival of a new threat. It never came. After two full minutes, he felt comfortable enough to get to his feet. He trotted to the terrorist he'd downed and checked him for ID. Nothing. He looked up and saw Lyons doing the same. Blancanales waited until he saw his teammate look up and shake his head to indicate like results on the ID check.

The parking lot abruptly became a hubbub of police activity. Squad cars and vans suddenly rushed into the combat zone, and officers from three separate jurisdictions exited their vehicles. Lyons began to bark orders. Something in his natural take-charge attitude had them complying. Nobody questioned the big blond man with the cold blue eyes—they just did as they were told. Clearly, they knew a leader when they saw one.

"Thanks for the save, Ironman," Blancanales said when he'd joined him. "I owe you one."

Lyons scratched the back of his neck. "You owe me way more than that."

"But who's counting? Right?" Blancanales grinned. "Me."

Blancanales stopped grinning and got serious. "We need to find Delmico."

"We need to hope he's alive. I've told them to do a room-by-room search."

"You!" Bowker roared, storming toward the two men. "You two boys have a hell of a lot of explaining to do!"

"*We* have a lot of explaining to do?" Lyons said. "Now look, Opie—"

"Sheriff Bowker, you'd best settle down," Blancanales cut in firmly. He readied himself to come between the two men if need be. "First of all, we don't answer to you. Second, you violated a direct order from a federal office with jurisdiction over matters concerning international terrorism. In effect, that means you ignored the orders of the director of Homeland Security, which means, sir, you violated the instructions of the Oval Office itself."

That gave the sheriff pause. He stopped in front of the pair, his big shoulders heaving and the freckles indistinguishable in the beet-red of his face.

"Now," Blancanales continued, reaching into his pocket and producing his cell phone, "I don't suppose you'd care to explain to the National Security Adviser what you happened to think you were doing when breaking all those rules and regulations, which you swore to uphold, by the way. Or no…let's just skip that and dial the White House directly. I'm sure the President of the United States has nothing better to do this evening."

Blancanales held the phone out to Bowker, who continued to stand there and breath heavily for another minute. The matchstick moved from one end of his mouth to the other, reminiscent of a Wimbledon tennis ball. After a very long moment, the man turned and soundlessly went about directing his men as if they hadn't spoken.

That issue resolved, Lyons began to get the reports back. Nobody had found Delmico. Not yet, anyway, although at this stage of the game Lyons didn't expect they would find him. The terrorists had either dumped him somewhere else before coming here to lie low, or he had somehow managed to escape during the attack.

One of the SWAT officers finally reported, "We finished our searches of both the first and second floors, sirs. We didn't find this man you're looking for."

"Sweep them again, Lieutenant," Lyons said. The SWAT officer looked at Bowker, studied the Able Team pair a second and then delivered a curt nod.

While the men began their search anew, Lyons said, "We'd better call the Farm."

DR. SIMON DELMICO couldn't believe his rotten luck.

When the police first arrived, he managed to convince his captors to let him hide in the bathroom of the cramped second-floor room. Little did the idiots know that he was small enough to squeeze through the roll-out window in there. As soon as the trio of guards who had been his constant companions attempted to confront their dreaded enemy, Delmico managed to slip through the second-story window and descend on several bath towels he'd knotted together.

The actual jump hurt like a bitch on landing, he recalled, but not like it would have if he'd traveled the entire two-story distance. The sounds of battle quickly faded as he merged with the long line of greenery and shrubs on the backside of the motel parking lot and crossed through the back lot of a strip mall. This led him onto a residential street. Much of the numbing between his prosthesis and the callused nub of his foot had dissipated by the time he hopped a bus to the airport. From there, he could rent a car and get wherever he needed to go.

So far, none of this had gone quite the way he'd planned it, which was due in large part to the lack of cooperation he'd received from the GFR leader. Choldwig Burke might have been intelligent—hell, a veritable genius, even—but the man didn't have a grain of patience. In fact, he'd warned Burke that the request to come up with an entirely original biotoxic weapon would take time and resources. Considerable resources, in fact, which Burke swore up and down he could provide.

"To produce a biological agent strong enough to do what you're talking about and yet stable enough, you'd have to develop something that can't be easily spread," Delmico had told him. "Most biological agents can also be transmitted from human to human. Once you're a carrier, the show's over."

"I have confidence in you, Doctor," Burke replied with an icy grin.

But as soon as he'd gained Delmico's trust, Burke sang quite a different song and turned into a tyrant. He seemed almost obsessed at times, and even spent the money to travel all the way from Germany to St. Louis once just to visit Burke and check on his progress. It had surprised and impressed the scientist that a man of Burke's reputation could steal in and out of the country right under the noses of an army of terror watch security measures. In fact, Burke had even somehow managed to bypass the infamous "no-fly" list, a purported document of espionage lore.

Delmico took his time in developing Shangri-La Lady, Burke's demands notwithstanding, and even derived pride and satisfaction in the knowledge the end product had performed greater than expected. What he hadn't planned for was a group of half-crazed Hezbollah fanatics snatching him from his campus.

Well, no point in bellyaching about it now, Delmico thought.

Yes, this would simply double his price. Fortunately, Delmico had thought ahead and made an extra batch of the bioagent, and secured it at a time-share town house in Tulsa. It wasn't much of a plan as plans went, but once the Feds figured out he'd escaped his captors they would expect him to return to St. Louis. Therefore, it only made good sense that he go south on Interstate 55 and head for Tulsa by way of Little Rock.

The route took him considerably out of the way but would make it that much more difficult for them to follow his tracks. When he arrived at the St. Louis airport, he told the clerk he'd be driving to Chicago, but an hour into his trip he called and said there was a sudden change in destination. A family emergency would now require him to go to Tulsa, and was there perhaps a place where he could drop the car instead of his original destination? That would throw off any pursuers, especially since authorities would probably monitor his charge-card transactions and any databases utilizing his date of birth, social security number and driver's license information.

"That shouldn't be a problem at all, sir," the clerk advised. "We'll let the Tulsa branch know you're dropping the car off there. Very sorry to hear about your family and if we can be of any further assistance, please don't hesitate to call."

With that little angle of his plan now addressed, Delmico could concentrate on his next move. He stopped at a large factory outlet along the highway and used cash to purchase a cell phone. He then called the number for Burke he'd memorized. It rang off the hook and he never got an answer. Some type of message finally came on in German but Delmico didn't speak the language, so he disconnected and tossed the phone next to him on the seat.

Damn it all to hell! How could he play a hold-out game with Burke if the muscle-headed kraut wouldn't even answer the goddamn phone? he wondered in exasperation.

Well, it didn't make a bit of difference. One way or another, Burke would try to contact *him* again, and as soon as he did he'd get the message. On afterthought, Delmico called his telephone company and asked the customer service unit to turn on his call-forwarding feature to ring the temporary cell phone. He'd thought about calling his home phone and doing it remotely, but he couldn't be sure if the Feds would be monitoring his lines. Better that he keep the automated or computer-based activities to a minimum. After all, he'd worked for the U.S. government a lot of years.

Nosy bastards had their fingers into everything, he thought. He knew it—hell, every citizen with half a brain knew it. Some would have called such a viewpoint paranoia, but Delmico preferred to think of it as just plain sense. All one had to do was look around to figure out what was really going on. It didn't take someone with acute inside knowledge or special powers of observation to know the government had the whole country under surveillance. Hell, he thought, the *Patriot Act* had practically opened the doors to unilateral wire-tapping and video taping of any individuals even remotely proved to have ties to terrorist groups or a "discerning or unusual interest in terrorist activities and groups."

Stoplights throughout cities all over the country now had cameras, and it wasn't all for the purpose of catching juveniles blowing red lights. If that were the case, why not simply take a picture? No, these were live video feeds that caught people doing everything at stoplights from sexual acts to putting on makeup. And then there were the cameras that weren't just at ATMs and in banks, but now posted at restaurants, motels, airports and shopping malls.

Well, they weren't going to fool the likes of Simon Delmico. The government had put the magnifying glass up his ass and those of the citizens around him long enough. He was about to give them something to look for. Something spectacular. And then he'd collect his rightful pension and go retire in some country like Bolivia, where basically they didn't care what you did as long as you had enough cash to make authorities look for better things to do.

Yeah, Delmico would have that and a whole hell of a lot more.

CHAPTER THIRTEEN

Choldwig Burke had expected an encounter with the American team of special operatives—he'd never imagined it would take place in the late evening on the Main River.

Standing at the upper deck area in the bow of the twenty-one-meter conversion trawler, Burke first detected the new arrivals from the sudden roar of their boat's engine. The enemy boat couldn't have been more than ten meters in length, but it had obviously been equipped with an engine well in excess of its recommended ratings. So, the Americans were not only resourceful, they were also apparently well equipped.

And well armed.

Burke watched as a pair of shadowy forms landed on the aft deck with weapons up and ready for action. Burke's men responded with enthusiasm, the sentries moving to repel the boarders. Within moments of the first two enemy commandos alighting on the rough-finish deck plates, the GFR mercenaries went into action and moved to block the assault.

Their efforts were in vain as they immediately fell under the unerring accuracy of enemy autofire. Burke drew the pair of MP-5 K machine pistols holstered at either thigh and moved without hesitation to join the battle. He would see to it personally that his enemy tasted the vengeance and ferocity of the GFR.

DAVID MCCARTER HANDLED the swift reaction of the enemy sentries with a swifter offense. The Phoenix Force commando dropped to one knee and triggered his MP-5 SD-6. The weapon chugged out a pair of 9 mm Parabellum slugs from its suppressed muzzle. The weapon's 3-round burst capacity had been modified to output only 2 rounds. Recent training statistics had left the Stony Man field units convinced that such modifications could increase control and accuracy ratings by a factor of thirty percent. The duo rounds took the first terrorist in the chest and drove him backward. His body struck the railing, went over and disappeared from sight.

Gary Manning caught the second terrorist with a shot to the head. The single 7.62 mm round from his Galil sniper rifle cleaved a furrow through the skull and blew a gaping hole out the back of the terrorist's head. The terrorist's body twisted sideways as he reflexively triggered his weapon. A flurry of 9 mm stingers from the Uzi SMG buzzed along a narrow path. One of them neatly clipped the big Canadian. Manning grabbed at the wound but kept on the move to avoid the certain death that would have come if he'd stopped to react. He made cover as a fresh volley from a terrorist above sprayed his area of operation with vicious salvos from twin machine pistols.

McCarter found cover beneath a wide metal table and tracked his weapon on the attacker but the silhouette moved backward before he could gain an accurate sight picture. The Briton broke cover and rushed to aid Manning. The two found refuge behind a large metal covering protruding from a far corner of the aft deck.

"You okay?" the Phoenix Force leader inquired.

Manning nodded. "Just a bite."

"Keep a low profile."

"I can operate."

McCarter's eyebrows rose. "You sure?"

"I'm sure."

McCarter nodded and the two pressed onward toward the entrance leading belowdecks.

James and Hawkins followed. Both men hit the deck running and proceeded in opposite directions. They skirted up the sides of the boat via the outboard walkways and headed directly toward the steps leading to the upper foredeck.

One of the terrorists rushed down the steps, eyes watching the narrow steps and unaware of the danger looming ahead. By the time the terrorist noticed James the moment to bring his subgun to bear with effectiveness had long passed. James had left the M-16 A-2 with Encizo in preference to an FN Herstal F-2000 Assault Rifle. Chambering 5.56 mm NATO rounds and equipped with an LV 40 mm grenade launcher, the F-2000 sported a forward ejection port and bullpup profile.

James made short work of his enemy and triggered the weapon on the run. The high-velocity slugs stitched the terrorist from crotch to sternum and slammed him against the steps. James vaulted over the man's sagging body and continued on.

Hawkins managed to get up the deck unmolested. As he alighted on the top step, a pair of terrorists whose attention had been focused on Encizo tried to react to the new and quite unexpected arrival. Hawkins brought the stock of his MP-5 to bear and squeezed the trigger. The weapon tapped out its violent retorts as a burst of 9 mm Parabellum rounds rocketed straight and true into the pair. The first terrorist did a grotesque dance under the onslaught as rounds cut a corkscrew pattern in his gut. The impact drove him into his partner, who had apparently experienced some type of jam in his own weapon. Hawkins finished the fight with a short burst that blew the better part of the terrorist's head from his neck.

ONCE RAFAEL ENCIZO had slowed the terrorist boat to a crawl, he took up a firing position with the M-16 and steadied the weapon's bipod across the fiberglass frame in front of him. The Cuban aligned his sights on a group of terrorists who had emerged from a canopy shelter at the bow of the converted trawler and opened up on them with lethal vigor.

The air-cracking report of the weapon nearly stung his ears as Encizo triggered one sustained burst after another, sweeping the muzzle of the weapon wherever a target presented itself. Despite the fact he was no longer steering the boat—a fact that didn't concern him since the pilot of the enemy boat was taking care of that small detail—Encizo had managed to bring the trawler to a near standstill.

The terrorists fell in numbers under the Phoenix Force commando's marksmanship. Blood and bits of flesh erupted into the chilled night air. The terrorists had stacked themselves too close together, and as a result the ones who managed to escape Encizo's wrath only faced some other painful demise when they tripped over their deceased comrades and fell to the close-range fusillade being laid down by James and Hawkins.

Encizo soon started to run out of targets, and he figured the time had come to remove the boat's mobility altogether. He abandoned the M-16 when the bolt clacked back on an empty chamber and raced down the steps to the cockpit. He reached to the satchel loaded with C-4 plastique, which Manning had left wired. Encizo extended the heavy gauge wire coated with a plastic and rubber sheath and heaved it across to the trawler. He then attached the pair of wire loops at the end to the positive and negative poles of the detonator, removed the safety catch and pumped the handle repeatedly. The detonator zinged as the internal magnets produced the electrical charge required to prime the blasting caps.

A moment of deadly quiet ensued just milliseconds before the explosion. The C-4 blew, and the concussion rattled Encizo's teeth hard enough to cause discomfort. Metal and wood shards erupted in every direction as the diesel line ruptured and engulfed the fuselage in hot flames. As the echo of the explosion died away, the massive trawler slowed significantly. Encizo had already made his way back to the steering tower. He cut the high-powered engines on the boat and all motion ceased.

MCCARTER AND MANNING realized the moment they reached the lower deck they'd walked into a dragon's den of terrorists.

A pair of GFR gunmen opened fire on them in the main entryway that ran through the center of the seventy-foot-long boat, and the narrow corridor left them with few places to find cover. Each man dived through a door off the corridor, thus narrowly avoiding the volley of high-velocity rounds intended for them.

"Only one way to clear a room!" McCarter shouted over the cacophony of reports.

Manning nodded, reached to the strap of his load-bearing harness and came away with a flash-bang grenade. The Canadian tossed it to McCarter, who yanked the pin and underhanded the grenade with a fast spin down the corridor. During the few seconds that followed, the pair of Phoenix Force warriors opened their mouths, clapped their hands to their ears and squeezed their eyes shut. Even protecting themselves, they could still feel some of the effects of the powerful flash-bang.

So did the terrorists, although they were hardly prepared for it. The blast and bright flash of the grenade stunned them long enough to cause a lull in the firing. McCarter and Manning moved immediately up the corridor. They neutralized the terrorists with well-placed shots and continued toward the interior of the vessel.

Following a cabin-by-cabin search, a door at the end of the corridor opened onto an open space that had probably served as the dining area before the boat was converted. McCarter and Manning burst through the door and split off in opposite directions. They searched the entire area but other than a few satchels of spare equipment and clothing, they found no sign of the LAMPs.

Suddenly a heavy explosion rocked the boat and threatened to knock the men off their feet.

Manning steadied himself against a wall, then looked at McCarter. "Sounds like Rafe's moving right on schedule."

McCarter nodded. "I was afraid these bloody things might not be here."

"We knew it was a long shot," Manning said as the two men turned and headed back the way they'd come. "That we could go bust on the whole thing."

"Yeah, I know it. But Welby lost his life for what? Nothing."

Manning didn't know exactly what to say at that. While McCarter had never been one to hold back in saying what he thought, he didn't talk much about personal issues.

"Your friend didn't die in vain, David," Manning reminded him. "He probably died because he wouldn't tell Burke whatever it is he wanted to know. He died making sure that whoever came after him would have the greatest advantage."

McCarter stopped a moment to think about it, then

clapped his friend on the shoulder. "Yeah, you're right. Thanks, mate."

"Sure, now let's get this thing finished."

"You got it."

THINGS HADN'T TURNED OUT exactly as Choldwig Burke planned. When the battle began, more than a dozen of his highly trained team had accompanied him. Now they were defeated and Burke found himself on the run. The chase began when a huge explosion at the back of the trawler caused him to lose his balance.

As Burke started to get to his feet, he saw two commandos charging toward him. A pair of GFR mercenaries opened up with their SMGs and scattered the pair rushing him. Burke triggered his own weapons once more, then watched as his men fell under the unerring marksmanship of the enemy. Burke realized in a heartbeat that not only had he lost the fight, he didn't know the names of either of the men who had risked their lives to save him.

The first fell under a steady burst from the SMG of the tall, lanky Caucasian with blond hair. The GFR mercenary staggered backward as half a dozen rounds or so punched through his chest and punctured his lungs. The other man died under a 3-round burst to the abdomen. The black man wielding the weapon didn't even appear to give his actions a second thought, as if cutting down an enemy gunner was as natural as breathing.

Seeing no options left to him, Burke turned and rushed to the point of the bow. The boat had come to a virtual standstill, and he leaped off the bow into the river twenty feet below. The chilled water felt like icicles pressed to bare skin as the murky black water swirled around him. Burke kept below the surface, aided by the weight of his machine pistols and equipment, and swam in the direction of the shore. He sincerely doubted any of the enemy would attempt to follow him. With any luck, the darkness would obscure where he came ashore. The most important thing now would be to escape so he could fight another day.

"WHERE'S RAFE?" David McCarter demanded of James and Hawkins.

"He went after Burke," Hawkins replied.

"Choldwig Burke. You're sure?"

Hawkins nodded. "No doubt about it. We nearly had him, but two of his boys got in the way at the last second."

"Went after him…where?" Manning asked.

James jerked an index finger toward the water.

"Alone?" McCarter demanded.

The Phoenix Force leader turned on his heel and trotted toward their boat. Flames fueled by the ruptured diesel line now licked hungrily at the fuselage of the trawler, and before long they would engulf it. It was time to get away from there. The quartet jumped into their smaller boat, disengaged the boarding ropes, then powered up the high-power engine. This part of the river wasn't particularly wide, so they stood a pretty good chance of catching Encizo before he made it to the shoreline.

"You guys find the LAMPs?" Hawkins asked McCarter.

The Briton shook his head. "Nope. They must be transporting them by ground."

"You think this was all a ruse?" James asked.

"Maybe, maybe not," McCarter said. "But I'd be willing to bet that wherever we find those LAMPs, we're also going to find Hezbollah."

Hawkins shook his head with disbelief. "Do you ever get the impression these things are sometimes like a soap opera? You know, get a little piece of the story a little bit at a time? What ever happened to the good old days where they just handed you the mission and it was all cut-and-dried?"

"That's the problem with you, T.J.," James said. "You want to go back to where we just point and shoot at whatever we're told. Where's your sense of adventure?"

Hawkins eyed James and let out a sigh of disgust.

Manning took the captain's seat as the rest of Phoenix Force prepared themselves and their weapons for a brand-new hunt. McCarter wanted to kill Encizo for taking off after Burke alone, although he couldn't really fault the Cuban for his dedication. Moreover, from childhood, Encizo had taken to water like a duckling to a pond.

Still, he'd gone off after a dangerous terrorist without backup or support. McCarter could only hope all that skill and training would be enough to keep his teammate alive.

ENCIZO HAD THE SCENT of his enemy, and he damn sure wasn't about to lose it.

A call to action had been made—almost like the bugler's call to join the fox hunt—and the prey had run. Encizo moved his powerful arms and legs through the water, surfacing only twice for air during the entire duration of his swim. As he felt the silt along the muddy shore sift through his fingers, he raised his head just in time to see the terrorist leave the water and scramble up the wooded embankment.

Encizo poured on the speed, crashing against the shore long enough to gulp air before he pushed up the hill in pursuit of the terrorist. The terrorist took the time to look back once, and in the moonlight scattered by the trees, Encizo couldn't really fully discern his features. Still, he was fairly convinced the man was one of the heads of the GFR, if not Choldwig Burke in the flesh.

The warrior pushed himself up the slippery, leaf-covered slope of the embankment and within a minute the pair was moving across level ground. The branches of willows and thickets cut at Encizo's clothes and face. He assumed his quarry suffered similar afflictions. At one point, he tripped over a tree root and hit the ground hard. The blow knocked the wind from him, but the Cuban ignored the burning in his lungs and got back in the chase quick enough.

The delay had cost him some ground, although it looked as if maybe the terrorist was starting to slow down. He appeared to be younger and more athletic than Encizo, and yet he didn't seem much for endurance. The Phoenix Force commando picked up speed and started to gain ground. It was as they got into a clearing that Encizo realized he'd underestimated his opponent. The terrorist had slowed purposely, giving the Cuban the false sense of advantage.

The man suddenly stopped, then turned and rushed him. Encizo slid to a halt, but the earth floor of the woods had become slick with autumn leaves and he slid just enough to be out of control. The terrorist hit him with a body check that took Encizo off his feet and nearly knocked him unconscious. A flash of stars danced before his eyes and a white-hot pain lanced through the back of his head.

Encizo rolled out of the fall and came to his hands and knees. He tried to clear his head, but recovery time was cut short by the flash of a boot sailing toward his ribs. He managed to twist in time so the side of the boot glanced off his ribs. The Cuban rose out of his hands-and-knees position and executed a well-timed leg sweep. The maneuver took the terrorist down hard.

Encizo shoulder-rolled to put distance between them and got to his feet. He turned to face his opponent, who was now up and moving toward him. At some point during the lull in battle, the terrorist had produced a large hunting knife. Encizo whipped his Cold Steel Tanto combat knife into action, which gave his charging opponent pause to reconsider. Encizo could now clearly see he was facing off with none other than Choldwig Burke.

The two men circled each other, each sizing up the other, then Encizo made the first attack. He feinted with an overhead stab but then went low and tried to stick the blade in Burke's gut. The German sidestepped and managed to lay open Encizo's right forearm with a three-inch gash. Blood immediately soaked the torn fabric of Encizo's sleeve. The Cuban danced away, assumed a defensive posture and pitched his knife to his left hand, concerned Burke would take advantage of the distraction. For some reason, the man hesitated and Encizo counted the reprieve good fortune. So, maybe Burke wasn't as experienced a combatant with the blade as Encizo first thought—although he'd underestimated the man once before and he wouldn't make that mistake twice.

Burke began to taunt him. "You Americans have made a mistake. It will cost you terribly."

"The only one who's made a mistake is you, Choldwig Burke."

"Ah, how nice," the German said with a genuine smile of appreciation. "You know my name. I take comfort in the fact you will know the name of he who has beaten you."

"You plan to talk me to death?" Encizo asked.

Burke let out a blood-curdling shout and lunged at Encizo. The knife blade flashed toward the Cuban's abdomen, but Burke's left hand snaked out at the last moment in a punch toward his adversary's right temple. Encizo saw the move, every sense alive, and adrenaline coursing through him like an electric charge. The Cuban executed an upper forearm block, stepped parallel to Burke, and slashed through the German's rib muscles. Burke reacted as expected, the right hand that held the knife wrapping around his stomach and covering his ribs to protect them from further injury while his left arm came down to trap it there.

Encizo drove the Tanto in a backward motion and buried the blade hilt deep in Burke's neck. The razor-sharp steel cut nerves and tendons, nicked the spinal cord and severed the left jugular. He then twisted and kicked out Burke's left leg behind the knee while tearing outward with the knife at the same moment. Hot blood began to spurt from the gaping wound in Burke's neck. Its coppery, sickly smell filled Encizo's nostrils as steam began to roll from the wound.

Burke emitted a gurgling, unintelligible noise as he dropped to his knees. His hand went to his neck to try to stop the blood flow but to no avail. Encizo stepped aside in time to see Burke's eyes look up at him in horror as the German realized the mortality of his wounds. He knelt there a few seconds more, then fell to his stomach, twitched a few times and lay still.

Encizo turned at the approach of rapid footfalls and the crunch of leaves. Four familiar shapes burst into the clearing.

"You okay?" Hawkins inquired.

"Yeah," Encizo said, still panting to catch his breath.

James noticed Encizo's bleeding forearm and immediately went to work on it while the rest of the crew gathered around Burke's body. McCarter stood over the dead terrorist's corpse and stared at it long and hard. Finally he looked at Encizo. "It's Burke?"

Encizo nodded.

"Good work," McCarter said. "But the next time you want to chase the likes of these characters through the woods, try to remember to take us along with you."

CHAPTER FOURTEEN

The drone of the truck engine coupled with the vibration of tires on the road threatened to lull Mukhtar Tarif to sleep.

The Hezbollah cell leader resisted the drowsiness that made his head and eyelids heavy. He hadn't slept well since the group became involved with Choldwig Burke. This ridiculous scheme to transport their secret cargo by truck while sending a decoy force over the country's waterways seemed overly complex. Not to mention, it put a good number of Burke's men at unnecessary risk. It simply demonstrated the man's ineptitude when it came to his leadership abilities.

Tarif wished the man good riddance. If Burke got himself killed in the process, what was that to him? Besides, he planned a reversal of fortune as soon as they reached Munich. Tarif hadn't bothered to tell anyone of his real plans, not even his father. He wanted it to be a surprise. While he'd endured a lot of school and learned military tactics, his father had never let him participate in any large operations. So Tarif had decided to take matters into his own hands, his father's approval be damned.

What puzzled him most, however, were the contents of the crates that had been loaded onto the trucks. The agreement had been to supply the terrorists the bio-toxin produced by Delmico. There hadn't been discussion of the exact quantity, but the three trucks in this convoy carried extremely large—not to mention oddly shaped—containers that couldn't have warehoused barrels of Simon Delmico's brainchild. This entire plan not only baffled him, it worried him just a bit.

Decisions had to be made, and since his father seemed unwilling or unable to support his own son over the GFR, Tarif had decided for him. There would be hell to pay. The Hezbollah leadership considered wanton insubordination intolerable, especially insubordination of its leader. Familial relationships made little difference in this hierarchy. They all answered to God in the jihad, and the fatwahs made it clear such activities were punishable.

Tarif didn't let any of it concern him. Once they saw the results of his minor coup, his father would have no choice but to pardon him. Mukhtar Tarif was about to become a hero for his people and the cause.

It wouldn't be easy to accomplish. Burke had insisted that Tarif and Harb travel together under the direct oversight of his hulking, blond lieutenant, Helmut Stuhl. Stuhl had a reputation among his own men as being nothing less than an uncivilized barbarian who seemed to thrive on blood and mayhem. Well, Tarif would make sure the German numbered among the dead before the dawn broke on a new day.

Due to weight restrictions, there was a section of the autobahn that they could not travel. Tarif's informants had managed to get him this information ahead of time, allowing them to predict the route as well as the best place to make their move. As they left the autobahn and made their way along an all-but-abandoned secondary road lined by trees, Tarif reached inside his shirt and keyed the signaling device he'd smuggled aboard the truck.

In a short while, all would be set right and he would be free to take the Hezbollah's holy war to their enemies.

HELMUT STUHL WOULD NEVER have admitted to being the kind of man who worried, but the fact that more than an hour had passed since Burke's last scheduled check-in gave him cause for concern. That left only one of two possibilities: he couldn't get through on his mobile phone or something had gone wrong. Given they carried fairly sophisticated satellite phone units Stuhl was convinced the latter scenario was the more probable one.

Stuhl had tried to convince Burke to let him lead the decoy unit, but Burke adamantly refused. "I need you to make sure the platforms get to Munich without problems. I need someone I can trust," Burke had told him.

Now, a hell of a lot of good the infernal machines would do them if they lost their greatest leader. Burke hadn't batted an eyelash when he extended his complete confidence in Stuhl's leadership abilities. They had talked about what would happen—the order of succession and the steps that would need to be taken—if Burke ever met his demise. Well, there seemed little reason to become concerned just yet. The fact remained Stuhl didn't really know what had happened to Burke. It wouldn't do either him or his men a spit of good if Stuhl worked up a lather because of one missed check-in. If Stuhl hadn't heard from Burke by the next scheduled check-in, which was less than two hours away, then he'd send a detail to find his friend.

Besides, Stuhl had a greater concern at the moment: babysitting Mukhtar Tarif and his motley band. Stuhl had worked with a lot of terrorist groups in the past, but he couldn't recall ever working with a sorrier bunch of fiends. Stuhl had collaborated with the Taliban, al Qaeda and Hamas. None of them had come close to the ineptitude and slovenly discipline of these Hezbollah fighters. In fact, their performance had first surprised Stuhl, given the reputation of Tarif's father, Kadils Tarif bin Nurraji.

In Stuhl's assessment, then, it came down to a single deciding factor: leadership. This Tarif just apparently lacked the discipline and natural charisma of his father. It took a certain type of man to lead the special men who followed. Stuhl had heard it proposed many times by allegedly "great" leaders of the world that the best leaders were only as great as the people allowed. Stuhl considered that complete shit. The best leaders were the ones who possessed a natural talent for it, the ones who possessed both the charisma and the complexities necessary to lead those with a variety of personalities and motivations.

Choldwig Burke was just such a man, and the sole reason Stuhl had chosen to follow him. He'd known Burke since youth. The two had become close friends, surprisingly after Stuhl protected Burke from some schoolyard bullies. They grew up together, and for a time they went their separate ways—Burke into college and internships and Stuhl into the military where he served with honor—but their paths were destined to cross. The friendship had never died; the embers kept burning by letters and phone calls or the occasional holiday together.

So, what now to do with Tarif? They couldn't watch out for this Hezbollah riffraff indefinitely. Stuhl didn't give a damn what the contract might have been. Burke held to being a man of his word, but Stuhl had always taken a more mercenary approach. Such rivalries had caused many a heated discussion between them, but it had also provided the balanced leadership their men so desperately required. The men of the GFR were motivated by profit, and that's all there was to it. If something *had* gone wrong, Stuhl wasn't sure how long he'd be able to hold the group together.

A moment later he realized it wouldn't really matter because the road fifty meters ahead exploded in a flash of light that rained red-hot asphalt in its wake. The pop of the explosion reached his ears a moment later. Stuhl slapped the arm of the tractor-trailer driver and ordered him to stop. The man didn't need any urging as he'd already started to put on the trailer brake intermittently to avoid a jackknife. When the truck had slowed considerably, Stuhl bailed from the cab.

Stuhl hit the pavement running and drew an H&K USP Tactical pistol from beneath his leather jacket. He banged viciously on the side of the large cargo trailer and accompanied it with a shout in German. At least he could give orders to his men without being understood by the enemy. And if they took him prisoner, he didn't speak Arabic. That's assuming he was correct about his attackers and they were members of Hezbollah. Burke had warned Stuhl of this possibility before they'd parted ways.

Men were already bounding from the small outlet door by the time Stuhl reached the rear of the semitruck. He'd cautioned his men to remain prepared for anything, and it looked as though they had heeded his advice. Although they weren't armed with explosives or incendiaries, Stuhl knew they possessed a substantial cache of firepower.

Autofire resounded throughout the predawn air in concert with muzzle-flashes winking from the trees on both sides of the road. Stuhl ordered his men to fan out and take up defensive positions. The other two trucks had stopped now, and more of Stuhl's men poured from the backs of trailers. The men who had been riding shotgun in those trucks—who also doubled as sort of lieutenants in the GFR—took charge of the units. Within less than a minute out of the cab, the lieutenant in the middle truck fell under a hail of automatic rifle fire.

Bullets whined close to Stuhl, and he decided standing in the open would get him killed. He grabbed cover behind one of the massive wheels of the semi-truck and began popping off shots with his .45-caliber pistol. Stuhl stopped to look at one of the men to his right who was sweeping the tree line with sustained volleys from and H&K M-21E machine gun.

"Slow your fire!" Stuhl ordered him. "Pick your targets! You burn out your ammo and barrel and you'll die, not to mention you'll take a few of us with you!"

"Yes, sir!" the GFR troop replied.

Stuhl returned his full attention to the battle. They seemed to be gaining some headway. He didn't see as many muzzle-flashes as he'd seen before, and there were fewer gun reports. Good, they were claiming the victory, just as he'd thought. At one point, Stuhl saw a pair break the lines and try to move in close. He managed to take one with a well-aimed shot to the chest. The other fell under autofire sourced from a position blind to Stuhl.

"Keep it up!" he said, slapping the shoulder of the man who was now delivering shorter, more controlled salvos from the heavy machine gun with considerable effect.

And then he looked to his left flank and noticed men running away from their ranks and rushing for the trees. Stuhl couldn't make out exactly who it was, but it had to be Hezbollah goons since it didn't appear any of them were falling under enemy fire. Stuhl was betting Mukhtar Tarif and his chief bodyguard, Harb, were among the fleeing, and he swore in that moment they wouldn't walk away from this alive for their treachery.

Helmut Stuhl would see to it. Personally.

As soon as Tarif—accompanied by Harb and a handful of his closest allies—made the tree line, the Hezbollah leader blew a sigh of relief.

So far, their attack had been a total success. Now all that remained would be to eliminate any remnants of resistance and then seize the trucks for their own. The sounds of battle continued to rage around him, although to a man like Tarif it was all just music to his ears. He'd spent so much time training in Afghanistan and other secret Hezbollah camps throughout the world that the sounds of battle were almost second nature to him.

Tarif began to order his men to join in the fight. Each of the warriors on the assault team had toted an extra weapon for the escapees. They passed out those weapons now as their comrades joined them. Branches snagged at Tarif's clothing as he navigated his way through the forest and brush to take charge from the leader of the assault team. At points throughout their trek, Harb ordered his men to break off and take leadership of their assigned squads.

The cell leader found the pair in charge of the team. They embraced briefly and then Tarif inquired on the battle.

"We've lost only a small number of men," reported Marwa Shazzad. He and Tarif had trained together at the wintry mountain camps of Kazakhstan. "Your plan is working, so far."

"We *must* take those trucks at any costs," Tarif stated. "I don't know exactly what's on them, but whatever they carry is of extreme value to Burke's people."

"Perhaps they will prove of use in our own mission," Shazzad suggested.

Tarif answered by way of a curt nod. "I will take charge from here. You have done well, my friend. You will be rewarded for this."

Shazzad bowed slightly and stepped back in a submissive gesture. Tarif let a smile play at the corners of his mouth. He couldn't say he minded the deference of his colleagues, despite the fact he counted many of them as peers and, in so doing, equals.

He turned to Harb. "Get your men ready for the final phase."

Harb nodded and left to do Tarif's bidding. Everything was happening in accordance with Tarif's plans. And soon they would deliver an ultimate blow against God's enemies.

HELMUT STUHL WATCHED another man fall under a shot from his USP Tactical pistol. He turned to the machine gunner and ordered the man to lay down a battery of covering fire. On a three-count, the man opened up, and Stuhl broke cover to rush for the line of the woods where he'd noticed a gap in the muzzle-flashes. It was still dark enough—with enough noise and distractions— that he felt he could make it to the forest unhindered. He guessed right.

The German broke through the line of tall conifers and crouched. He felt more than heard his heartbeat. The autofire continued to rage around him, peppered with the occasional explosion. One thing he'd noticed was how the attackers seemed to take care not to damage the trucks. Had Tarif somehow learned of their cargo and staged this coup to take the booty? It seemed like the most plausible explanation, particularly in light of the fact Burke hadn't made his last check-in on time. Maybe Tarif had arranged for his demise, too.

Either way, Stuhl wasn't about to let the Hezbollah fanatic get away with it. His men would fight until they were victorious or dead—there could be no other outcomes. Stuhl pressed through the woods and encountered his first enemy up close in less than a minute. The dawn sun had now broken through and illuminated the man's face enough for Stuhl to see his was of Arab descent. Stuhl dived milliseconds before the terrorist opened up with a Czech-made Model 61 Skorpion machine pistol. He heard the buzz of rounds overhead but pushed out thoughts of his near-fatal encounter.

Stuhl hit one knee, raised his pistol and triggered two rounds before the terrorist could adjust his aim. Both bullets struck center mass. They perforated the chest and deposited the Hezbollah gunner on his back. Stuhl rose and commandeered the Skorpion. He hefted it for a moment and attempted to assess its balance. He hadn't seen one of these in ten or twelve years. They had once been popular among terrorists, but with the advancement in weapons technology the vast majority had gone out of circulation through confiscation or destruction by authorities. Well, he could make good use of it. He would need every advantage if he stood even a remote chance of hunting down and eliminating Tarif.

Stuhl advanced about thirty meters before he en-

countered fresh resistance in the form of three terrorists whose attentions had been diverted in another direction until he almost walked into them. The first fell
instantly under a short, hip-fired burst from Stuhl's
SMG. The other two managed to swing their weapons
around before Stuhl cut them down with a sustained,
sweeping burst. Blood and bits of flesh erupted in a
geyser of destruction, and Stuhl gave no quarter to his
enemies.

This was a fight to the death and Stuhl planned to
emerge victorious. He proceeded on his original path
but soon the sounds of battle started to die. Occasionally he could hear a short burst of autofire followed by
a shout, even occasionally a scream of terror mixed
with pain, and then he heard nothing for a long time.
Stuhl stood in the semidarkness of the woods listening,
but heard nothing. Then he could make out the rumble
of tractor-trailer engines as they revved up.

The nightmare suddenly came alive for him as a new
realization crawled over his skin like a legion of fire-
ants. Hezbollah terrorists had succeeded and were now
stealing the semi-trucks. Stuhl whirled and headed back
the way he'd come. As he neared the edge of the woods,
he saw the trucks heading away from the road. He
crashed through the tree line just as a semi passed by.

Stuhl rushed onto the road, then turned toward the
roar of the last truck as it advanced toward him. He
rushed the monstrous tractor-trailer, raising the Skorpion on the run and triggering the weapon. Sparks
marked the impacts and ricochets of the 9 mm rounds
on the thick metal body of the cab. A few even shattered

the windshield, but the truck continued to lumber forward as it gained momentum. Stuhl had to dive to the shoulder to keep from being run down.

One of the Hezbollah terrorists leaned out the window with a carbine and tried to gun him down, but the rounds fell short of their intended mark. Stuhl lifted his own weapon and triggered it until the bolt fell back on an empty chamber, but the truck had passed too far for it to be effective. Stuhl watched helplessly as the red taillights of the truck faded.

For a long time the German mercenary stood there and watched. Even after the trucks had completely gone from view, he simply stood and watched the ever-lightening horizon. Eventually he shook himself back to reality. He walked along the roadway amid the bodies of his men, strewed along the shoulder. Some had even made it as far as the tree line before falling under the weapons of the enemy. The smoke of gunfire hung as a low haze and the smell of battle stung his nostrils.

Stuhl noticed that the trucks had run over a couple of his men, including the machine gunner who had provided cover fire for him. He grimaced at the thought that some of his men might have died as a result of being run over. Such a death would have been painful and horrific. Well, he couldn't do anything about it now. Somehow Hezbollah had beaten them; Tarif had managed to outsmart him. They had escaped with valuable equipment and slaughtered the men who were originally hired to protect them. All for what? Their beloved jihad?

"We never should have trusted them," Stuhl muttered under his breath as he inspected the site where they had blown up the road. He saw no real damage, just a bit of surface burns and flash residue. So they had simulated blowing up the road to make the convoy stop. The entire thing had been planned in a cold, calculated way. They had made a fatal mistake, however. They had underestimated the GFR's resources. Stuhl would take back the LAMPs and his honor and all else that rightfully belonged to his people.

And they would meet again at the final battleground. A city called Munich.

CHAPTER FIFTEEN

"Chicago was Delmico's last known destination," Aaron Kurtzman advised Carl Lyons.

"Chicago? Sorry, but I don't get the connection."

"We didn't, either," Kurtzman said. "He has no known relatives or associates there. In fact, near as we can tell he's never been there."

"Then what's the angle?"

"We decided to keep our eyes open for anything unusual," Kurtzman said. "The phone at his residence didn't receive any calls, and he hasn't used the cellular registered in his name. Finally, I cracked into the database of the rental agency and extracted its GPS key."

The thought brought a smile to Lyons's face. Kurtzman had to be one of the most ingenious men in cyberspace. Not only did he serve as chief architect of Stony Man's entire information and data storage network, he could also hack through any security barrier in existence. The massive computer servers and other advanced equipment buried deep in the Annex helped that cause, but it would have been so much worthless junk without the brains behind its smooth and efficient operation. Kurtzman was a man who knew how to leverage every available byte of information-processing power.

Kurtzman continued. "We just pinpointed his vehicle one hundred miles due east of Little Rock, Arkansas. We think he's headed for Tulsa."

"Rather than Chicago," Lyons concluded. "Anything in Tulsa?"

"He's got a town house there on time-share. Jack's standing by at the airport."

"I thought he was on convalescent leave."

"Doctors cleared him for duty." Kurtzman's voice moved away from the phone a moment and he said, "What's that? Okay." His booming tone came back full strength. "Barb says to pick up Gadgets on your way."

"Gadgets is under a doctor's orders to stay put," Lyons reminded him.

"Maybe, but he called Barb and told her he's not contagious and there's no point in him sitting there polishing a stainless-steel bedpan."

"This is really to say he's tired of sitting around on his ass, missing out on the action. That it?"

Blancanales heard Lyons's side of the conversation and flashed the Able Team leader a wicked grin.

"That's it," Kurtzman replied.

"All right, we'll grab him. He's probably driving the hospital staff to suicide by now, anyway."

"Understood."

Lyons disconnected the call. He rode in silence,

looking out the window, but eventually got around to giving the details of the conversation to Blancanales.

"None of it made a damn bit of sense," Lyons said. "Delmico makes a biotoxin for a German terrorist smuggler. He gets grabbed by those being smuggled, allegedly members of Hezbollah, and then it turns out he escapes from them only to run away from the people who saved him—members of his own government, to boot."

"You have to remember, Ironman," Blancanales said, "that Delmico has every reason in the world to hate the U.S. government. Not only did they turn him out on his ear after he violated safety protocols and blew up a building, but he also took a pretty bad mark on his record. We can't be sure if Delmico even knew about Burke's association with Hezbollah."

Lyons looked glum. "I don't know why any American would want to associate with known terrorists after 9/11."

"Because they forget," Blancanales said. "They put their trust in others instead of putting it in themselves. They don't push their elected leaders to tighten security, they just push them away. And by the time any of it gets to the point where the legislation comes up for a vote, most of them have forgotten what the big push was to begin with."

"Ah, the wheels of democracy. They grind slow, don't they?" Lyons did nothing to hide his sarcastic scowl.

"Well, I know better than to veer too closely to the subject of politics with my friends."

"I guess that's why we call you the Politician."

Blancanales grinned. "I guess so."

IT TOOK LYONS AND Blancanales thirty minutes to get back to the hospital and retrieve Schwarz, another hour to the airport, and by midnight Jack Grimaldi had put down the Gulfstream C-21 in Tulsa. A car awaited Able Team and they loaded it with weapons and equipment from the plane. They had encountered a number of hostile forces in unpredictable places, and none of them felt like a repeat performance. This time, they planned to be well prepared for any eventuality.

"What's the plan?" Grimaldi asked. "Any need for air support?"

Lyons nodded toward the Gulfstream parked on the tarmac behind him and said, "Not unless you can get that thing to hover."

"Hey, this is Jack we're talking about," Schwarz cut in. "If anybody could do it, he could."

"Thanks for the vote of confidence," Grimaldi quipped.

"Just stand by here," Lyons said. "We'll be in touch as soon as we've got Delmico in hand. And we're going to need a quick lift back to St. Louis so he can develop an antidote."

Grimaldi nodded with a thumbs-up.

Schwarz took the wheel of their Toyota 4-Runner after insisting for the twelfth time that he felt fine. Dr. Corvasce had reiterated his original sentiment that it would be approximately forty-eight hours or more before Schwarz began to show symptoms. Already, representatives from the CDC and at least a half dozen other agencies were converging on St. Louis to assist Corvasce and Kingsley's team with the small epidemic they had on their hands. The site of their original battle with the GFR terrorists had been fully contained, but for safety's sake the campus had been quarantined and the student body billeted on Army cots wherever they could place them. It wouldn't be long before the press got wind of what was happening.

Schwarz pulled to the curb down the block from Delmico's time-share, killing the lights and engine. The car windows were down. They figured Delmico would likely approach from the other direction, never even passing them, not to mention the warm, humid air of Tulsa had dissipated to something on the edge of tolerable.

"Been a while since we were here," Blancanales remarked.

Lyons nodded but said nothing. The blond warrior's attention remained focused on the street ahead. Schwarz snapped the wad of bubble gum in his mouth. Blancanales could see neither of his compatriots felt much like small talk, so he went about the task of checking their weapons.

Lyons had taken the AS-3 along as his preferred weapon. Stony Man's cache brought along by Jack Grimaldi had included two fresh MP-5 40s and a SIG 551 carbine. Manufactured by the Swiss, the SIG sported a high-end, night-vision scope and three magazines connected by a stud-and-slot system. This allowed a much faster magazine change out, as well as tripled the firepower capacity. At a 700 rounds-per-minute cyclic rate of fire, the SIG 551 was perfect for this kind of mission.

Blancanales barely completed the weapons check

when headlights appeared at the end of the street and swung into the driveway of Delmico's town house. Lyons focused a monocular NVD on the vehicle and watched as a man climbed slowly from behind the wheel.

"Hard to tell from this distance," Lyons finally said as he lowered the NVD. "But I think it's Delmico."

"Car matches the description according to Kurtzman's data from the rental company," Blancanales said.

"All right, it's him," Lyons decided. "But let's do this quick and quiet like."

The three warriors went EVA, but before they could move out a custom van raced over the hill at the far end of the street and screeched to a halt in front of Delmico's residence. Blancanales let out a curse and reached back inside the SUV. He handed the AS-3 shotgun to Lyons, tossed an MP-5 40 over the roof to Schwarz and procured the SIG 551 for himself.

"Go!" he said. "I'll be your cover."

Lyons and Schwarz nodded and raced up the street to intercept the new arrivals. Blancanales engaged power to the scope of the SIG, braced the weapon between the A-post and front passenger-side door, and put his eye to rubber. The van's occupants poured from the vehicle, illuminated in the blue-green light of the scope. Blancanales aligned the red hue of the sighting reticle on the nearest target and confirmed his distance with two clicks on the horizontal-align dial.

The Able Team warrior took in a deep breath, let half out and squeezed the trigger. The weapon barked a sharp report as the 5.56 mm round left the muzzle at a velocity over 900 meters per second. Blancanales saw a blood spray where the bullet entered through the passenger's neck. The man tumbled from the van and slumped to the ground just outside his open door. Blancanales next took the driver, who remained behind the wheel. The high-velocity round punched through the windshield and wiped the look of shock from the man's face as it entered just below the left temple. The right side of his skull exploded in a gory mess against the back of the cab.

Blancanales laterally panned the target zone and through the scope he saw that his teammates were almost on top of the van. Lyons took the first one to exit from the rear with a shotgun blast from the hip. The mixed shot blew a grapefruit-size hole in the man's stomach and the close-range impact lifted him off the ground. The enemy slammed onto his back, and the SMG he'd toted skittered across the pavement.

Schwarz dropped to one knee and fired a rising, sweeping burst from the MP-5. The .40-caliber S&W rounds ventilated another pair of gunners who had emerged from the back. The first one caught a swathing batch of slugs across the chest, and the second gunner took twin shots to the face. His upper lip caved under the impact, and another round managed to enter his mouth at an angle, blowing off the top of his skull.

Blancanales didn't wait to see them fall. Whatever happened, Simon Delmico held the key to curing a lot of sick college kids—not to mention his closest friend—and Blancanales intended to make sure the guy didn't manage to slip through their fingers again. He only hoped Delmico didn't hold the mistaken impression Blancanales was an enemy. Worse yet, there was still a chance the GFR or Hezbollah could get their hooks into him again before Able Team did.

In any case, it would be hard to keep him alive.

SIMON DELMICO COULD remember better days.

First Hezbollah kidnapped him, then government agents tried to "rescue" him. Instead, they nearly managed to get him killed. Now a vanload of goons whom Delmico immediately suspected to be members of Burke's entourage had arrived at his town house—he couldn't figure out how in the hell they even knew it existed—and tried to punch his ticket. That didn't make a lot of sense, either, since they didn't have the Shangri-La Lady yet, or the antidote, so it would make more sense to try keeping him alive.

But before they could even make their intentions known, the Feds showed up. Well, he sure didn't plan to stick around to find out what was what. It made better sense to get the hell out of here. Once he was free and clear, he'd contact Burke and tell him he'd give the guy what he wanted just as long as the steroid-loaded, homicidal maniac left him alone once and for all. He wouldn't even ask double for the biotoxin. Hell, at this rate he would have settled for half his original fee and free passage out of the country. Argentina was pretty nice this time of year. And he could evade extradition, as well, since most of South America demanded to operate independently, and particularly free from U.S. interference.

Delmico managed to reach the front door of his town house and finally got inside after nearly a minute fumbling around with his keys. The scientist raced to the safe behind a painting on the wall of his study and quickly dialed in the five-number combination. The heavy safe door snapped open to reveal a plastic case approximately eight inches long by five inches tall. He flipped up the safety catches and opened the lid. Six glass vials of greenish liquid were wedged securely in the precut foam and a seventh with a cherry-colored substance: the antidote. Delmico snapped the case closed. He reached into the safe again and withdrew a .38-caliber snub-nosed gun, then headed for the back door. He crossed through the sliding doors and stepped onto the ten-by-ten concrete patio. Delmico wound his way through the matching set of bamboo patio furniture and stepped onto the lawn. The rear of the town house opened onto a strip of manicured grass that separated the quadruple units across the way identical to his own. A fresh burst of gunfire reminded him to put it in gear.

Delmico remembered that there was a convenience store a few blocks distant. He could probably catch a cab from there and head for the airport. He needed to get out of the country as quickly as possible. He could stash the biotoxin in a locker at the airport, contact Burke with arrangements to deliver the key, exchange it for the money and be out of the country by dawn. The intensity of gunfire increased, and Delmico moved swiftly toward freedom.

HERMANN SCHWARZ HAD EXPECTED resistance, but not quite at this level. It seemed for a moment as if the bodies pouring from the back of the van would go on forever. Schwarz gritted his teeth and steadied the MP-5 in his fists. He triggered another short burst that took one of the GFR terrorists in the face. The 210-grain, .40-caliber S&W rounds decimated the man's head and showered some of his colleagues with blood and gray matter.

Schwarz rolled from his kneeling position and went prone as a flurry of autofire buzzed around him. They needed to level the odds on the battlefield and real fast.

Schwarz opened up with the MP-5, this time sweeping the area with a thick salvo of fire. The rounds cut through the hoard of gunners still trying to untangle themselves and spread out. They had made one critical mistake in that they came out of the van together and failed to disperse. By sheer numbers, which Schwarz estimated at nearly a dozen, they could have easily overcome the pair. Instead they jumped from the van into the wide open and had succeeded only in getting in one another's way.

Schwarz didn't even wince as three more fell under his marksmanship. The men let out screams of pain mixed with surprise as bullets cut through their arms, legs and bellies. A couple even took some rounds to the chest.

Interspersed with his own fire, Schwarz could clearly detect the heavy boom-boom-boom of the AS-3 shotgun wielded by Lyons. The Ironman had smartly grabbed cover behind a telephone pole, which afforded him the option of taking his targets by more selective methods. Still, nobody could have accused him of not pulling his weight.

Lyons dropped one of the GFR enemies with a 3-round burst to the head. Each shot that hit tore more bone and skin away from the gunner's skull. The man's corpse was practically headless by the time it hit the ground. Lyons blew off another man's kneecap, followed by part of his left hip and finally the center of his chest. While the rise was natural in the muzzle of such a shotgun, Lyons knew how to handle it well. His well-conditioned forearms kept total control of the AS-3, despite the significant recoil.

"Keep one alive!" Schwarz reminded his comrade.

Lyons followed through on the request, snapping off a single shot that caught the last enemy gunman in the right shoulder. The force of the blast nearly tore the man's arm from its socket.

Silence fell on the scene as the echoes of gunfire died away in the night. The ringing in Schwarz's ears started to dissipate and almost immediately he could detect the wail of sirens in the distance. They would have to stick around to explain the situation. They couldn't just leave the scene, especially since they were supposedly acting as officials with Homeland Security.

"Hey, Gadgets," Lyons called as the Able Team electronics wizard climbed to his feet.

"What up?"

"What happened to Pol?"

Schwarz turned to see that his friend had disappeared.

Rosario Blancanales looked down at a jab of pain in his left arm and saw blood starting to soak through the bandage.

He forced thoughts of the weeping gunshot wound from his mind and continued in pursuit of Delmico. He could barely make out the shadowy figure as it sprinted across the lawn and up a slight rise to the town house units on the other side. He'd abandoned the SIG 551 and retained only his P-239 sidearm. He was fairly confident that Delmico wasn't armed. Even if the scientist had been packing, it was probable he couldn't be that proficient with weapons.

Blancanales stepped up the pace, intent on keeping Delmico in sight. The guy had a pretty good head start on him, but he wasn't sprinting like Blancanales. He also knew the scientist had a prosthesis, which would make it more difficult to outdistance his pursuer. Finally, Blancanales had the cover of darkness to help conceal his approach.

The chase continued up the street of the town house units, and at the intersection atop a hill, Blancanales got to within twenty yards of his quarry.

"Hold it, Delmico!" he said.

The scientist stopped at that, and as Blancanales got closer he could see something tucked under Delmico's arm. It was a little plastic case. What the hell was it? But Blancanales made no mistake about the item in the scientist's left hand. The stainless-steel finish of the .38 revolver gleamed oily silver under the streetlight.

Blancanales looked around quickly to ensure there weren't bystanders that might be hurt by a confrontation. Blancanales considered reaching for his pistol, but he decided not to do anything yet to make Delmico itchy. He'd hoped it wouldn't come to this but the possibility it might, however slim, had been there from the beginning.

"You won't get away from this, friend," Blancanales said calmly. He raised his hands to show he wasn't armed, and then lowered them. "It isn't worth it."

"You don't even know the reasons I'm doing this… *friend.*" Delmico expressed a sneer that contorted his otherwise smooth and handsome face.

"It doesn't really matter," Blancanales said. "Whatever your reasons might be, they aren't worth it. Now you can go ahead and pull that trigger, but if I die there will be five more to replace me. And if you get them, then they'll send ten after you. The more you run and resist, the worse your odds."

"You're right. Why not just kill me now?"

"Because I need you alive to help my friend. There are a lot of sick kids at the hospital in St. Louis. *They* need you, too. We need the antidote to the toxic agent you created. Is that why you made this terrible stuff? You wanted to kill innocent American college kids?"

"They're casualties of war."

It was Blancanales's turn to sneer. "Bullshit. You don't believe that any more than I do, Delmico. What you need to ask yourself right now more than anything is what happens when Burke's people catch up to you? Or some fresh, young fanatics with Hezbollah. You think you'll be safer with them, then go ahead and shoot me. Or you can come along peaceably and—"

"Don't you get it?" Delmico screamed. He reached up with his right hand and pulled the plastic case from under his arm. "*This* is the only bargaining chip I have. It's the power of life and death all in one package."

Although Blancanales knew what Delmico meant— that the case most likely contained the toxin and the antidote—he could say little more because of his surprise at the sudden appearance of Able Team's 4-Runner. It topped the hill behind Delmico, traveling at a good clip. What Blancanales didn't hear was an engine, nor did he see any lights. The 4-Runner swerved suddenly and headed directly for the scientist. At the last second, just after it jumped the curb, the driver steered to the right while opening his door. The door caught Delmico from the rear and knocked him to the ground.

Blancanales let out a shout and rushed Delmico's position to intercept the case that was dislodged from his hand. The Able Team warrior dived, but despite his best attempt he fell short of the mark and the box cracked nosily against the pavement. Fortunately, the lid stayed secure. Blancanales rose, rushed to Delmico's side and scooped the gun from the sidewalk where it had fallen near its owner's groaning, semiconscious form. Blancanales looked up to see Lyons and Schwarz emerge from the 4-Runner they had stopped at the curb.

He nodded toward the case. "We'd better hope whatever's in there survived."

CHAPTER SIXTEEN

David McCarter looked upon the smoking hull of the GFR's converted trawler and considered their situation. He'd just completed his report to Stony Man, and Price had reconfirmed Brognola's directive to utterly decimate the GFR, Hezbollah and anyone else who might be involved. McCarter's eyes roved over the smoldering deck—the remnant of Manning's handiwork with demolitions—as smoke curled upward from the charred edges and danced in the sunlight that peered through the trees. The smoke cast shadows on the green-brown waters of the Main River, maybe two miles west of the Rhine tributary.

A combination of Manning's assessment on the boat when instructing Encizo to place the explosives combined with the lower seals had isolated flooding to the engine compartment. The fact that compartment had been the only one to take on water was the chief reason the converted trawler remained afloat.

Not finding the LAMPs had disappointed McCarter most about the mission. He now had to wonder if they hadn't been purposely misled by the men Burke left behind at the auto plant, or if the boat had been a decoy. Either way, he'd fallen for it hook, line and bloody sinker; the death of his friend had clouded his judgment. McCarter wondered, if only for a moment, whether it might not be wiser to turn over the lead on this particular mission to Encizo.

Then again, the Cuban warrior had his own load to carry. Burke had been their only lead to finding the LAMPs. With the GFR leader out of the picture, they had very little to go on. Hell, not that he blamed Encizo— McCarter would have done the exact same thing in that situation. He wouldn't start second-guessing his comrades now. Phoenix Force hadn't found any written documents that might give them a clue on the location of the LAMPs up or down. Wherever they were, McCarter knew one thing: the GFR had some plan for the platforms and they were bloody well running out of time.

McCarter tossed the satellite phone to Hawkins, who immediately stowed it in the commo bag.

"What'd they say?" James asked him.

"Keep looking," McCarter replied with a shrug. "I told Barb and Hal we didn't have much to go on, but they said to do the best we could. They're going to look into it on their end in the meantime. See what they can come up with."

"So I don't think the plan's for us to just sit here," Hawkins replied in his usual drawl. "What's our next move, Chief?"

"I've been thinking about that and I'm drawing a blank," McCarter said. "Anybody who's got an idea, I'm all ears."

Encizo cleared his throat and spoke up. "Maybe we've been looking at this wrong from the beginning."

"How so?" Manning asked.

"Well, up to this point we've assumed the GFR's calling the shots. And maybe they are. But it seems probable Tarif will move on his own now that Burke's out of the way."

"You figure he's got plans?" McCarter interjected.

Encizo shrugged. "Why not? The Farm already told us he had no qualms about sending a team to the States to snatch up Simon Delmico. We also know that whatever reason Burke had for wanting the biotoxin, it had nothing to do with any operation the GFR had planned."

"That's true," Hawkins added. "Acts of terrorism in the conventional sense aren't the GFR's style. These guys are strictly in the business to make money."

"So maybe they contracted Delmico to make this biotoxin to sell to the highest bidder."

Encizo nodded. "And let's not forget that this whole thing first got started by Tarif's father. According to the intelligence we have, Tarif's never been linked to a single terrorist act. Sure, Hezbollah has caused plenty of trouble. But in those cases, there was somebody else masterminding the whole thing."

"Rafe's right," Manning said. The big Canadian had a trapdoor mind when it came to terrorist activities worldwide, and everyone in Phoenix Force would have agreed Manning remained their resident expert on such matters. "It was only recently that Tarif first entered the picture."

McCarter nodded slowly, confident he was beginning to see their direction. "So you think maybe Tarif's ready to strike out on his own. Maybe they convinced the GFR to take them in because they already had a target in mind from the beginning. They just needed the right opportunity."

"And by this," Encizo interjected, waving his arm to encompass the remainder of the boat, "we just *gave* it to them."

"It's the best theory I've heard yet," McCarter said. He didn't try to keep the enthusiasm from his voice. "But how would they know we eliminated Burke?"

"You think a guy with Burke's background wouldn't have checked in regularly with his counterparts?" James asked.

"Wherever they are, they've probably got Tarif's crew *and* the LAMPs," Hawkins said.

McCarter frowned and nodded. It almost made him ill to think about the sheer magnitude of it, but he couldn't shake the sense his friends were right on the money. It was entirely probable Burke had missed a scheduled check-in with the transport team. That left two possibilities, assuming it was true. Burke's men would either proceed with their plan for the LAMPs and the biotoxin, or Tarif would see that the GFR had reached the end of their usefulness and eliminate them.

McCarter retrieved the secure satellite phone and contacted the Farm once more. He ran the theory first by Price, then recapped for Brognola at Price's insistence.

"It's a strong possibility," Brognola said. "How can we help you?"

"Have Bear pull everything you can get on any major events happening in Germany this week."

Manning said, "Have them run it against known target profiles for Hezbollah, David. That should narrow the search parameters some."

McCarter gave him a thumbs-up and passed it on to Brognola. Kurtzman had now joined the call and they ran through the various possibilities. Kurtzman also passed geographic parameters, which would also help to narrow their choices. It seemed likely Hezbollah would hit a major population center. Most of their attacks in the past had been intended to create the widest devastation. They were infamous for hitting areas that contained large crowds like public transportation, museums and tourist centers.

"Got it," Kurtzman's voice chimed in. "There's an American delegation in Munich this week for an anti-terrorist summit."

McCarter grunted. "That's exactly the kind of thing that would interest our Hezbollah friends."

"Exactly," Brognola said. "How soon before you can get there?"

"A few hours, if you can have air transport waiting out of Frankfurt."

"Shouldn't be a problem. We'll contact you with the details as soon as it's arranged."

"It's going to be close," Kurtzman said. "You'll only have a few hours to locate them before it all falls apart."

"We've got some Interpol connections in Munich,"

Price told McCarter. "We'll sound the general alarm and see if they can assist."

"Thanks, Barb," McCarter said. "We'll take any help we can get at this point."

"Take care of yourselves," Brognola said. "And if I failed to say it before, nice job taking down Choldwig Burke."

"You did fail to say it first time around," McCarter said. "But I think we can overlook it this time."

"Just bring yourselves home in one piece," Price said. "That's an order."

"Got it. Out."

McCarter passed the phone back to Hawkins and flashed the group a broad grin.

"Well?" James asked.

"Let's get this boat moving, mates," McCarter said. "We got a plane to catch."

MUKHTAR TARIF STUDIED the contents of the crate they had broken open upon their arrival in Munich. His men had managed to procure safe haven in an abandoned sewage station on the outskirts of the city. The sun rose higher in the sky by the minute, and a quick check of his watch told him they wouldn't have much time to get the devices operational.

The Hezbollah cell leader looked at Marwa Shazzad and Harb. "Do we have anyone who could operate these vehicles?"

"I suppose it would depend on how they work," Shazzad replied. "They don't look like much more than discs constructed of a thin alloy. I'm not even sure how you know they're mobile."

"Because I've had my spies gathering as much intelligence as possible on our former benefactors." Tarif purposely injected a sharp sarcasm in his tone. "This operation has been in the planning phases for months. Do you think my father decided to solicit Burke's services on a whim?"

Shazzad lowered his eyes. "I apologize, Mukhtar. I wasn't trying—"

"Forget it." Tarif waved the matter away. "We don't have time for this. I want you to find as many engineers among our team as you can. I want to know how these machines operate by midday."

"But that…that's only a few hours!" Shazzad stammered.

"Then they had better get started."

Tarif whirled, gestured sharply for Harb to follow, and the two men moved away from the semi-trucks. Tarif knew that probably all of the devices weren't operational, but he had it on good authority that Burke's crews had managed to retrofit at least two of them for operation. It was simply a matter of process by elimination. He had total confidence his men would figure out how to operate them. Then they could move forward.

Once they were out of earshot, he said, "What's the status on the American, Delmico?"

Harb shook his head. "I'm afraid it's not good. We haven't heard anything from our men since they last had him stowed away."

This news took Tarif by surprise. "They were instructed to put him on a plane out of the country as soon as possible."

"I understand, Mukhtar, but there has been no word from them."

Harb splayed his hands to emphasize the complete helplessness of their situation. Tarif wasn't ready to accept such a defeat. Thus far, the Americans had demonstrated an impressive resolve where it concerned Delmico. He had to admit he hadn't expected this type of proficiency from their intelligence agencies. Usually they ran around like bumbling fools, always one or two steps behind the attacks, left only to clean up and scratch their heads at the tragedy of it all. He'd clearly underestimated the abilities of these individuals this time, although he had no intention of mentioning that fact to Harb or anyone else.

"Perhaps it's time we take a more aggressive posture in America," Tarif said. He folded his arms and stared at nothing in particular. "I think an alternative exercise might be in order. If we cannot obtain results through more conventional methods, then we must revert to an unconventional plan."

"And that is?"

"Since this scientist may have intimate knowledge of our operations, he's a liability we cannot afford, in spite of his biotoxin." Tarif replied. "Find him and eliminate him."

HELMUT STUHL HAD MANAGED to reach the highway and flag down a passerby. It hadn't really been that difficult. Picking up hitchhikers had always been less dangerous in Germany, for some reason. The people were more easygoing, and they didn't have as high of violent crime statistics as the U.S. or Great Britain—or even other European countries for that matter.

Once in Munich, Stuhl reached out to the Germanic Freedom Railroad's two main contacts in the city. After relating his tale of the ambush on their convoy and the betrayal of Tarif's Hezbollah fighters, he didn't have to urge them to rally to the cause.

Deep beneath the heart of Munich ran a subterranean waterway system of some renown. The vast majority remained in active use—predominantly accessed by public works personnel for the purposes of maintenance—but there were some areas long abandoned. The mercenaries of the GFR had set up a base of operations in one of those areas. Mostly, it served as an area to store their equipment such as firearms and other materials, or to hide their own people from authorities. They had never used it to stow away clients, so it had the distinct advantage of being known only to select members inside the GFR.

A number of men had gathered around Stuhl, who was studying maps of the city on some stacked crates of grenades converted to a makeshift table. The men were drinking steaming cups of coffee.

"What makes you think Tarif is even here in Munich?" one of the men asked Stuhl.

"Trust me, he's here."

"But how do you know?" the man persisted.

Stuhl stopped his perusal of the city maps and stared the man in the eye. By all rights, he was Burke's second in command, and in Burke's absence that put him in charge. Stuhl wanted to lash out at the guy for even daring to question him, but he realized that wasn't how Burke would have handled the situation. Then again, he wasn't Choldwig Burke. At the same time he knew that it wouldn't serve any real purpose. He had enough things on his mind without adding to them by causing a rift between him and the men. Stuhl knew he'd need every one of these guys to support him. After all, they weren't soldiers—they worked for sheer profit.

In many cases, that was how they made their living and fed their families.

"Tarif knew what he was taking," Stuhl said. "Otherwise, he wouldn't have planned the ambush for where he did or how he did it. Believe me, he has every intention of striking right here in Munich."

"And you know this how?" asked another man.

"Because it's my job to know," Stuhl replied. "Now, listen up. There is a conference that begins tonight. It's being held at the Hanns Seidel Conference Center in the downtown area. We're certain this is Tarif's target, based on our intelligence. I intend to make sure he doesn't succeed."

"What are we going up against?" asked Howe von Ruden, one of Stuhl's closer friends and supporters. "Do you have numbers?"

Stuhl nodded. "There were at least forty at the ambush site, or at least it seemed like that, and possibly more."

"I'd say based on where they attacked you, that guess is probably a bit inflated," von Ruden pointed out. "It would have seemed like a larger force than in reality. I'd say we're dealing with more like twenty."

One of the men agreed with von Ruden. "That's probably right. Any larger a group than that would draw too much attention, Helmut."

Stuhl nodded to concede the point. The attack had been swift and particularly brutal. There probably *had* been less than thirty of them. He considered the possibility there were more that hadn't accompanied the ambush team but then dismissed the notion. Tarif wasn't smart enough to have left one of his teams behind in the event he failed. The guy wasn't much of a tactician, as far as Stuhl could tell, anyway.

"Okay, let's assume a maximum of thirty before the ambush," Stuhl said. "We took out a few of them. So if we're talking about somewhere between twenty and twenty-five men, and assuming they use the platforms for their attack, that would leave approximately ten on the ground, since each platform is only capable of transporting about six men in full gear."

"I thought they stole all of the LAMPs," von Ruden interjected.

"They did. But our engineers only managed to get two of them operational before Burke ordered us to pull out."

"Has there been any further word from him?"

Stuhl shook his head once and looked absently at the map. "No. And I'm not sure there will be."

"You think he's dead," von Ruden stated simply.

"Yes."

"Then that means you're in charge now."

Stuhl's eyes narrowed at his friend. He did nothing to conceal the malice in his tone. "Just because I think he's dead doesn't mean he is. We must continue to assume he's alive until we know otherwise for certain. I'm only pointing out that if Burke were alive, he would have found some way to contact us by now."

"Maybe he's been captured," offered one of the other cell leaders. "Surely law enforcement would keep his detainment under secrecy and prevent his communicating with us."

Von Ruden's eyebrows rose. "It was never Burke's intention to be taken alive. I believe Helmut's right. If he believed the police were closing in, he would have tried to escape. And if that failed him, well…"

Von Ruden chose not to finish the thought and Stuhl was glad of it.

"The fact still remains we have no information on Burke right now," Stuhl said. "Until we do, we assume he's dead and proceed with our plans. Those were his last orders to me and I intend to follow them. So we need to get to doing what we came here to do and quit discussing it further."

He directed their attention back to the maps. "Now, as I was saying, I believe they'll attempt their attack here, at the Hanns Seidel Convention Center. This particular conference will be attended by at least a couple dozen diplomats, a large number of them Americans and British."

"Not a particularly large conference," von Ruden remarked, the surprise evident in his tone.

"I don't think it's meant to be. In fact, I think they

were hoping to keep a very low profile for this one. This only makes it an even more perfect target for a coward like Tarif. It gives him the sensationalism Hezbollah seems to want to achieve in every attack. Not only do they get to kill a number of Westerners, they will achieve a decisive blow against the antiterrorist movement.

"I'm certain their strategy will involve using the LAMPs to plan some sort of air-based campaign. It's possible they even plan to use the biotoxin under development by Simon Delmico. This is why Burke felt it was so important that our people get to him first."

"And what's their status with that mission?" von Ruden asked.

Stuhl shook his head. "I haven't heard from them, so I assume they are either still trying to locate him or they've encountered the American agents again. Either way, we must prepare ourselves for this attack. We know it's going to come."

"How do you want to proceed?" von Ruden asked.

"We should probably position six-man units here, here and here," Stuhl replied, pointing to specific points on the map near the perimeter of the convention center grounds. "I think we also might need a couple of two-man teams in cars for forward observation."

"And the rest?"

"We'll have them inside the Seidel. Get them positions catering, cleaning and busing…whatever they must do. But we must ensure that we can respond to any attack, whether it comes externally or from the inside."

Von Ruden's chuckle betrayed his discomfort with

the plan. "And exactly how do you propose we protect our men against these chemical agents?"

"They should pack protective gear," Stuhl said with a shrug. "If they keep a set of chemical gloves and a protective mask close at hand, that should reduce the risks of exposure. Besides the fact we don't have any evidence Tarif's even managed to get his hands on the agent."

"We should still prepare ourselves for that possibility," von Ruden replied.

"Agreed."

"We'll start getting the men into position. Within the hour, if possible."

"That should be more than sufficient." Stuhl's countenance darkened. "We will teach Mukhtar Tarif the price of spilling our people's blood. And I intend to collect on that debt. Personally."

CHAPTER SEVENTEEN

True to Hal Brognola's words, a plane awaited Phoenix Force at a private hangar. Once airborne, the men of Phoenix Force discussed their next move.

"Make no mistake about it, the numbers are ticking on this one, mates," McCarter told his crew.

"You're sure this summit is the target?" Encizo asked.

"Can't be much sure of anything at this point," McCarter replied. "But it's our best lead and it happens to fit the modus operandi of our Hezbollah friends."

"So what's the plan?" Hawkins asked.

McCarter kicked his feet against a fold-out table, leaned back in the seat of the Lear jet and folded his arms. "The summit is scheduled to take place inside the Hanns Seidel Convention Center in the central downtown area of Munich. Barb's managed to get three of us some cover credentials as maintenance crew that'll put us inside for it. We'll pick up our uniforms at the maintenance chief's office. That should allow us access to the areas we need. You and Rafe will work the exterior grounds in civvies. You blokes won't have any official creds, so you'll be on your own in staying under the radar of security and law enforcement."

"What about weapons?"

McCarter let out a deep sigh. "Sidearms only."

"What?" James expressed incredulity. "That's nuts."

Hawkins shook his head and drawled, "More like suicide."

"Maybe so, but that's the way it'll have to be. Everybody coming into or out of that place will be screened by security staff, both for proper ID and search by handheld wands. As it is, we won't have access to our weapons until we're inside the building."

"So we'll make entry unarmed," Manning remarked.

McCarter nodded.

"Any idea what we'll be up against in the area of numbers?" Manning asked.

"Not yet. I'm still waiting for additional intel from Aaron and his team," McCarter replied. "Given how many of Burke's people we've already taken down, and our original estimates, I'm guessing no more than ten."

"Those aren't such bad odds," Encizo said.

"No, but—"

The PDA on McCarter's belt warbled for attention. The Phoenix Force leader let his feet down and snatched it from its holster. He keyed in the code to disengage the key-lock and adjusted the earpiece, then engaged the video screen. "McCarter, here."

"It's Bear," came back Kurtzman's deep voice, followed by static and then his picture. The pair communicated over a secured, high-speed microwave data frequency enabled for picture and voice. "We've got some updates for you, but I'm afraid you're not going to like what you hear."

"Why not?" McCarter said. "My day's already started off with such good news. Can't imagine how it can't get anything but better."

"I'll pass your sentiments on to Santa. Anyway, we just got word some sort of major deal went down on a secondary road between Wiesbaden and Munich. The details are still sketchy, but there was talk of dead bodies, military-grade demolitions and automatic weapons. Right now, the *Bundespolizei* are keeping things under wraps."

"Makes sense," McCarter interjected. "The last thing they need is the press poking their collective noses into it."

"Maybe, but given the nature of this thing they're taking this one *very* seriously. We received word less than half an hour ago that because of the weapons used, they've activated the GSG-9. And in light of what's happened so close to the start of the antiterrorist summit, they're dispatching MEK to the Hanns Seidel as an additional security measure."

Kurtzman had been right: McCarter didn't like it. The GSG-9 had started as an elite border guard unit with strong ties to the military. Now, as a subunit of the German federal police, GSG-9 maintained the credibility as one of the finest official antiterrorist units in the world.

What had discomfited him even more was hearing

of the German government's decision to involve the *Mobileinsatzkommandos,* or MEK. Operating under the direction of the German federal states, the MEK answered to a Präsidium at the capital headquarters for that given territory's *Landeskriminalamt.* The SEK were the uniformed version, and McCarter would have much preferred to see them involved.

The Phoenix Force leader shook his head. "It's going to get tough real quick to tell the good boys from the bad."

"You won't get any argument from me," Kurtzman said in way of empathy. "You'll just have to be doubly careful, I guess. Sorry, David."

"Not your fault, mate," McCarter said.

"Hal's here. Wants to talk to you."

"Sure."

Brognola's face filled the screen immediately. "David, we just got word from Able Team. They caught Delmico, so you won't have to worry about anything on your end relative to the biotoxin."

"That's good to hear," McCarter said.

"I thought you'd like to know. Also, we're convinced that despite the fact you didn't find the LAMPs Burke's people had time to make them operational. Our best guess is maybe he'd have brought up half on the outside."

"What are their capabilities?"

"Bear's sending the more technical specifications now, but we're fairly convinced their main propulsion would be caged rotary blades."

"Sort of like the hover boats they use in swamplands like Miami and Louisiana?"

"Exactly like that, yes," Brognola said.

"Anything else?"

"Maximum weight capacity would be no more than four men plus two pilots."

"Two?"

"One steersman and the other on propulsion. Our technical consultants at MIT think the LAMPs are still too much in the prototype stage that Burke's people could have figured out how to utilize them with only a single operator."

"So they'll be functional but unstable," McCarter concluded.

"Correct."

"Fine, then it shouldn't be too hard to bring them down."

"You have the information on your IDs and such?" Brognola asked.

"Yes."

"Okay then. Out, here."

McCarter disconnected the call and a set of technical specifications replaced Brognola's face on his PDA. He didn't bother to study them. It was all a bunch of technical mumbo jumbo to him, and he didn't see how it would help them, anyway. McCarter had to stop a moment and ponder his grumpiness. He'd experienced an increasingly foul mood since the start of this little adventure.

Cut yourself some slack, mate, he thought. You just lost a close friend. "Bloody hell."

"None of that sounded good," James remarked.

"Calvin and his flair for understatements," Hawkins cracked.

"It's not going to be," McCarter replied. "Something major went down while we were chasing Burke. Hal thinks it involved either the GFR or Hezbollah. I'm betting on the latter. They also think at least some of the LAMPs will be operational, unstable but operational all the same. And they've eliminated the possibility of a biological attack. Either way, the German government's now involved GSG-9. And MEK will be present at the Hanns Seidel Convention Center."

"At least these LAMPs won't be an issue," Encizo said, steering them back to the topic at hand. "That's got to count for something."

"I don't like this at all," Manning cut in. "Not even a little."

McCarter knew exactly where the big Canadian was going, but he didn't comment. Instead, it was Hawkins who prodded him for an explanation.

"What are you talking about?"

Manning shook his head. "Didn't you hear him? The MEK will be at the convention center."

"Well, forgive my ignorance, but who is the MEK?" Hawkins asked.

"Civilian special forces," Encizo said. "Pretty much like American SWAT teams."

"Except they're trained in military tactics dating back decades," Manning said, "and those tactics have proved very effective. They've been emulated by agencies all over the world, including Delta Force."

"What bothers me most is that we won't be able to

identify them," McCarter said. "I don't want to get into a firefight with the wrong crew."

"I don't know how we can avoid it, David," Encizo replied. "There's no way we can be selective if the shooting starts, and I doubt an appeal to the German government would help us much at this point. And it's not exactly like we can go in there and say, 'Hey, fellas. Just your friendly neighborhood covert-ops team here to help out. Please don't kill us.'"

Hawkins nodded. "You can't argue with that. They see guns and they're going to defend themselves, whether our pistols are pointed at them or not."

"Not to mention the fact we'll have double the trouble to watch now, and only one-third the required firepower," James added.

That caused McCarter to look sharply at each man in turn. He visualized the wheels turning inside his head. "Maybe we won't have to."

Manning's eyebrows rose with inquisitiveness. "What?"

"Maybe we won't have to," McCarter said. "We have an opportunity here. Maybe we should exploit it."

"And how do you propose to do that?" Hawkins asked.

McCarter sat forward in his chair with increased intensity. "We've assumed up to this point the mission would be to defend the convention center from whatever threat the terrorists pose. Instead, what if we change tactics by focusing our efforts to simply remove the ones threatened?"

"Wait a minute," Encizo retorted, "let me get this straight. You're suggesting we evacuate the summit attendees."

"Why not?" McCarter countered. "We're only talking a couple dozen bloody diplomats here. It's not like hundreds. Maybe if we get them out of harm's way first, that'll slow them down and give the MEK boys a chance to react."

Hawkins cocked his head, scratched his neck and said, "That's not a bad idea, boss. Not bad at all."

"Agreed," Manning said. "And then once we've staged them in a safe zone, we can go to work on taking out the LAMPs. Besides, it just occurred to me that I might know someone who could help us out on this. It'll take a little time to track her down, but I can sure-fire guarantee she'll help us if I ask."

"Well, then, gentlemen, I'd say it sounds like we have a winner," Calvin James said. He looked at Mc-Carter and grinned. "Cigars for the Canuck and the limey."

McCarter's eyes rolled skyward. "God save us from the Yanks."

SHADOWED BY HARB and Shazzad, Mukhtar Tarif watched with great interest as his engineers rendered their first demonstration of the Low Altitude Military Platform's abilities. The flared front made the LAMPs appear more like wedges than their oblong, oval shapes. They were equipped with a low-slung seat at the back, just forward of the propulsion rotor. Two smaller rotors inside cages along either flank added to the steering abilities.

The one problem they had encountered were the magnetic gravities themselves. Because they worked on the principle of polar opposites, they generated a gravity field from which they could not shield the riders. This completely restricted the wearing of metal by any occupant. It wasn't something anyone in the group had thought of and to come up with a countermeasure had turned into nothing short of an engineering nightmare. That left them with two possibilities: send in unarmed men or use the platforms only to provide cover for their attack plan. Given their low numbers, Tarif elected to follow the latter plan out of sheer necessity. He couldn't afford to lose a single one of his men in this operation.

As the LAMPs buzzed back and forth across a desolate stretch of field bordering the Isar River—their speed and capabilities being measured and recorded by engineers—Tarif considered their plan. They had no biotoxic weapon to distribute. That left munitions and demolitions, of which they had managed to procure plenty. His connections had been in Munich months ahead of time, awaiting his signal. They were prepared to load the weapons on board the LAMPs once they had been proved by Tarif's team.

By now, he figured word had reached his father of their little coup d'état against Hezbollah's plans for the Munich summit. Tarif bin Nurraji had eyes and ears in nearly every country on earth. Surely he'd already been told of their success in overthrowing their German captors—not that this hadn't already been part of the plan—as well as Tarif's actions to accelerate operations. Tarif knew the risks; he knew there might be a heavy price to pay. But he just didn't give a damn. To him, it seemed more important that he make a name for himself and restore the pride of his countrymen—*and* his father.

Bin Nurraji could not be angry when his son returned with complete victory in the palm of his hand. And that was exactly what Tarif knew would happen. He'd already foreseen it. While the Hezbollah leader didn't necessarily subscribe to the egomania of some men in his position, he did believe each man was born to fulfill a destiny.

Tarif considered this one his and only his for the living.

"Very impressive," he told Harb and Shazzad after watching the engineers put the LAMPs through their maneuvers for a few minutes more. He turned on his heel and the men fell into step behind him. "Although I believe it would be better if we consider a way to maneuver them remotely."

"Remotely?" Shazzad asked with hesitation.

Tarif stopped and looked at him. "You said that almost as if you believe the idea is impossible. Do you think I'm mad?"

"Of course not," Shazzad replied. "I just didn't think—"

"No," Tarif cut in. He sighed. "You didn't. I think what many of you have failed to understand is the importance of maximizing our resources to effect. We took some rather significant losses in our assault on the GFR, despite the fact it was, in my assessment, an overwhelming success. We must take every precaution to conserve our numbers so we may engage a similar success in this operation. While it seemed like a good idea at first, I now think it's unwise to allow them to ride on such unstable vehicles. So, I want you to find a way to pilot them remotely."

"But we only have a few hours!" Shazzad protested. "There's no way we could retrofit them in time."

Tarif, who had started walking away, stopped dead in his tracks. He turned and pinned his subordinate with a baleful stare. He'd never liked Marwa Shazzad, and this experience was leading him to liking the man even less. Had this been another time, he would have simply ordered Shazzad's beard shaved and his ears cut off. Then he'd tie him in the desert and leave him for the hungriest of its beasts. Unfortunately, Shazzad possessed both the understanding and the loyalty of the majority of men, and any such action in this environment could have very undesirable results.

"Very well. We will suspend the operation for twenty-four hours."

"Mukhtar, I don't think that's a good idea," Harb said.

"And why not?" Tarif asked, hands on hips.

"Because every minute we wait will simply give our enemies that much more time to prepare. They will have to scramble to put in adequate resources on short notice."

"Exactly. And your statement makes my very point. Inasmuch as they are expecting us to attack tonight, it will come as some surprise when we don't. That will likely cause them to relax their guard and slacken their defensive posture. And then, when they least expect it, we strike!"

Tarif slammed his fist into his hand for emphasis as he returned his gaze to Shazzad. "Now get started."

Shazzad turned and departed in haste to follow Tarif's orders. Harb got back into step behind his protectorate. "We have another issue of which I think you should be aware."

"Why is it you always bring these things to me at a time like this?"

"There is the matter of our men in America and your intent toward Delmico."

Tarif smiled as they reached the small, makeshift camouflage shelter nestled in a copse of trees bordering the field. "You're wondering why I've ordered him eliminated. You think it's a waste of resources when it's obvious the Americans already know we're partly behind some of the recent activity. Yes?"

Harb didn't hide his surprise. "That's exactly what I was thinking."

Tarif nodded and shook his finger. "It's a good question, but I would think to a man of your experience, Harb, that the answer would be plain. As long as we keep the Americans occupied with chasing Delmico, we take the focus from our operations here. If our men are captured there, it would be, while tragic, acceptable losses. But here, at the heart of our operations, we cannot afford to fail. And we certainly cannot afford to lose any more men."

Harb nodded in understanding. "A very clever way of handling it. I'm impressed. I think you'll succeed your father well one day. Although I still think you have some maturing to do. I hope you may forgive what might seem like insolence, but is actually little more than an observation."

Tarif stepped over to Harb and laid hands on the giant's beefy shoulders. "From any other man, I would. But you, my friend, will never have reason to fear repercussions from *me*. And your point is valid. It will be some time before I have fully acquired my father's wisdom. But the point is, I will eventually gain it, and we both know that."

Harb nodded and the pair embraced. Tarif trusted Harb with his life. He was counting on Harb's complete loyalty and support in this operation. After all, Harb stood to lose his life if any harm actually befell Tarif. Bin Nurraji might also subject Harb to unspeakable punishments because he'd allowed the man to proceed without the blessing of the Hezbollah's grand leader.

Still, Harb couldn't help himself. He held a special place in his heart for the young firebrand, and Tarif knew it.

"I do have one mission for you," Tarif said.

"Anything for you, Mukhtar."

"When the operation here is complete and when the opportunity presents itself, I want you to kill Marwa Shazzad."

Harb didn't so much as twitch. "It shall be done," he replied evenly.

CHAPTER EIGHTEEN

Able Team took every precaution accompanying Simon Delmico back to St. Louis. Rather than tamper with the container and risk a major biological incident, they called in the Oklahoma State Police hazardous material unit to take charge and quarantine the scene. Assuming the vials were intact, the virus would be secured and transported separately to Our Lady of the Resurrection Hospital.

Aboard Stony Man's plane, Blancanales studied Delmico with interest while the scientist slept. He pondered what kind of trauma it might take for him to betray his government. What could drive any man or woman to do such a thing? In some ways, the entire psychology of it fascinated Blancanales. He thought back to the time around the birth of the country when Samuel Johnson had declared, "Patriotism is the last refuge of a scoundrel."

He would have called Delmico anything but a patriot.

But part of him couldn't help but feel sorry for the guy. He'd once been working on the same side as Blancanales. Delmico had made one ill-fated mistake—a mistake that cost several hundreds of thousands in property damages, sure—and they had put him out to pasture for it. A single mistake that anyone could have made. Blancanales wondered for a moment if one day he could possibly suffer a similar demise in his own career. He'd known better guys who'd received worse for doing less.

Yeah, maybe he'd waste an innocent person by mistake, tap the wrong phone at the wrong time, somehow unintentionally betray a Stony Man secret he shouldn't have. The difference was they couldn't convene some official tribunal. Blancanales would answer to a court of his peers, not the court of public opinion. The President of the United States simply couldn't afford that kind of publicity. In fact, one mistake by a member of their group could result in the unemployment line for all of them.

Blancanales shook it away. He bent over, checked to see that Delmico's shackles were secure, then moved to one of the seats in the forward compartment ranged around a small table. Schwarz had leaned back in the chair, resting his eyes, although Blancanales could tell his friend was still awake. Lyons was hunkered over a bottle of water, half a ham-and-cheese sub with the works and the latest report from the Farm.

"What's the word?" Blancanales asked.

Lyons looked up. "Our guest asleep?"

Blancanales nodded as he dropped heavily into the seat. "Yup."

"Well, it looks like Phoenix got Burke," Lyons replied, returning his attention to the report. "Says here they took him out along with about an estimated half of his crew. No LAMPs, though."

"So they're still out there."

Lyons nodded. "They also think this Tarif's somehow managed to get his hands on them."

"None of this still makes much sense," Blancanales said.

Lyons leaned back in his seat and clasped his hands behind his head. "Such as?"

"This whole thing," Blancanales replied. He waved his hand at the report. "All of this stuff with the GFR and Hezbollah. The theft of the LAMPs and this biotoxin the GFR contracted Delmico to make, but was actually for Tarif who has now, apparently, gone rogue and turned on his benefactors. The whole thing just smacks all wrong to me."

Lyons nodded. "It's messy."

"It's more than that. There's an unusual layer of complexity here that seems overdone. In fact, it almost seems clichéd, doesn't it?"

"You think too much, Pol," Schwarz piped up, his eyes still closed.

"Still, you've got to admit he's right," Lyons replied. "Seems a bit crazy a group like the GFR would try sinking their teeth into something like this."

"But that's just it. I don't think they were." Blancanales scratched his chin and considered his next words. "Even if Tarif and Hezbollah had planned this from the beginning, they wouldn't have known of Burke's plans to steal the LAMPs. Sure, so they knew about the bio-toxin because they probably convinced Burke to approach Delmico. But how would they have known Burke was planning to bring down that plane? In fact, how would they even have known about the LAMPs at all?"

"Maybe someone inside Burke's group told them," Lyons replied.

"Or maybe somebody on the outside of the whole thing told them."

"Well, either way, they've got it under control for the most part. Barb says they already have Tarif's target figured and McCarter's ready for them."

"Good deal. And what do we do with Sleeping Beauty in there?"

"We get him to help those sick kids. With any luck, no more will die before he can treat them."

Schwarz lifted his head. "And if he refuses to treat them?"

Lyons didn't bat an eyelash when he said, "I'll put a bullet in his brain pan."

Blancanales raised his eyebrows. "That's a bit of an impassioned response, Ironman."

"I'm not much for someone who kills innocent college kids," Lyons replied. "In fact, innocent people of any age."

"I don't think you'll have to worry about it," Schwarz said. He opened his eyes and raised his head to exchange looks with the pair of concerned friends focused on him. "What? You guys are looking at me like I'm on my deathbed."

"No offense, but you may not be far from it," Lyons said. He tried to chuckle away the offhand retort, but it sounded unnatural.

Schwarz had known Lyons way too long to take umbrage. "Could be."

"You just said we won't have to worry about it," Blancanales said. "Why?"

"Because I don't think Hezbollah will stop trying to kill him."

"Who?" Lyons asked.

Schwarz frowned and jerked a thumb in Delmico's direction. "Who do ya think? If they can't use the biotoxin for this operation the Farm thinks Tarif's planning, then they'll just try to eliminate him. Face it, as long as the guy's alive he's a liability to them. Not only does he possess the biological agent they hired him to concoct, he also holds the only known antidote in existence."

Blancanales splayed his hands. "Yeah, but as far as we know they haven't been able to get their hands on the agent."

"That we *know* of," Lyons reminded him sternly.

"Either way, I don't think Hezbollah will give up so easily. We already know the likelihood they'll go forward with their attack on the Munich summit, this Shangri-La Lady or not. All I'm saying is I think they'll take the same view toward our little biochemist friend in there and I think we should be ready for it."

"We'll be ready for it," Lyons replied. "We'll be ready like it's nobody's business."

As FAYED SAROUT replaced the phone receiver, elation coursed through his body.

At last, after many hours of pensive waiting, the order had come through to proceed with the operation full force. Really, he had been waiting more than hours for this moment. The past year had been spent planning this entire operation, and at long last he'd received authorization to execute their plan. And it would start with the assassination of the American scientist who had failed to meet the deadline.

This part of the operation hadn't exactly gone as Sarout planned. Tarif should have acted earlier and simply had Delmico eliminated instead of costing them more than half a dozen able-bodied soldiers of the cause. Clearly, Tarif was acting on his own. He couldn't possibly have been receiving his instructions from bin Nurraji's headquarters. Sarout had already heard rumors of Tarif's actions in Europe. To his way of thinking, this constituted bad faith on the man's part.

Well, it wouldn't serve any purpose to mourn it now—what was done was done, and Sarout had what he needed to proceed against his enemies. Now it came down to a matter of simple logistics. They had never attempted this kind of attack on American soil on such a grand scale. He'd received reports that the team that defeated his agents at the motel had somehow managed to track down Delmico. Word had it they were returning to the hospital with the scientist in tow.

Sarout couldn't allow that to happen. Not only would this negate all of the work his teams had done to get to this point, it would also give the Americans a way to counteract the biological agent. According to his intelligence, samples of Delmico's creation were still in existence.

"You are to steal it if you can," Harb had told him. "But your greater priority remains Simon Delmico. You will exterminate him at all costs. Do you understand?"

Yes, he had understood that perfectly and moreover, he considered it the right decision. They had already wasted entirely too many resources trying to rein in Delmico and acquire his biowarfare concoction. Sarout considered himself a man of action, and he didn't deem this waiting an activity worthy of a man of his talents, not to mention the waste of his men. Waiting to take action instead of acting tended to make men soft, even freedom fighters who had been forged in the battlefields of Lebanon and Iraq.

As soon as he received the order from Harb—a man for whom he had little respect but tolerated as he was the official spokesman for Tarif—Sarout began preparations for the assassination of Delmico. It wouldn't be easy. The man would be under constant guard, and security at the hospital in St. Louis would be very tight. The penetration of the American college had proved much easier.

Sarout left the study of their large cabin nestled among the woodlands outside of St. Louis. As he passed through the foyer of the front door and into one of the large living areas, the raucous sounds of gunshots blared from the large television. It was another one of those pathetic American Westerns. Sarout didn't ponder why none of his countrymen took the Americans seriously.

Despite their increased, albeit ineffective, security measures, they were still predictable. Their jihad had been affected more by the traitors the CIA had coerced into talking of their operations than any internal operations.

Lieutenant Dwight Maebrook sat with his feet propped on a leather ottoman, his hands laced behind his head and a half-empty beer wedged in his crotch. The beefy, red-faced cop looked in Sarout's direction with disinterest and returned his attention to the television. Sarout had found the American to be as slothful as he was greedy. Any man who had sold out to his country didn't deserve the attentions of a soldier like Sarout, let alone the blood money for which he'd contracted. Still, it wasn't his call. The orders had come straight from Tarif bin Nurraji's headquarters that he *would* work with Maebrook. Bin Nurraji believed in honoring his contracts and Sarout, whether he liked it or not, had to follow his master's wishes or face certain death.

"I have just received instructions," Sarout said.

"Uh-huh," Maebrook retorted without letting his eyes off the blaring television.

"We have been ordered to proceed with our operation."

That bit of information got Maebrook's attention enough that he muted the blaring sounds of horses, gunfire and cavalry trumpets. "What does that mean, 'proceed with our operation'? What operation?"

"We are to eliminate the scientist at all costs."

"Who? Delmico? You've been told to kill Delmico? Says who? That was never a condition of my contract." Maebrook got on his feet. Sarout prepared for a tantrum, the third in as much as two days. "I told bin Nurraji I wasn't going to kill no one!"

Sarout resisted the urge to pull the pistol dangling from a holster beneath his arm and shoot the infidel between the eyes. He wasn't really that interested in what Maebrook had to say. He had his orders, and that was all he really needed. He shrugged with indifference. "Whether you agree with it or not does not change a thing. Besides, American, it's not like you're getting your hands dirty. You've been paid to help sow disinformation. That is all. In fact, I would prefer you not to involve yourself in any of this, but that is not my decision. Just as it is not your decision whether Delmico lives or dies. You have been paid the agreed-upon price, and you are expected to honor that agreement, for if you do not, then I am authorized to kill you, burn your body and scatter your ashes into a muddy pit of swine. And in my mind, this would be a most fitting death for you. Do you understand this?"

Sarout waited for Maebrook to speak out again, but he saw something change in the American's eyes. He'd seen this same thing in others before: defeat. So the man was nothing but a coward, after all, a soft and spineless rodent with neither the courage nor the capacity to face an enemy under even odds.

Maebrook still tried to pass off his bravado with his preposterous ranting. "Oh, I understand perfectly, camel boy. But that don't mean I've got to agree with you. And don't forget who's feeding you all this intelligence."

Sarout stared at Maebrook a moment and then shook his head. "Don't press me, American. I'm not amused or impressed. Now, you will need to tell us exactly the best way of getting to Delmico."

"Is he under protection?"

Sarout nodded, and Maebrook paused to think about that. He turned and went back to his seat, returning to his exact former position. Maebrook finally lit a cigarette, and Sarout wondered if the guy expected him to stand there all day and wait for him to get around to expressing his thoughts. Either way, they wouldn't have much time to complete the operation.

Maebrook took a few drags from his cigarette, scratched the back of his neck and belched.

"Seems to me," he finally said, "they'll probably use their own to guard him. That means that cocky blond one will be in charge, more than likely."

"You're speaking of the men from the FBI."

"FBI, shmef-BI. There's no way those guys are run-o'-the-mill Feds."

Sarout had to admit this observation interested him. "What makes you think so?"

"You're kidding me. Right?" Maebrook looked at the man with disbelief. "For one, they're too goddamn competent. I talked to witnesses who saw them shooting it out with your teams. Those guys operated like nothing I've ever heard of before. Those students said it was like watching something out of the movies. I'd say CIA—it's allegedly illegal for spooks to operate inside U.S. borders, even under the newer laws. Some kind of black ops… Delta Force types, maybe."

"Could they be from your NSA?"

Maebrook shook his head. "Don't fit the profile. Too much brawn, too few brains."

"Either way, they are going to present the same problem they have presented before."

"Don't count on it," Maebrook said. "You forget, you've got an inside man."

The statement didn't make Sarout feel any better, although he knew Maebrook was right. It only made sense. They would need to get him inside that team, somehow, and then he could lead them to Delmico. They'd do the actual job. He didn't trust Maebrook beyond simply providing the information. And in doing it this way, he could use Maebrook until he didn't need him anymore and then cancel his contract as a liability, similar to the fate they planned for Delmico. He could easily explain away the entire incident to bin Nurraji and Tarif.

"You have a plan?" Sarout asked Maebrook.

"I always have a plan," Maebrook said, and he returned to watching television.

As soon as Able Team touched down in St. Louis they proceeded directly to the hospital. The trip took only twenty minutes by vehicle from the airport. Delmico rode in the back of the SUV, wedged between Lyons and Schwarz. Blancanales had taken the wheel this time out of concern the time gap had closed between Schwarz's initial exposure and Corvasce's prediction of the onset of symptoms.

As the early light of dawn broke the horizon, the Able Team warriors began to feel the effects of their vigil. They'd been going full-bore since the previous morning with little time to rest. Schwarz especially had begun to feel the effects, which were exacerbated by the biotoxin. To make matters worse, they still hadn't been apprised of the HAZMAT team's progress in either the clean-up or salvage operation. The whole thing had them nervous.

Lyons felt it especially although he was generally the last to complain about it. Even among his closest allies he'd always made it a point not to grumble about the job, although sometimes he couldn't help but wonder how much of a difference they really made. Then again, he didn't take much of an impassioned view toward the work—Lyons wasn't a crusader. He viewed this as more of a duty. He owed his country, and he believed in defending those who were incapable of defending themselves. Well, there wasn't much point to thinking about those kinds of things. Ultimately, they served only to put him in a foul mood and that was exactly the kind of distraction that got guys killed in his line of business.

Corvasce greeted them at the entrance to the Communicable Diseases Ward. He kept his eye on Schwarz as he said, "Gentlemen. How you feeling, Agent Black?"

Schwarz nodded. "A little stiff."

"Yes, muscle stiffness is one of the early symptoms. I think you're probably just about done running around. I received information from your superiors that you've found a potential antidote."

"Yeah," Blancanales said, giving Delmico a gentle shove. "Meet Dr. Simon Delmico."

"Otherwise known as Dr. Doom," Lyons growled.

"The good doctor here is also the concoctor of this biotoxin that's giving everyone the nasties," Blancanales added. "We caught him trying to sneak it, along with the antidote, out of Tulsa. Came from his own private stash, you could say."

Corvasce did nothing to hide the utter contempt in his eyes upon hearing that. He stared hard for several seconds at Delmico, a look that could have caused even hardened men to shrink. "You barely have the right to call yourself a doctor, sir."

"That's your opinion," Delmico mumbled.

"Whether it's his opinion or not doesn't much matter," Lyons said in an ominous tone. "Because either way, you're going to help him cure what remaining kids here are alive, and you'll do it quickly. Otherwise I'm going to exercise a little street justice of my own."

Delmico looked surprised. "Is that an ultimatum?"

"It's a choice," Lyons said. "You either help get these people better or I take you somewhere they'll never find you. How do you want to play it?"

"It doesn't even matter, you fool," Delmico said. "That antidote, if it even survived your Machiavellian heroics, is just that—an antidote. It's not a cure."

"You're saying it's strictly prophylactic?" Corvasce asked.

"Yes."

"Then you've got a lot of work to do, sonny," Lyons said. He shoved Delmico in the direction of the ward and added, "So get to it."

Schwarz pulled Corvasce up short as the rest headed through the doors. "Listen, um, Doc...what's going to happen if he doesn't come up with a cure? What's that mean for me and the kids? I mean, how will I know if—"

Schwarz couldn't seem to find the words to finish his sentence. For the first time in a while, he'd begun to experience fear. He'd spent the vast majority of his career fighting an enemy he could see. This time around he was up against something for which he had no tactic, no quick way out; neither brawn nor brains would serve him this time. He felt helpless.

Corvasce smiled and put a comforting hand on his shoulder. "We'll figure it out, Black. I won't let you or the kids in the ward die. If there's anything I can do, I will. I won't rest until we figure this out. Deal?"

"Yes, sir."

"Good. Now why don't we get some additional tests done on you. I may not be able to stop this thing, but we've come up with some drugs that might help us slow it down considerably."

And with that, the two men headed for the ward.

CHAPTER NINETEEN

Magda Flaus, special police investigator for the *Bundes-polizei,* decided to accept a call from a man who insisted he speak only to her. She wasn't accustomed to such calls since she'd left fieldwork some time ago following her promotion. That eliminated any informants, and she had better odds being struck by a cabbage truck than to receive a call from former colleagues. Sadly, there remained a chauvinistic view toward women, particularly if they held officer-level rank as she did.

"Hallo?" she said into the receiver.

"Guten tag, fraülein," came the greeting. The caller then switched to English. "I suppose you're fairly busy these days. Do you have a minute for an old friend?"

It took her only a moment to recall that voice and she could hardly believe her ears when she did. "Gary?"

"Right!" Manning replied.

"My God. How are you?"

"I'm okay. And you?"

"I'm okay, too. I'm surprised to hear from you." She paused, kicked herself for the almost coquettish way in which she'd reacted. She caught her breath and steadied her nerves. "Where are you calling from?"

"Right here in Germany," Manning replied. He paused, then added, "Munich, to be more precise."

Flaus heard the tone in Manning's voice and immediately caught the reference. Their short relationship, although she really considered it more of a brief romance than a relationship, had been more about mutual need for companionship than anything else. Still, this unexpected call from Manning had caused her some giddiness, and she had always wondered what might have happened if their careers hadn't pulled them apart. She'd told herself when he'd gone, "Be practical, Magda. You're from two different worlds." So maybe her head had heeded her advice, but obviously it had taken her emotions some time to catch up. But it had been enough of a connection she could read the meaning behind his words.

Being a ranking case officer in the *Bundespolizei* had its definite advantages. One of those happened to be information access. The Frankfurt Präsidium of *Landeskriminalamt* kept Flaus well informed of all activities in and around their jurisdiction. In just a few hours they would be holding the summit on terrorism in Munich, and already both civilian and antiterrorist units had been dispatched to multiple locations.

"I take it you're in Munich on business?" she asked.

"Yeah, you could say that." His rather cryptic reply told her that his mission, whatever it might be, had been approved by whoever oversaw American secret operations. But Flaus knew enough to understand Manning wouldn't be working in Germany with either the knowledge or official sanction of her own government. Now she faced a choice. She knew he'd only call for one reason: he needed help of some kind. They had gone through weeks of antiterrorism tactics training together, had a bit of a romance and had kept in touch over the years. Of course she'd help him.

"When can I see you?" she blurted before her brain seemed to know what her tongue had just done.

"I'd like to see you," he replied. "How soon can you meet me?"

She looked at her watch and said, "Two hours?"

He told her it would be soon enough, gave her a number to call him when she got to Munich, then hung up. Flaus grabbed her handbag, slid into her overcoat, left her office and headed for the train station.

MAGDA FLAUS hadn't changed much.

Neither had Gary Manning. Sure they were a bit older than the last time they had seen each other, but Manning could feel the energy between them, and he knew Flaus could, too. He couldn't find exactly the right choice of words, at first. They had purposely kept their conversation cryptic on the phone. Through postcards and letters, Flaus knew Manning wasn't with the RCMP anymore, and his activities these days were in a higher order of importance *and* secrecy.

They decided to meet at a small pub in an uptown square of Munich. Manning took in the surroundings.

He had decided not to tell Flaus that his teammates were scattered throughout the bar. McCarter had managed to engage a fellow Briton in conversation. Encizo and Hawkins remained together at the bar, nursing beers and watching everyone carefully while making small talk like a pair of businessmen. James had ordered food and sat where he could get a full view of the entrance.

"You look good," Manning told Flaus when she came through the door and walked directly to his table. He hesitated a moment, then gave her a quick kiss on her cheek.

"You, too." Her tone was noncommittal although she smiled.

Manning remembered that smile, a pleasant smile. God, she was still as lovely as ever—he wondered why they had never hooked up. Not that marriage for either of them would have been practical. Working for an ultracovert, elite unit and flying around the world to kill terrorists didn't exactly make for romantic dinner conversation.

And Flaus had elected to focus on her career, which left her with no time to think about a husband and children. Manning wondered a few times over the years what drove Flaus but quickly realized he already knew the answer. The very same things that drove him drove Flaus—duty, honor, country, a sense of right and wrong.

Manning held her chair out. She inclined her head with a half smile and sat. He reached out and grabbed both her hands as soon as she stripped off her gloves.

"How have you been?" he asked with genuine interest.

She studied him for a moment. "I've been well, thanks. And you?"

"I've had my moments, but mostly I'm doing well."

"I am glad to see you," she said with abrupt exuberance in her mischievous brown eyes.

Manning felt his face flush slightly and averted his gaze. Damn her, she had a way of taking him off his guard. She had always been that way, and Manning wondered what it was about her that left him feeling like a shy schoolboy. Here he was, a conflict-hardened vet who could still go soft over a woman with whom he'd had a fling more years ago than he cared to recall. Manning let the moment pass in favor of getting down to business.

"Look, um…Magda, I— That is… Look, we have a big problem. I need your help."

She nodded. "Does this have anything to do with the summit at the Hanns Seidel?"

Manning looked around to ensure nobody appeared to be eavesdropping on them, then nodded. "We think Hezbollah is going to try to hit the convention."

"When?"

"Tonight. Or at least, we have to assume it's going to be tonight."

"What happened on the autobahn," she asked. "Are these two things connected?"

"Yes, we believe so. Are you familiar with a group calling themselves the Germanic Freedom Railroad?"

"Of course," she said, consciously lowering her voice. "We've been attempting to find something that will allow us to arrest Choldwig Burke, their leader. Something more than just a petty charge that will have him out of jail before our paperwork is complete."

Manning heard the frustration in her voice and tried to decide whether to tell her about Burke's demise. He couldn't officially say a word about their operations. It had nothing to do with trust. Manning trusted the woman almost as much as he trusted his teammates. But to disclose what they had been doing in Germany for the past thirty-six hours probably wouldn't play well with the upper brass. Then again, he didn't have time to pussyfoot around on this deal. They needed her help if they wanted to succeed in the operation, and that just damn well meant they would have to trust someone. Manning couldn't think of a better candidate.

"Burke's no longer a worry."

"My God," she said, sharply inhaling. "You killed him?"

"Not personally, but I can definitely confirm he's dead." Manning shook his head. "You didn't hear that from me. And anyway, it's not important right now. What's more important is that we think he was betrayed by Hezbollah. That's what all the shooting was about on that back road out of Wiesbaden. Pretty soon, you'll probably hear someone's discovered the smoldering ruins of a boat with a whole bunch of dead men on board."

"You again?" she interjected.

Manning gave her a curt nod. "That's when Burke went down. It's also when we discovered there might be an attack on this summit. Magda, we're dealing with some pretty nasty customers here. These aren't your average criminal types. Hezbollah is being led by a man named Mukhtar Tarif. We think he's taking orders from his father of El Tarif bin Nurraji, the most powerful and influential Hezbollah sect in the world."

"I see."

"There's something else you need to know. Because Tarif betrayed Burke, we think the GFR plans to retaliate."

"Do you believe they know of Tarif's plans to attack the summit?"

"We can only assume they do since they were helping them out. Beside the fact, there wasn't any other reason for Hezbollah to be in Germany. They could've hidden in any number of countries much better suited until they chose to implement their operations. Instead, they chose Germany and put a splinter cell in the United States, and now we think they're about to make their move."

Flaus sighed. "You know I trust you. Right, Gary? You *do* know this?"

"Of course. I don't think you'd be here if you didn't."

"Then you must also know that I could lose my job if I was caught meeting with you like this. In fact, I could be held accountable for not arresting you on the spot. Simply knowing that you are operating illegally in my country and doing nothing about it would be grounds for my immediate dismissal and arrest. I'm afraid the Präsidium is not very forgiving about such things."

"I understand you took a risk," Manning cut in. "And

I appreciate it. But we need your help or a lot of people could get killed in this thing. It's not just about Hezbollah or the summit anymore. We think the GFR's going to be looking for a payback of some type. We don't think they'll be really discriminate when the shooting starts."

For a long time she didn't reply. Manning knew what he was asking her to do was… Well, he hadn't asked her to *do* anything yet. That didn't mean she didn't know it was coming. She'd worked hard to get where she was. She had a good career. To betray all that now went against the very grain of her own professional code of conduct. And yet, he knew she would do it.

"I will help you, Gary. You fight the good fight. I believe in you and in what you do. And I believe that to turn you in would be the greater sin to my country. So I will help you unconditionally as long as you promise something in return."

"Of course."

"Whatever you're about to ask me to do…do not ever ask me again."

"I understand."

She replied with a sharp nod, then leaned forward. "Okay, then. It's settled. Tell me what you need me to do."

CHAPTER TWENTY

Helmut Stuhl listened with interest as his informant told him of the increased activities by the German federal authorities in the past twelve hours. Little doubt remained in Stuhl's mind that the GSG-9 would soon learn of GFR's involvement with Hezbollah, assuming they didn't already know. They had processed the site of Tarif's betrayal and identified a number of his people; these were men the *Landeskriminalamt's* records indicated had direct ties to the GFR. It wouldn't take a genius to eventually make the connection to Tarif.

But the most disturbing report was confirmation of Choldwig Burke's death. This confirmed Stuhl's worst fears—his friend and leader had fallen for the cause of the GFR. Burke would be missed, and as long as Stuhl had breath in his body he would never allow their members to forget Burke. Now, however, they had no time for mourning. Reports had reached him that Tarif had fresh reinforcements secreted away somewhere inside Munich.

Stuhl intended to find them.

"What about the Americans who killed Burke?" Howe von Ruden asked.

"Yes," another unit leader echoed. "How about the Americans?"

Stuhl studied the faces of his unit leaders in turn. "We don't have time to worry about the American commandos right now. We have bigger problems. We need to find out where Tarif is hiding his men and destroy them. That's the only thing that matters. If we do this, we can prevent him from any further damage as well as protect ourselves. We must defend what little we have left. Perhaps we can even recuperate some of our losses."

"Nonsense," von Ruden snapped. "You don't believe that any more than the rest of us do."

"It doesn't matter what I believe, now does it?" Stuhl said. "Our people are watching the Hanns Seidel Convention Center. I don't believe they'll hit them tonight. I think Tarif will wait. I think he'll let some of this blow over, wait for the police to let down their guard before he strikes."

"And what if the Americans *do* happen to get in our way?" von Ruden asked.

"Then that will be their problem, Howe," Stuhl replied. "If they get in our way, they'll simply wind up as collateral damage. And who's going to ask questions? Any operations the Americans have going on inside our country right now would hardly be sanctioned by the German government. Especially after they agreed to host this antiterrorist summit."

"It still may not be that easy to discover where Tarif's people will be operating," von Ruden said.

"What do you mean?"

"Oh, come now, Helmut. We all know our government doesn't exactly take the threat from terrorists seriously. German citizens have rarely been the targets of terrorist activity, and in fact we are seen by a large part of the world community as more of a haven for terrorists than a bane. How else may those like the Americans view us as an evil and perverse nation, willing to sell out our very mothers for the latest cause we deem fit to meet the end needs of a solution."

Stuhl raised his hand in defense. "Please, Howe! Spare us your pitiful views of our still undergoing punishment for the Third Reich. It's an old story."

"Maybe, but still a true one."

"Whether it's true or not isn't really the point. We're here to settle this situation once and for all. I don't know about the rest of you, but I intend to seek retribution for Mukhtar Tarif's betrayal of our leader and people."

Von Ruden's countenance took on a scarlet hue. "We are here to make money. That's why most of us joined this pitiful band. Your personal little vendetta against Tarif is solely yours. As long as we stand to gain from it, I'm willing to go along out of respect for our friendship and Burke's memory. But the minute this looks like it's going to stop being profitable, I'm out of it. Understand?"

The sting of von Ruden's words left Stuhl aghast. He couldn't believe his ears, although it really should have come as no small surprise his friend would take this attitude. After all, they had all joined the GFR for money, and so far he hadn't demonstrated how obtaining vengeance on Tarif would accomplish those ends. He would have to do that before he could hope to gain their respect or support. For that matter, he would also need some means by which to live once this thing came to an end. He hardly doubted he'd continue Burke's business.

Stuhl chewed his lower lip a moment as he thought furiously about his reply. He needed some type of leverage—something that would appeal to more than a sense of honor but also to a sense of greed—and it didn't take him long to spin the same profit motive Burke had originally spun when first getting them into this deal.

"Has it occurred to any of you that there *is* money to be made in this operation?" Stuhl asked.

"How much money?" von Ruden asked, cocking his head.

"More than you could dream possible," Stuhl replied quickly. He leaned forward and looked around to add the conspiratorial effect. "Think about it. That equipment Tarif stole from us, the LAMPs? They are worth a considerable amount of money to the British."

"How do you know?"

"Burke was interrogating a pilot from the RAF plane we brought down that was transporting the things from CERN to Portsmouth. The guards told me they overheard the pilot tell Burke their estimated worth. We're talking billions of British pounds. That's what Burke *really* wanted them for. He'd planned to sell them off to the highest bidder once they were operational."

"And now you're saying that if we get them back, we can still make that kind of money?"

Stuhl had to sweeten the pot by reining back their expectations. If he spun the tale too good now, they wouldn't believe him. "Maybe not as much as we initially expected, since we don't have the resources to make the damn things work. But they'll still be worth enough to make it worth everyone's while, and then some."

There was a bit of truth to his statement. One of Burke's plans had been to make all six of the devices operational, to prove their value, before selling them out to the highest bidder. Burke had talked of retirement with that final job, but Stuhl had questioned his friend's volition on that particular point. There had always been something relentless in Burke's personality, something inevitable that had destined him to be a soldier of fortune and remain one. Beneath that keen intellect and genius IQ had lurked baser instincts.

Stuhl couldn't be sure if Howe von Ruden and the rest of this band would even believe him. The LAMPs were an engineering feat certainly beyond his comprehension. Only Burke and a handful of their engineers had really understood the devices, and now they were all dead. Nobody remained who could make good use of them. Von Ruden knew this and he knew Stuhl knew it, as well, so there wouldn't be much fooling his colleagues. For now, he could tempt them with tales of fortune and hope it stood the test long enough to locate Tarif and finish him.

"You had better be right about this, Helmut," von Ruden finally said.

Stuhl felt like challenging his friend but opted against it. He could not risk putting enmity between them. They had already lost Burke, the only one who'd seemed able to bring a sense of cohesion and unity to the GFR. If Stuhl alienated his only other ally now—an ally who had garnered a significant amount of local support while Stuhl and Burke were absent—he risked driving further wedges between him and what remained of the GFR's resources. He simply couldn't afford that at this point.

"I am right" was all Stuhl could think to say. "You must trust me on this."

Von Ruden nodded. "What's your plan?"

"We must assume that Tarif will split his forces. I never thought he would have left some of them behind, but the reports I'm getting back from our contacts would lead me to think otherwise."

"Such as?"

"Well, there are reports of activities just outside the city." Stuhl directed their attention to the map. "Here, near the Isar River."

"This makes sense," one of the unit leaders interjected. "I know the area fairly well. I used to hunt quail and pheasant all along those banks with my father when I was just a kid."

"And it would be the perfect place for Tarif to test the capabilities of the LAMPs?" von Ruden asked.

The man nodded.

Von Ruden looked Stuhl directly in the eyes. "We should send a team to check it out immediately."

Stuhl nodded. "I agree. But my contacts have also told me there are several places right here in the city that may require further investigation."

"Such as?"

"They supposedly have staging areas set up in Altstadt, Haidhausen and Schwabing. They are small units, allegedly, with no more than five or six men each. They are storing weapons and equipment, and have been ordered to stand by in case Tarif needs them."

"How do you know all of this?" von Ruden asked.

"Do you think we take on just any business partner so callously? Burke insisted on finding out everything he could about his enemy. We inserted a spy into their ranks long ago, one of the Hezbollah men who owed us a favor for hiding him from Interpol. This man is simply returning the favor."

Von Ruden grunted with dissatisfaction. "It apparently didn't do you much good to have this spy when Tarif's men were cutting you to ribbons on the abandoned road. I wouldn't doubt it if he arranged to lead you there. Maybe he was even found out, and they offered him his life in return for betraying you."

"Then why are we still getting these reports?" Stuhl countered. "And there may have been no way he knew about the attack of our convoy."

"Why don't we just say what we're really thinking?" Hans Gewalt remarked. "None of us trusts these Arab bastards, so let's just admit it and get on with our plan. We need to hunt down these fuckers and eradicate them. It's as simple as that. And if we don't give our men the opportunity to do that and make some extra cash on the side, well then, none of this is really worth our trouble. I know you liked Burke, Stuhl. Hell, we all liked him. But the reality here is that we hate the Arabs more than we liked Burke, and it's high time we start doing something about that. So I say we break into units and go hunt them down like the animals they are!"

A long silence rippled through the men gathered around Stuhl. For once, everyone nodded in agreement. This wasn't really about getting revenge for the betrayal and murder of Burke. They could make it sound like that all they wanted—coating it like a frosting on a cake so it would taste better—but in truth these men were simply looking for some action and blood. Stuhl worried about this, in part because he wondered when it actually came down to executing their plan if they could operate like the well-oiled machine they were.

"I think Gewalt's plan sounds rather good about now," von Ruden agreed. "It *is* time for us to take back our honor. We're wasting time talking about it. It's time to get on with it."

"Fine," Stuhl said. He folded the map and slipped it inside his field coat. "We begin operations in two hours."

Yes, Mukhtar Tarif was about to feel the unbridled wrath of the Germanic Freedom Railroad.

CHAPTER TWENTY-ONE

The mission had started out simple enough, but it sure hadn't stayed that way, and all the skullduggery put David McCarter in a foul mood.

Nonetheless, as soon as Manning finished his pitch, Magda Flaus contacted her people and arranged to get them some local transportation. Apparently, Flaus also had enough loyal connections inside the *Landeskriminalamt* that it wasn't long before the men of Phoenix Force found themselves inundated with an entire accordion folder full of dossiers on all known GFR members operating in Munich. They studied the contents of the files and pictures now laid out on a large table in the hotel suite they shared.

McCarter checked his watch. "We need to leave here in the next half hour. The dignitaries will already be arriving. We won't get another crack at this, so we'd best be on the numbers all around."

"How do you figure this'll play out?" Hawkins asked.

McCarter frowned. "I don't think they'll make their move tonight. It's too soon. It will be best for them to hit in broad daylight to maximize impact and confusion."

"Midday, I'd say," Encizo added. "Probably right after lunch when everyone will be filled on food and wine, and off their guard."

"I still think my idea's the best one," Manning stated. "If Hezbollah betrayed them and stole the LAMPs like we think, I can guarantee you the GFR's going to be looking for some payback. They're probably already scouring the city, looking for Tarif's men."

"And according to this intelligence, they'll be operating from a safe house that could be located anywhere in this city," Encizo pointed out.

"So let me get this straight," James said. "Manning's now solo inside the convention center while the rest of us go on this little scouting party to look for the GFR."

Manning nodded. "I'll have Magda there to help identify the friendlies."

"Well, I'm more than happy to do it however you think's best, David," James replied. "But I got to say what I think, and I think that's a bit risky."

"Noted, mate," the Phoenix Force leader replied. "But we've also agreed that evacuation is the best plan if anything goes down. Plus, we'll be in two-way contact with him at all times. If he needs our support, we can be their most ricky-tick."

"What about the exterior watch at the convention hotel?" Hawkins inquired.

"Won't matter," McCarter replied. "Between MEK,

local police and GSG-9 there'll be plenty of coverage on the exterior. That can only stand to benefit us."

"Those cops will be easy targets," Hawkins interjected. "They'll be the ones most conspicuous because they'll be busy trying to look anything but. A few well-trained fighters from either the GFR or Hezbollah wouldn't have any trouble taking them out."

"Don't underestimate this bunch," Manning cautioned the most junior member of the team. "The *Bundespolizei* are some of the very best at what they do. They've got a lot of years of success behind them, and they're more than capable of pulling this off."

"Agreed," McCarter said. "And besides the fact, we can't police the whole bloody country. We need to choose our priorities carefully. If we're going to pick a fight, I'd rather it be on our terms where we can control the situation and minimize our exposure. I don't relish getting our arses blown off by the cops, nor do I want to have to worry about innocent civilians in the line of fire. Plus, I trust Gary and his friend."

"We'll be fine," Manning added in support of McCarter's confidence.

"Well, we'd best get cracking, then," Encizo replied. "We've got a long night ahead of us."

"YOU KNOW, the only problem we're going to have with this deal is figuring out where the GFR might try to hit first," McCarter said as he stared at the city maps Flaus provided. "A half dozen potential targets and we don't have a bloody clue which one it could be."

"I don't think there's any way we can make those

kinds of decisions logistically," Encizo said from behind the wheel of their rented sedan.

"Well, we can't very well sit around here and wait for something to jump out," Hawkins drawled. "I say we get busy."

James nodded as he checked the action on the Austrian-made Glock Model 18C. The time crunch hadn't allowed Stony Man to procure more than that since they had originally thought only handguns would be allowed inside the facility.

All five men were carrying the exact same piece. This particular model featured single-round or autofire mode, and to compensate for the lack of more powerful weaponry, the arms dealer had thrown in extra 9 mm Parabellum ammunition. James liked the Glock, not only for its durability but also its reliability. He'd rarely experienced a jam with one, plus they were well balanced with good trigger pull. The extended 19-round box magazine also made them the better choice under the circumstances.

Each of the Phoenix Force warriors checked their weapon in turn, then McCarter and James went EVA. Their target was a known safe house for GFR mercenaries who worked under one Howe von Ruden. James had done a brief study of the guy's dossier and it left an impression.

In fact, the credentials of a good number of the men in the GFR stood out above the average mercenary. Many were college educated, a number with trade skills and quite a few more with families. This fact had James concerned—like all the rest of his comrades—that they might encounter innocent bystanders. James wasn't exactly keen on the idea of shooting some guy who was just trying to make a living and feed the mouths of three young daughters. Still, they had made their choices and decided to throw into the lot of thugs and murderers. A soldier of fortune was still just that, no matter how many letters he had behind his name.

James had to forget about those realities and concentrate on the ones that would keep him alive in the heat of a firefight or hand-to-hand skirmish.

McCarter crossed the darkened street in front of the two-story, wood-and-cobblestone home in the district of Arabella Park. According to Flaus, only the extremely wealthy lived along this stretch of estates, and the neighborhood remained one of the nicest in the city. Despite the luxurious surroundings, the place still had a small-village quality to it and reminded James of places he'd visited under much more pleasant, certainly less ominous and morbid terms.

McCarter reached a waist-high wall of limestone that butted against a rolling green front lawn. Night had finally settled on Munich, and the streets were practically deserted. James came up next and took the area on the opposite side of the walkway that emerged from the steps that descended directly from the house to the broad sidewalk. McCarter and James remained for cover as Encizo and Hawkins burst from the car, sprinted across the street and ascended the flagstone steps.

Once they reached the door, McCarter and James climbed after them and split off to find alternate paths of egress from the house. Flaus hadn't been able to provide them with architectural plans to any of the suspected GFR operation locations; not that they would have had time to study them. They were going in blind on this one—blind on all of them really—and this would prove especially tough on unfamiliar ground under cover of darkness. The men of Phoenix Force planned to give themselves every possible advantage.

McCarter had barely rounded the back corner of the house when four men emerged from the porch carrying submachine guns. The men wore alert expressions, almost as if they knew their security had been compromised, but they didn't immediately notice McCarter. Neither did they notice James, barely visible at the opposing corner. James read it as a signal to engage when McCarter stepped from the shadows, raised his Glock 18C and squeezed off a short burst.

James sighted down the slide of the Glock pistol and triggered his own volley. The SMG-toting terrorists were unprepared for such a vicious cross fire. McCarter scored the first hit with a 3-round burst to an enemy gunner's head. The man staggered under the barrage, then teetered off the back porch steps. His corpse struck the manicured lawn with a dull thud. James got mercenary number two with a double-tap to the chest. The 9 mm slugs entered at about the level of the heart and lodged in his spine. He collapsed in place on the porch.

The other pair nearly ran into each other as they bumbled their only chance to find sanctuary from the marksmanship of the Phoenix Force duo. McCarter got the third gunner through the neck. One of the rounds struck the man's carotid artery and sent a hot fountain

of blood skyward. The man lost his balance as his partner collapsed into him, courtesy of Calvin James's burst
to the man's abdomen. The pair of GFR gunmen hit the
ground simultaneously and lay still.

McCarter keyed up his mobile headset, the words
crisp and clear in James's ears. "Red Team to Blue.
Four bogies down here."

"Roger," Encizo replied. "We're making entry
through the front now."

McCarter nodded in James's direction and the pair
left cover simultaneously and headed for the back
porch. They scooped up the SMGs on their way through
the back door. The extra firepower might come in
handy.

ENCIZO AND HAWKINS WASTED no time in their entry to
the house.

On a three-count, Hawkins put all of his weight behind a kick to the front door six inches below the lock.
The old, flimsy door splintered on its hinges before
swinging inward with a crash. Encizo went through
first in a shoulder roll and came to one knee. His intui-
tion on a possible ambush saved his life as a steady buzz
of autofire burned the air overhead.

The little Cuban tracked the muzzle of his pistol toward
the source of the gunfire and triggered off rounds before
verifying target acquisition. His combat instincts paid off
a second time as Encizo was rewarded with a scream. A
gunner toppled from behind a curtain dangling from a
pole in the adjoining room and hit the hardwood floor.

T. J. Hawkins came in high a moment later and engaged someone lurking at the end of the hallway to the left. The enemy gunman was actually down on one knee and too busy aligning his sights on Encizo to notice Hawkins. The former Delta Force member sucked in a breath, let out half and squeezed the trigger twice. The double tap caught Encizo's would-be assassin full in the face. Both rounds plowed through the man's jaw and left very little below the cheekbones.

The entire downstairs area got deathly quiet. Encizo and Hawkins held position and waited but no further threats presented themselves. Activity toward the back of the house broke the stillness but the arrival of McCarter and James a moment later allayed their concerns.

Hawkins's eyebrows rose at the sight of the SMGs his colleagues toted. "Looks like you picked up some old friends."

McCarter nodded and tossed one of the autoweapons to him. Hawkins caught it with his left while simultaneously stowing his pistol in shoulder leather. Through a quick inspection he identified it as an HK-53. The appearance of the weapon took him by surprise. As yet, no military force had officially adopted it, an oddity given the fact it chambered 5.56 mm rounds. Despite the appeal of such harmony between special-operations weapons and most standard assault rifles, the HK-53 hadn't garnered as much favor among military units as the MP-5 or FN series.

"She ain't a Cadillac, but she's got the same spirit," Hawkins remarked with a wink to his comrades-in-arms. "An oldie but a beaut, this one is."

Encizo grinned as he checked over the MP-5 McCarter handed him. "Ah, he waxes poetic."

McCarter remained all business. "Check your guys for ID and spare ammunition."

The men moved to follow orders while McCarter and James watched their backs. They didn't have time for a lot of banter.

"Nothing for ID," Hawkins replied. "His pistol is no match for the Glock, but I did manage to grab a spare clip for this baby."

Encizo reported similar findings and McCarter nodded. "Let's move out."

The men went up the narrow staircase one at a time with James on point and Encizo taking rear guard. Five large bedrooms and two bathrooms comprised the upstairs. They counted a total of twelve made beds in all, which meant they were short by a count of six, which left half the GFR force that had been holed up there as unaccounted for.

"There has to be an explanation," McCarter said once they had gathered downstairs. "I'm not chalking it up to bloody coincidence."

The two-tone sirens of police vehicles echoed in the distance.

"Well, we best not get caught standing around here discussing it," James pointed out.

Hawkins started to turn under the assumption they were leaving when he spotted a door in the sitting room he hadn't noticed before due to the poor lighting. His eyes had adjusted enough that he noticed a faint, reddish glow coming from underneath it. The Phoenix Force warrior crossed the room quickly, and as he got close he motioned to the others. They fanned out, weapons leveled to provide him sufficient cover. Hawkins pressed his ear to the door, then grabbed the handle, twisted and stepped back quickly to avoid being ventilated by friend or foe.

A dim, red lightbulb dangled from the ceiling and barely illuminated the wooden steps that descended into a gloomy unknown. McCarter took a couple of steps forward, then stopped, looked at James and pointed at the door. The team medic nodded and moved up immediately to take point. McCarter sent Hawkins next, then followed and ordered Encizo to keep their flank covered once more. McCarter and Hawkins waited for James to move ahead of them before following. If ambushers waited below, it wouldn't do much good to make all of them targets simultaneously.

The stairs led deeper and deeper into the bowels of the earth, too deep to be a normal cellar. Hawkins could immediately sense they had stumbled onto something important. He looked back and could only perceive the outlines of Encizo's chiseled features in the faint light. When they finally reached the bottom, Hawkins let out a deep breath in the realization he'd held his breath during their descent. The bottom of the rickety stairs opened onto a tunnel, and the men detected a pungent odor of mustiness and disuse.

Hawkins wrinkled his nose and whispered, "Smells like someone ate something that didn't agree with them."

"Yeah," James replied.

"Quiet," McCarter ordered. "Keep alert for enemy."

The quartet moved on into the tunnel until it widened at a circular opening lined with rusty metal. James halted at the mouth of it and peered over. He reported back, "Opens onto a sewer tunnel."

"Dry?" Encizo inquired.

James nodded.

"All right, mates," McCarter said. "Looks like maybe we bloody well lucked our way into something here. Maybe Magda's information will pay off, after all. Cal and Rafe will take the left side. T.J., you're with me on the right. Don't anybody get in the open or you're likely to get your arse shot off."

"Guess we're not out of the woods yet?" Hawkins replied.

"Not by a long shot."

They traversed the sewer line for nearly twenty minutes and all they saw were more lines branching off. Encizo had proposed investigating them at one point, but McCarter nixed the idea. Hawkins could understand McCarter's reasoning. They stood a better chance of tracking down the GFR if they stuck to the main path. The idea the mercenaries would have established any significant operations in the subterranean tunnels seemed unlikely; it just wouldn't have been practical. No, if they stuck to the main path, they would eventually come upon their enemy.

Not that Hawkins was itching for a fight. He could feel the exhaustion right down to his bones. They'd been pushing themselves for more than twenty-four hours straight without much of a break. They managed to grab a little bit of shut-eye on the flight from Frankfurt to Munich, but not more than an hour on the outside. All of them were getting a bit punchy and as a result Hawkins was as ready as the rest of his teammates to get this over with.

The Phoenix Force warriors slowed as the first sounds of activity reached their ears. Somewhere ahead, invisible for the gloom, were men working—moving heavy equipment from the sounds of it. There were maybe three, possibly four, distinct voices Hawkins could make out, and it sounded like they spoke German. Okay, so now they were getting somewhere with all of this. McCarter signaled for them to fall in on him, and they huddled in the shadows to discuss it.

"Those are probably our missing GFR men," McCarter said.

"It doesn't make much sense," James noted. "Why conduct operations in the sewer system?"

"Makes perfect sense," Encizo replied with surprise. "These characters have been fugitives from the law, some of them for the better part of their adult lives."

"All right," McCarter cut in. "We can assume there are at least six of them, so we'll do this by the numbers. Once we engage, fan out and don't stand still in any one place. That will get you killed the fastest, mates."

"Maybe we can get in for a closer look first," James offered. "Check things out before rushing headlong into trouble."

"No time," McCarter said with a shake of his head. "We have to do this and do it now. It won't take those police we heard long to find this place, and we certainly don't want to be around when they show up. It'll be tricky getting out of here with our skins intact as it is."

Phoenix Force broke and moved into position like

the offensive line of a football team. McCarter was right, Hawkins thought. It would take split-second timing and they would only get one shot at it. He took a deep breath and let it out slowly. The time had come to take the fight to the enemy once more, and Thomas Jackson Hawkins was ready.

CHAPTER TWENTY-TWO

Dwight Maebrook hadn't always hated being a police officer.

Once, long ago, he could recall his chest swelled with pride, when he told exciting stories about being a cop to anyone who might care to listen. Then again, that had also been a time when people had a hell of a lot more respect for cops. These days, he thought, the vast majority of American citizens held about as much reverence for the badge as a public toilet. And occasionally they treated the toilet better.

For more than twenty years now, Maebrook had put up with all of the ass-kissing and departmental regulation he could take. He'd come to the point in his career where he felt they were watching him every second of the day and night. Looking back, he had nothing more to show for it than a lousy thousand-dollar-per-month pension and a commemorative plaque for twenty years of service. Big fucking deal.

So when Fayed Sarout approached with the story of Simon Delmico, a scientist who'd apparently fouled up and damn near killed a bunch of people, Maebrook saw opportunity knocking. Sarout hadn't even blinked when Maebrook named his price of a quarter million dollars. Maebrook had thought about upping the ante, but he knew the kind of group he was dealing with and he had no suicidal tendencies. In a way, Maebrook felt like he was betraying his oath but in another way he felt like the oath had betrayed him.

These days America had sown so many bad seeds that they now paid for the harvest of public corruption rife throughout her larger cities. Everyone walked through the halls of power with the mask of piety—that holier-than-thou attitude was probably what pissed off Maebrook the most—and yet the vast majority of officials were either protecting a closet full of dirty little secrets or simply on the take.

Everywhere he looked, Maebrook had seen the spoils reaped by others as they manipulated the system for personal gain. Not a day went by that Maebrook didn't witness some type of corruption among public officials. From the streets of his very first beat to the office of the mayor, there existed everything from prostitution for political favors to outright extortion and bribery. Maebrook had even considered becoming a cop in a smaller town, but he knew that wouldn't have been profitable to him.

So he had a choice: either get with the program or get out. Maebrook opted for self-preservation. He didn't view himself as a hero or patron saint of causes. No,

Dwight Maebrook had learned long ago that he should watch out for Number One because nobody sure as hell else was going to do it. There were times Maebrook wished for a "normal" life, but those came few and far between. For the most part, he was happy with his situation and he didn't put his nose in the business of others. In return, he expected they didn't put their noses in his.

Unfortunately that philosophy didn't seem applicable to Sarout and even less so to the eagle-eyed blond man staring at him now. Agent Irons of the Justice Department had made it clear fairly early on in this that he didn't trust Maebrook, and now the cop had to admit to a mutual feeling. In fact, he wasn't even convinced Irons held any official position with the Justice Department. Maebrook had gleaned a hell of a lot of good sources over the years, and according to all the chains he'd rattled in Washington, nobody named Irons worked for any branch of the DOJ.

Maebrook had requested a private conversation in an adjoining waiting room off the main wing of the surgical ward. Irons hadn't seemed cooperative at first—in fact he expressed his irritation in no uncertain terms— but he finally managed to convince the guy to give him five minutes. Now all he had to do was pump the guy for information—no easy task to achieve—so he could formulate the plan he promised to have for Sarout no later than noon.

"So what's this all about, Maebrook?" Lyons asked.

Maebrook did his best to look annoyed, deciding he'd start with righteous indignation to see how far it took him. "This is about how you just walk into my jurisdiction with a prisoner and don't even have the god-damn courtesy to keep me informed of what's going on," Maebrook said.

"What's going on? You're putting me on, right?" More evenly, Lyons said, "Take a look around, Mae-brook. We're up to our asses in sick kids who have very little time left here on the third rock from the sun. Delmico's in there right now working with Dr. Cor-vasce's lab boys to come up with a cure before we lose any more. That's not to mention my partner and friend is in there, also infected, and I can guarantee you that if he dies we won't rest until every last man responsible is caught."

Maebrook tapped a finger on the man's chest. "That's too bad, Irons, but you—"

The cop stopped short as suddenly something clamped on his wrist like a vise and threatened to tear his arm off. Maebrook blinked through the sudden sting of tears in his eyes and saw it was Irons who had him in a wrist lock. A damn painful one at that. Maebrook tried to re-sist, but the more he struggled the more pain he experi-enced, pain like he'd never felt before, and suddenly he feared if he moved another inch in any direction—even resisted Irons in any way—the Fed would simply break his hand off.

"I'm going to say this just one time, Maebrook," Lyons said, leaning close to his ear. "You ever touch me again, and you'll spend the rest of your days in one of the rooms upstairs here, sipping your food through a straw. You got it?"

Maebrook could only nod before he finally emitted

a groan of pain that reverberated in his ears. The pressure suddenly released and Maebrook grabbed his wrist protectively. Pain continued to burn, radiating through his hands as ferociously as the blood did through his cheeks. In that moment, Maebrook swore he would make sure to kill Irons before all of this was over.

"I ought to have you taken into custody for battery on a police officer!" Maebrook's face flushed fully now and he could hear his pulse quicken.

"Oh, I didn't come even close to battery, Maebrook." Lyons's grin could have made ice. "Now your team did a pretty decent clean-up job at the university, which is the only damn reason I'm still here talking to you. But you'd best understand this, and good. We're in charge of the operations here until they're concluded. This biotoxin is a terrorist act. We know Delmico's affiliated with at least one criminal group from Germany, and we also have evidence Hezbollah is involved in some way."

So, they *did* know about Sarout's people. That complicated matters a bit, since he'd hoped they wouldn't be able to differentiate one from the other. It also made things more complicated for Maebrook. If Irons had enough connections that they could pinpoint Hezbollah as being involved, they were astute enough that Maebrook's name would eventually come up connected to them in one way or another. That meant he'd have to come up with a fast way for Sarout's men to kill Delmico so he could get his money and get out of the country while he had the chance.

"I'm just looking to help here, Irons," Maebrook

said, making his tone more conciliatory. "There's no need to get violent."

"You want to help?" Irons asked. "Do what you can to get some extra bodies over here. We need to beef up security, especially when it comes to Delmico. We've got a couple of sides who have already shown they'll do whatever's necessary to take him down or take him out, including open confrontation. We don't want any repeats."

"How many bodies you need?"

"As many as you think your department can spare right now. Call in reserves if you have to, but get us some more men. This place is a security nightmare. It's too big for us to police by ourselves, especially since I have one guy who's all but out of commission."

Maebrook nodded and without another word he left the ward. It seemed better to placate Irons by making himself appear as the subordinate rushing to do his master's bidding over exacerbating an already volatile situation. Let Irons fume for a while—that was the type of distraction he needed. And thinking about that very thing as he rode the elevator to the parking garage of the hospital brought a smile to Maebrook's face.

That's what he needed to do! Provide distractions. Little distractions here and there. He needed to find things that would divert security away from the area, leave that ward open and vulnerable. After all, what else did they really have protecting Delmico outside of a pair of flimsy doors? Sarout had a veritable army of trained Hezbollah soldiers who were looking for any reason in the world to fight their jihad against the Westerners.

Yeah, that was the answer he sought. He'd distract and divert, and when they thought they couldn't handle it, he'd divert some more. And by the time Irons and his people realized what was actually going on, they'd be faced with a group of screaming Arab fanatics armed with submachine guns and explosives. Then he wouldn't be so tough. So Irons's team had taken down a few of Sarout's lesser groups. So what? In the final analysis, they'd overcome their enemy with sheer numbers.

And by the time the smoke cleared, Maebrook would be long gone.

As soon as Lyons finished with Maebrook, the cell phone on his belt rang for attention.

The Able Team leader answered midway through the second ring. "Yeah."

"It's me," Hal Brognola answered. "You alone?"

"Yeah, for the moment," Lyons replied.

The tone in Brognola's voice said he wasn't calling with good news. "The HAZMAT crews finished their decontamination procedures in Tulsa."

"It's not good," Lyons said.

"No. None of the vials survived the impact," Brognola replied. "I'm sorry, Cal."

"I'm sorry, too."

"What are you going to tell Gadgets?"

For a long time Lyons said nothing because he couldn't really concentrate. In fact, the words had echoed inside his head as if Brognola might be talking through a cup and string, or maybe even in a fishbowl submerged in five feet of water. How he would ever break the news to his friend moved beyond his comprehension. It would be an even tougher task to explain to the host of worried parents who would soon start arriving at the hospital in droves. Since there was nothing to indicate the virus could be spread by purely human contact, it would be difficult to find a reason to keep the parents away from their children, particularly those who had maybe a few hours to live.

"I'm not sure yet," Lyons said. His own reply sounded lifeless and hollow to him. "I'll think of something. Is there anything else?"

"No, other than to let you know that Phoenix has stepped into the thick of it in Europe."

"It should be mostly a mop-up job left now that Burke's out of the way," Lyons said.

"Hardly." Brognola gave him the short version of Phoenix Force's activities over the past few hours.

Lyons whistled when the Stony Man chief had completed his tale. "Sounds like a tall order. Wish we could be there to give them a hand."

"I know, but you've got your hands plenty full there," Brognola reminded him. "I'm sure David's got things well in hand."

"Well, I'd better get back to it," Lyons said.

"You sounded hesitant just now. What is it?"

"I'm having a tough time imagining what it would be like without Gadgets here," Lyons said. "I know it's morbid, but it's right there in front of me, and I can't deny it."

"I understand," Brognola replied quietly. "But let's not put any nails on the coffin yet. Just sit tight and give modern medicine a chance to work."

"Sitting tight isn't exactly what I'm best at, Hal."

"Then consider this a training exercise."

"I'll do my best. By the way, do me a favor and check out a cop here named Dwight Maebrook." Lyons spelled out the last name for him.

"You looking for anything in particular?"

"Just find what you can on him. I'm not really sure, but something about this guy just rubs me the wrong way. We just had a little spat here, and he was acting pretty damn strange."

Brognola laughed. "Compared to you, Carl, I'm sure everyone *is* strange. But we'll check it out and I'll have Bear send the information to you within the hour."

"Thanks. Out, here."

Lyons disconnected the call and headed back toward the ward where Hermann Schwarz had just started undergoing a fresh set of tests. Lyons couldn't put his finger on it, but something was definitely wrong with this Maebrook. The Able Team leader could almost smell the trouble rolling off the cop. The guy almost reeked of it. Yeah, something wasn't right in good old St. Louie, and Lyons would have to make doubly sure he kept an eye on Maebrook.

It was possible all their lives could depend on it.

LIFE OR DEATH: it would go one of those ways for Hermann "Gadgets" Schwarz.

The thing that bothered Schwarz more than all else—other than the hospital gown that barely covered his buttocks and the fact Corvasce had assigned him to bed rest and IV fluids—was the idea he'd faced death a thousand times but never like this. He stood to gain nothing and lose everything on this one. And what stung him most of all—the thing that frustrated him so utterly he couldn't find words to describe it—was that he couldn't do a damn thing about it. Schwarz had never known such helplessness until now.

"Had I been given a choice," Schwarz told Lyons and Blancanales, "I would have preferred to face bullets and bombs instead of this."

"It may sound like a platitude, Gadgets, but don't sweat it none," Blancanales replied.

That's the one thing that made it somehow less frightening and terrible to Schwarz. He had his two best friends in the world to see him through it. He couldn't remember a time when they hadn't been there for him.

Schwarz had come through a lot in his life. He'd experienced traumas and pain severe enough that it would have potentially killed lesser men. Despite all of those experiences, however, a man could never be asked to take a philosophical view toward an uphill battle against a raging disease. Sure, maybe quoting Socrates or Plato could work as a short interlude in the brief span of time man was actually allowed to exist, or prayer to the Divine could provide some measure of comfort and even, on occasion, a miraculous healing. But none of those ideas appealed to Schwarz at that moment. He would have liked to blame himself for where he was at—taking more responsibility on his shoulders than any one human could bear was at the center of Schwarz's quid-pro-quo mentality—but he knew that didn't devise any better a prognosis for his sad state of affairs.

"Yeah, well, I'd be sweating it a lot, if I were you," Lyons said.

Blancanales fired a scorned look in his direction, but Schwarz merely laughed it off. "Don't get too hot under the collar, Pol," Schwarz told his furious friend. "Ironman's just never been one to beat around the bush. And he's damn right, I should be sweating this one some. Maybe next time I'll be more careful."

"It's not your fault," Blancanales insisted.

"And that's not what I meant," Lyons added quickly, the tone in his voice genuine.

"I know, boys," Schwarz said. "And if I have to lie in bed, fight a fever and suffer my last few hours of life through cold sweats and shortness of breath, well, I can't think of two uglier guys to have around for such a dreadful experience as you turkeys."

"We're going to see this through no matter what happens," Lyons said. "You hear me?"

Something in Lyons's eyes told Schwarz he didn't find the topic humorous anymore. Schwarz couldn't really blame him. The man's morose, sometimes morbid, sense of humor had gotten him into more than one pickle, and through it all there were times Lyons still hadn't learned when it was best to shut up. That was okay, though, since neither Schwarz nor Blancanales minded the Ironman's candor.

Hell, he wouldn't have been the Ironman they knew without it.

Schwarz decided no time like the present to change the subject. "What did Maebrook want?"

"The same old crap. Wanted to whine at me about

jurisdiction and how we weren't keeping his team informed, yada, yada, yada."

"I don't like that guy," Blancanales said.

"Not you, Pol," Schwarz cracked. "The last greatest social worker on the face of the planet? Say it isn't so!"

"I don't blame you," Lyons interjected. "In my book, we've all got plenty of reasons to hate that guy. Outside of the help he brought to the university when we got into the fireworks with those GFR goons, Maebrook's been holed up in the dictionary between the words incompetent and lazy."

"Don't hold back, Ironman," Blancanales quipped. "Tell us how you really feel."

"I don't like the guy," Lyons continued. "I didn't like him when we met him and I like him even less now."

"What did you say to him?"

"I sent him on busywork errands, for now. I figured maybe we could get him to do something useful instead of standing around here and wringing his hands like an old woman."

"Maybe you should have put him on a short leash where you can keep an eye on him."

"Pol's got a good point," Schwarz said. "If this is a dirty cop we're dealing with, you might be able to get him to tip his hand, see what he's up to. It obviously sounds like he thinks you trust him."

"That's exactly my point," Lyons countered. "He *knows* I don't trust him. I didn't make any secret of how I felt. The guy knows where he stands, and he also knows what will happen to him if he crosses us."

Blancanales cleared his throat. "Oh, that will never do. We all know how difficult it is for you to be clear and direct. Maybe we should have a chat with him, as well."

"Oh, you're a regular laugh-riot," Lyons said, but he quickly got back to business. "Either way, I asked Hal to check him out. There's just something I don't trust about this guy, and I'd rather make sure we keep the upper hand if anything should go wrong. Actually, I hope I'm wrong about the guy, so if everything goes as planned he should be returning soon with as many extra cops as he can muster for security detail."

"You're bringing in more personnel?" Blancanales asked.

He looked at Schwarz with an expression of mock amazement. "I think maybe Ironman's getting a little paranoid in his old age."

"What are you talking about?" Lyons asked in a more serious tone. The time for banter had passed. "This place is as wide-open as a French whore on a Friday night. A sniper could take all three of us through that open window right now. Not to mention all the security holes and the multiple entry and exit points."

"What do you think they're going to try doing to us in here?" Blancanales asked. "And especially Maebrook. He's just one cop. A little strange, maybe a bit of a loner, but still just one man."

"It only takes one to bring down the curtain. We have to ask ourselves if we can afford that kind of exposure. Maybe Maebrook's just as he appears and maybe he isn't. But whatever happens in the next twenty-four hours, I plan to make sure we're ready for him. And he just better hope he doesn't try to cross us. Because we'll be ready and waiting."

CHAPTER TWENTY-THREE

Dr. Simon Delmico wanted to die, but they wouldn't let him.

It wasn't as if he'd taken some sick pleasure in seeing the suffering Shangri-La Lady had caused so many people. He'd never intended to start a widespread plague right here in his own country. Why would any sane individual do that? Oh, that's right, he thought. They didn't really consider him sane, anyway, so it made little difference. And he'd never really planned to be here when any of this happened, either, which merely proved the adage "The best laid plans of mice and men…"

No, at this point in time he was contemplating suicide. He'd die a quiet death. They'd bury his past sins with his carcass, unwilling to risk exposure that some crazed scientist had developed his own form of the Black Death and tried to poison the entire student body of a college for purposes of nothing more than personal gain. Yeah, they could spin it just about any way they wanted to. And given his past record while still working as a biochemist for the Department of Defense, nobody would give it a second thought.

But death apparently wouldn't come this day. Dr. Corvasce had put staff on him, and armed security officers watched him every second of every minute. He wasn't even allowed to relieve himself alone. Well, they couldn't keep him here forever. Maybe the sooner he came up with a cure, the sooner they would get him out of here. He had to admit the lab facilities were most impressive. Of course, the government had subsidized everything to provide Delmico with whatever he wished. He probably could have convinced them to bring a blowtorch and bazooka if they really thought it would help him find a cure for Shangri-La Lady.

Dr. Corvasce pushed through the double doors of the isolation lab adorned in protective gown, mask and face shield. Delmico actually admired the man. He was an excellent doctor and had even managed to deduce that the only mechanism for contracting the infectious agent in the biotoxin was by direct exposure. Delmico knew it would have taken a number of other doctors twice as long to figure that out, which only proved he wasn't dealing with an idiot. There would be no stalling Corvasce. Delmico's only recourse, then, was to cooperate and maybe he could come out of this with some semblance of his dignity intact.

"How are you coming?" Corvasce demanded.

"Slowly," Delmico replied truthfully. "But we're getting there. I've finished building the suspension liquid. It's a mix of lactated Ringers in a ten percent sugar solution."

Corvasce nodded. "Makes sense. You want something that can push the antibodies directly into the cells. That kind of electrolyte and sugar suspender should do the trick."

"Sort of," Delmico replied. "Since we're dealing with a virus, there's no real cure, as you know. But it is still a biological viral agent, and as such it is designed to attack the bloodstream. In this way, it acts much like HIV but on an accelerated path. Let me suppose your patients have experienced sudden onset of symptoms, usually beginning within twenty-four hours of exposure."

"Correct," Corvasce said with a curt nod.

"This is because direct exposure is absorbed into the body slowly but then attacks very suddenly. The virus mutates, waiting until it has reached a sufficient size to make the human-immuno system of null effect. Then it attaches itself to red blood cells."

"So it deprives them of proper nutrients?" Corvasce interjected. "Things like sugar and water? Base elements like oxygen and magnesium and other critical electrolytes?"

Delmico shook his head. "No, it doesn't stop anything from passing through the cell membrane, and it doesn't stop the cell from doing its work. What it *does* do in this case is block the cell's ability to expend the waste products of cellular metabolism."

"So the patient experiences many of the same symptoms of septic shock," Corvasce concluded. "Hence the high fever, chills, nausea and vomiting, seizures and then eventually coma and death. Oh, Christ! It's been there all the time in front of us. So obvious. Then maybe we can prolong lives and decrease the damage through dialysis."

"No, that won't work," Delmico said.

"Why not?"

"Remember that I said the virus mutates. Because of this fact, dialysis only filters the blood of waste products. But it doesn't kill the virus. And every time you pump the clean, filtered blood back into the patient, you're simply feeding the mutation and allowing it to grow faster and more virulent."

"Then how do we reverse it?"

"We develop an antibody that gives the virus something to attach itself to. Then we let the body's own immune system take over and kill the virus once it's become dormant."

"And you think you can do that before more of these kids die?"

"I don't know, but I've given you my word as a scientist that I will try, and I keep my word."

Corvasce looked Delmico in the eyes for a long moment, and he could immediately tell what the physician was thinking. He'd already cast judgment on him when they first arrived at the hospital and he was doing it again. To a man like Corvasce, Delmico could hardly be viewed as a hero. Delmico was simply doing what any decent human being should do by trying to reverse a horrific mistake that could cost dozens of innocent people their lives. Delmico took a much less impassioned view toward it. He was doing whatever was necessary to survive. If he was going to die, then he wanted it to be on his own terms. The last thing he needed was to fail and see the American agent die, and experience a whole new world of pain at the hands of the big blond Fed with the hard blue eyes. He knew the guy named Irons would make good on his threat if his friend died.

"No offense, Doctor, but your word as a scientist really doesn't mean a lot to me at the moment," Corvasce said.

Delmico raised a hand. "Spare me another lecture on the platform of righteous indignation. It's gotten old very quickly. I know you think I'm scum, and you're entitled to your opinion. In fact, I would probably have to agree with you in some respects. But I never intended for this to get out of hand."

"What you intended doesn't really matter now. Does it?"

Corvasce was a fairly tall man, and as he leaned in Delmico felt a bit intimidated. Well, he would have much rather suffered the punitive bantering of Corvasce's meager self-effacement than even the thought of Irons wrapping those massive hands around his neck and strangling his life from him. For the moment, he couldn't die by his own hand, and they weren't about to let him go, so all he could do was focus on the task at hand and hope his cure worked.

"We could stand here and debate all of the moral implications of my actions for the next decade, Dr. Corvasce," Delmico said quietly. He stepped back. "However, that isn't going to help me get an antibody synthesized any faster. So I would suggest that you leave me to my work and go check on your patients."

For a moment Delmico saw something in Corvasce's eyes, and he thought the physician might actually take a swing at him, but finally Corvasce whirled and stormed out of the isolation chamber. Delmico looked at the pair of guards who watched him with the bare hint of sneers on their chiseled features before he returned to his work. No, this wasn't going to work as a long-term solution. Simon Delmico still wanted to die.

And he swore he'd find some way of doing it.

DR. MICHAEL CORVASCE never considered himself a violent man, but he teetered on the edge of the bare-handed murder of Simon Delmico. How a man could ever have done the things that man had done he would never understand. What drove men to commit such atrocities? In many ways, Corvasce didn't see his work much differently than that of history's other malevolent figures, men who killed the most helpless of all victims by the whim of their medical skills. To use knowledge of the body to then destroy that very thing they swore to preserve made those men the worst kinds of wicked villains to Corvasce's way of thinking.

Well, there wasn't anything he could do about it now. He doubted Delmico would come up with a solution before more young people died, if at all, and yet he felt utterly helpless. He hadn't slept in more than twenty-four hours, and if one more kid came in sick he wasn't sure he'd be able to handle it. So, a dozen victims plus one dead, and two more whose deaths were imminent. That didn't bode well for Delmico. He'd overheard the threat made by Irons against Delmico, and he knew the fatality of the man he knew only as Mr. Black would most likely drive Irons to keep that threat.

Corvasce tried not to think about that eventuality as he stripped the mask and gown from his body and deposited it in the biohazard disposal bin. The physician checked the charts of a couple of his patients, did a little paperwork over paper cups of premixed coffee from the snack machine, then headed for Black's room. Upon entering, he found the man jovial and upbeat as ever, his two friends standing vigil near his bedside like a pair of stone lions at the entrance to a mansion.

"How are you feeling?" Corvasce asked as he measured his patient's pulse and respirations.

"A little chilled," Schwarz replied. "But otherwise I seem to be okay."

Corvasce nodded. "The chills are caused by your fever. It's low-grade right now, and I've ordered some antibiotic and fluid therapy along with aspirin. That should help temper some of it for a while longer."

"Just putting off the inevitable?" Schwarz asked, but he did so with a smile.

"Now listen to me, we're not going to lose you. You understand? I just came from Delmico in the lab, and he's hopeful we'll be able to develop an antibody in short order. We already have the suspension liquid necessary for delivery."

Lyons folded his meaty arms. "Yeah, but you don't actually trust this guy, do you, Doc?"

Corvasce shrugged as he put the stethoscope in his ears. "It's not about whether I trust him. It's about the fact we need him to come up with a way of reversing the processes of this biotoxic agent. And I have to assume Delmico can do that. I owe my patients that much."

Before he could say anything else, the door to the room burst open and a nurse rushed inside. Corvasce pulled the stethoscope from his ears and opened his mouth to scold her for not knocking but she didn't look at him. A sheen of sweat danced along the skin of the woman's forehead and her eyes were as round as saucers. She looked straight at Lyons.

"There's a problem downstairs in the Juniper Annex," the nurse said. "Security is asking for all the help they can get from any law enforcement here."

"What sort of problem?" Corvasce asked.

"A fire, Doctor." She turned back to Lyons. "They're evacuating everyone now, and they're asking for volunteers to assist in clearing the wing until the fire department can get here."

"You guys go ahead," Schwarz told his friends. "The doc and I will be fine here."

The men exchanged glances and then left the room on the nurse's heels. Corvasce had noticed the exchange between the pair and asked Schwarz about it.

"They suspect someone might try to break into the hospital and take Delmico again before he can come up with a cure."

Corvasce expressed surprise. "What makes them think that?"

Schwarz frowned. "Let's just say we've been to that party before."

AT ABOUT THE MOMENT Lyons and Blancanales reached the Juniper Annex—a building connected to the main wing of the hospital by a fully enclosed glass walkway—smoke became visible just aft of the foyer that housed an information desk and seating area off to one side. This foyer led out to the main entrance for the annex, as well, and a crowd of patients in wheelchairs or ambulating with IV poles were being escorted by hospital staff through the double glass doors. The buzz of the fire alarm droned at almost deafening levels.

Blancanales immediately grabbed the arm of the nearest security officer. "What's the story with this fire? Where's it coming from?"

"We're not sure yet," he said, keeping one eye on the crowd as they evacuated the building. "We think it might have been one of the staff smoking in a laundry room."

"Of a hospital?" Blancanales asked with disbelief.

The guard nodded. "It happens. Hopefully the fire department can arrive to contain it before things get out of control."

The guard's radio blared something and he had to put his head close to the speaker to make out what was being said.

"What is it?" Lyons asked.

The guard expressed puzzlement. "They say the power just failed on 2 East in the main wing."

"What's on that floor?"

"The cafeteria," the guard replied with a shrug. Another call came in on the radio and caused him to scowl. "What the hell's going on today? Is it a full moon or something?"

"What now?" Blancanales asked.

"Just got a report of a fifty-five-gallon drum in the basement leaking chlorine bleach. Apparently, the fumes are so bad they're moving up into the main lobby and choking people out. They're pulling everyone out right now. Man, SLFD's going to have their hands full when they get here."

Blancanales looked at Lyons, who returned the look, then pulled his friend away from the fire area so they could hear one another. "Something's very wrong here."

"Yeah," Lyons agreed. "A minor fire started by a careless employee smoking, and now power failures and chemical spills in nonessential areas? Seems like a design for distraction."

"You think something's about to go down?"

"I think it's a pretty good bet."

Blancanales nodded. "I'm going to head for our wheels, get our equipment."

"Fine. I'm going to head back to the isolation ward. If the GFR or Hezbollah are about to make their play, that's where they'll do it."

"Agreed."

The men split off, Lyons heading back to the ward and Blancanales bounding for their vehicle in the underground parking garage one level down. The warrior opted to take a service elevator, since the stairs and regular elevators would likely be crowded with evacuees. The doors opened onto the parking garage and Blancanales sprinted for their SUV. He managed to get their equipment bags out of the back before something tripped his combat instinct and sent hairs upright on his nape.

Blancanales reached inside the nearest bag and wrapped his hands around the handle of his MP-5 A-3. He ripped the weapon from its hiding place and ducked as he spun to face the threat he sensed. The back window shattered under the maelstrom of autofire that burned past his head. Four Hezbollah terrorists in camouflage fatigues and black keffiyehs with masks drawn across their mouths stood side by side, weapons chattering, clearly bent on destroying their opponent.

Blancanales responded in kind with a one-handed, corkscrew burst from the MP-5 40. A hoard of .40-caliber S&W slugs rocketed toward his targets and scored a number of vital hits. Two of the terrorists dropped with rounds to the knees and thighs. Blancanales could hear their shouts of anguish even over the echo of his weapon. The third terrorist took a 3-round volley to the chest. Bullets ripped through lungs and heart and drove him against the tail of an old Buick. The man slid to the ground, leaving a bloody smear in the wake. The last gunner fell with a single bullet to the forehead. The round caved in the front of the man's skull and blew out the top of his head.

Blancanales waited nearly a minute—making sure no further threats would present themselves—then got to his feet. He scooped up the equipment bags and headed for the elevator. As he rode toward the first floor of the main wing, he considered their situation. Somehow Hezbollah had tracked them here, which meant they knew what was at stake. That meant they knew about Delmico. What Blancanales couldn't figure was how. Only a select few even knew about their current situation, and most of them had been cleared. Somebody close to the operation had obviously leaked it to Tarif's men, and now they were bound and determined to see it through with a vengeance.

Where they had made their critical mistake was in underestimating the resolve of Able Team. The trio would ensure the protection of the sick and that Delmico stayed alive—at least long enough to help devise a cure. There were more than just the lives of innocent civilians at stake here. The security of an entire nation now hung in the balance. If word got out that terrorists had managed to successfully attack innocents right inside a hospital, it would be difficult to convince people they could ever be safe anywhere.

Well, damage control wasn't his problem, and he had to stop thinking about this in diplomatic terms. It was his job, just like that of Lyons and Schwarz, to inflict damage and to make sure they confined it to the enemy. The doors opened on the first-floor lobby and the almost overpowering odor of bleach filled his nostrils. An invisible haze stung his eyes and made negotiating his way to the main elevator difficult through the profuse tearing.

Blancanales reached the surgical ward a minute later and headed straight to Schwarz's room. He pushed through the door and immediately noticed the IV tube that had been in his friend's arm now dangled uselessly from the bag. Corvasce sat in one corner of the room, his arms folded, and a look of pure disgust across his face. Blancanales looked at Corvasce with a questioning gaze.

"He's refusing further treatment," Corvasce said.

"He threatened to rip out the IV himself if I didn't disconnect it."

"And you believed him?" Blancanales asked.

"Pol," Schwarz said quietly, "this is as much my fight as it is yours. If I'm going to fight for my life, then I'm going to do it on my terms."

Blancanales looked into his friend's eyes and saw only a mask of steely resolve. In fact, he couldn't remember a time when he'd seen his friend so intent on anything before. He could hardly blame him. Nobody would have ever dared accuse Hermann Schwarz of cowardice, and Blancanales couldn't call himself a friend if he didn't let Schwarz conduct his life as a warrior however he saw fit.

"As long as you say you're fit enough to pull your weight, then I believe you," Blancanales said. He zipped open the bag, removed the other MP-5 40 and tossed it in his teammate's direction.

Schwarz quickly checked the action and then slung the weapon over his shoulder. He reached beneath his pillow and produced his Beretta 92-F. He checked its action, as well, before nestling it into the shoulder holster he'd kept with his clothes.

"I'm glad to be out of that gown," he remarked. "Hell of a draft."

"You guys," Corvasce said hesitantly, "uh, you aren't really average federal agents. Are you?"

Blancanales smiled. "We never shoot and tell, Doc. Where's Ironman?"

The door opened as he asked the question, and Carl Lyons entered. He'd shed the oversize flower-print shirt he'd been wearing, leaving a black sport T-shirt beneath. Rock-hard chest and six-pack abdominal muscles pushed against the sheen of the fabric. He also wore the .44 Magnum Colt Anaconda now fully exposed in a nylon holster rig beneath his left arm.

"I'm right here," he said. "Went to lock down Delmico."

"Where is he?" Corvasce asked.

"Safe," Lyons replied as he took the AS-3 shotgun Blancanales proffered. He loaded a shell and then asked his comrades, "Ideas?"

"I ran into four Hezbollah gunners in the garage," Blancanales said. "Barely got away with my skin intact. I'm sure there are more. But how they found out we were here, I haven't got a clue."

Lyons's eyes narrowed as he said, "Maebrook. I'll kill that son of a bitch."

"That leaves us with two choices then, way I see it," Schwarz said. "We can wait for them here, or we can meet them wherever fate dictates."

Blancanales said matter-of-factly, "The farther we keep them from this area, the easier it'll be for security to protect Delmico. I'm sure he's their real target."

"Agreed," Lyons said. "Well, now that's settled, it's time to finish this."

"Well, then, a-hunting we will go," Schwarz replied.

CHAPTER TWENTY-FOUR

Phoenix Force hadn't realized that the lair of their enemy would turn into quite the stingers' nest that it did. The warriors immediately sought cover as about twenty GFR mercenaries brandished their assortment of weapons and opened up on the intruders. McCarter had expected maybe a dozen terrorists, at most. Thus the cacophony of thunderous autofire in the confines of the tunnel threatened to disorient and deafen his team. Phoenix Force responded like the professionals they were.

McCarter got the first pair from behind an empty steel barrel he'd found for cover. The Briton ignored the angry hum of rounds or the whine of their ricochets around him as he leveled the Uzi he'd procured from the house guard and triggered a series of short, controlled bursts. A trio of 9 mm Parabellum rounds found their mark and punched holes in the chest of one GFR gunner. The impact lifted the man off his feet and slammed him into a nearby wall. Another fell when a pair of rounds from McCarter's SMG entered the man's right pelvis and shattered his hip. The guy collapsed with a scream of agony.

Hawkins went prone, locked the stock of the HK-53 against his shoulder and aligned his sights on a trio of GFR gunners huddled too close together. The target proved most viable as Hawkins opened up with a sustained salvo. The 5.56 mm NATO rounds made short work of his foes, taking the first with a sustained burst to the chest. The flesh-shredders ripped holes through him as the high-velocity slugs punctured heart, ribs and lungs. Another took rounds in the neck and jaw. The impact spun him into his comrade, and the third crouched gunner lost his balance. He collapsed into a seated position and dropped his weapon. The look of surprise came moments before Hawkins triggered a second, shorter burst that blew the merc's head from his body.

One round cut a furrow through Rafael Encizo's fatigue blouse, but somehow missed the vital flesh beneath it. Encizo dropped and rolled to position behind an abutment that lined the sewer canal. He identified his would-be killer quickly by the way the guy frantically triggered off a couple more rounds from his pistol in Encizo's direction. The Cuban snap-aimed the MP-5, his selector already set to 3-round bursts, and squeezed the trigger. A trio of 9 mm Parabellum rounds scored hits in the man's abdomen and chest. The merc hollered in pain mixed with shock as the impact lifted him off his feet and slammed him to the unforgiving concrete floor of the abandoned sewer.

James encountered a bit more trouble as half a dozen GFR gunmen seemed intent on concentrating all their firepower on his position. Thankfully, a protruding wall saved him from being ventilated by the fury of 9 mm and .45-caliber rounds directed his way. James had managed to lift an Italian-made Spectre M-4. The Spectre boasted the unique quality of being the only double-action SMG ever manufactured. Added to that distinction was a four-column magazine, an ingenious design that permitted a 50-round capacity. In the hands of a veteran like James, the Spectre M-4 became a formidable weapon.

James broke cover, knelt and triggered a fusillade of 9 mm Parabellum death as he swept the muzzle across the path of his enemy. The gunners were surprised by the ferocity of their opponent's attack, and the confusion proved their undoing. Men twisted away from the hot flurry of rounds drilling through flesh. Blood sprayed against the nearby walls as a couple fell under James's counterattack. A few danced a crazed dance of death as slugs struck their joints in some cases. In short order, James took down all six of the GFR gunners, the bodies falling one atop another to build a literal broken and bleeding stack of corpses.

A shout resounded from behind their position, audible during a lull in the shooting, and McCarter turned to see the illumination of flashlights dancing on the walls in the distance. He could also hear the bark of dogs.

"Looks like the cops made good time," Hawkins said from nearby.

"Bloody marvelous," McCarter said.

The Phoenix Force leader ran down the scenario quickly in his head. The team couldn't head in the direction of the police, as they'd cut down any armed men on sight. Meanwhile, still more than a dozen GFR enemy gunners were ahead, now having found time to reconnoiter and take up secure positions. With the road ahead and behind blocked, McCarter knew they had to take their chances. The shadows of holes in the wall a dozen meters or so behind them, which also happened to be out of the enemy's line of sight, gave him an idea.

McCarter whistled at his teammates and gestured for them to retreat to safety. When they were out of sight, the Briton gestured toward the diversion pipes and indicated they should try to make their way around and flank the enemy troops. The warriors knew immediately their leader had devised a brilliant solution to the problem. The police would keep the GFR occupied long enough to give Phoenix Force time to come up on their backs. The GFR wouldn't be looking for trouble from that direction, and with their enemies' attention on the police, Phoenix Force would be able to grab the upper hand.

McCarter signaled for James and Hawkins to take one tunnel while he and Encizo grabbed the other. They scrambled into the shadows and disappeared far enough into the darkness that they should be able to escape detection by the police. As they hunch-walked through the massive piping, McCarter began to wonder if it would have been better to just let the police battle it out with the mercenaries while Phoenix Force found a way out of the mess entirely. He quashed the idea almost as soon as it came to him. The men of Stony Man weren't the kind to shirk their responsibilities.

After nearly five minutes of traversing the pipe, McCarter's legs began to ache. It seemed they had already gone a long way with no end in sight. Somewhere along the path he'd sensed the pipe starting to turn. Most of the light had dispersed and now a mere black maw loomed ahead. McCarter stopped to relax and he felt a reassuring hand on his shoulder. He could hear concern in Encizo's voice.

"You going to make it?" his Cuban friend asked.

McCarter grunted. "I was just stopping to let *you* rest."

"Uh-huh." Encizo chuckled. "I figured as much. I was only asking."

"Just make sure you keep up," McCarter replied, and he set off once more.

After another few minutes, the tunnel started to lighten again and the edges became discernible along with the slippery muck beneath their feet. McCarter kept his arms to his sides, and his hands pressed to the sides of the pipe for balance. The echoes of sporadic shooting now reached their ears, along with shouts in German over what sounded like a bullhorn. McCarter quickened the pace, intent to lessen the chance of police casualties.

By the time McCarter reached the mouth of the pipe he could make out the silhouettes of two men crouched on the walkway below. McCarter dropped to the ground and Encizo followed him a moment later. The foursome congregated in the shadows and discussed their plan. McCarter opted for the swiftest approach possible.

"We'll go in leapfrog fashion. Strictly fire and maneuver on this one, mates. And let's try to preserve any information they might have in their possession. Understood?"

The Phoenix Force warriors nodded and they fanned out with McCarter taking the lead. One by one they advanced quickly up the sewer, keeping close to the walls and providing a wide span of cover for whoever led the chain. As they got close there was a shout from the bullhorn again and the sporadic fire increased with intensity. True to McCarter's belief, they were concentrating fully on the enemy ahead and completely oblivious to the much greater threat on their flanks.

The GFR mercs were now fully exposed. Phoenix Force brought them to that awareness with perfectly executed charge. Encizo and Hawkins went left, triggering one controlled burst after another that began to drop their opponents at an alarming rate.

McCarter took the right flank, bracing himself against a large crate and popping off rounds against his target with a control and accuracy that demonstrated his sharpshooter skills. He caught two of the men close together with single shots through the head. One of them had turned in surprise when the skull of the man he'd been talking to exploded in a fountain of blood and gray matter. The guy turned in McCarter's direction and the British commando pumped a single round through the man's upper jaw. The maxilla fractured under the impact and blood filled the man's throat in such volumes he audibly choked to death on it.

James advanced straight up the middle, the Spectre M-4 held tight and low. He triggered a volley that took out three of the GFR mercenaries at one time. The first one got it through the stomach. The slugs effectively eviscerated him and his guts spewed from the tattered stomach cavity. James caught a second man with twin Parabellum rounds to the chest. Pink blood bubbled from a sucking chest wound and flipped the man over a small abutment he'd used for cover. The last man suffered a single round through the head. Blood poured from the wound as he dropped to his knees, froze there for a moment, before toppling to the concrete.

The odds had now thinned considerably. The few remaining gunners dropped their weapons, rose and rushed toward the police. McCarter knew they had a minute, maybe less, before the mercenaries were able to efficiently explain the reason for their surrender, and then they would be out of time. If they'd had Flaus with them, it might have been easy to explain away the entire situation, but to the police these four foreigners would be viewed as just as dangerous as the members of the GFR.

McCarter looked over the top of his cover and noticed a stack of documents on the crate. He scooped them up, tucked them inside his clothing and signaled for his men to retreat. Phoenix Force dashed down the walkway at a full sprint, intent on escape. If the German authorities realized they were making a getaway, they gave no sign of it. They continued at their breakneck pace for better than ten minutes, then McCarter signaled for them to slow down.

As they walked it out, panting and sweating with the exertion, Hawkins spoke up. "Anybody got an idea how we get the hell out of here?"

"I'd guess this probably leads to either a groundwater pond or a processing facility," Encizo said.

"Right-o, mate," McCarter said. "And seeing it's no longer in use, I'd be willing to wager its terminus is abandoned."

"What did you find back there?" James asked. "I noticed you pulled something from that crate."

McCarter grinned and produced the papers he'd shoved beneath his fatigue blouse. "Don't know yet, but they looked important. I think we got lucky and caught the GFR with their pants down back there."

"Well, once we get that information safely back to our hotel, it shouldn't be hard to decipher what they're really up to," Encizo remarked.

McCarter silently agreed with his friend's observation. If the information he'd stolen revealed the GFR's real plans, they would be able to neutralize the group permanently. With the GFR out of the way, Tarif would consider that an invitation to move forward with his own plans, which would simply draw him into the open. If they played their cards right, they could have the entire situation wrapped up within the next few hours and be on their way out of the country before anybody got wise enough to figure out what happened. Of course, that all depended on how Manning and Flaus were faring at the summit. McCarter looked at his watch and grinned. Yeah, right now the big Canadian would be standing in the thickets of a diplomatic forest.

And McCarter didn't envy Gary Manning one bit.

GARY MANNING DIDN'T ENVY McCarter and his teammates one bit.

They'd been pushing themselves since the start of this mission. Not that they weren't used to that kind of thing, but they were now going into the thirty-ninth hour of the mission and the sleep they'd grabbed thus far hardly bore a mention. Not that it mattered all that much to McCarter. Manning grinned as he thought of the fox-faced Briton thumping his chest and telling the rest of Phoenix Force in that Cockney accent, "I'll get all the bloody sleep I require when I'm six foot in the soil outside London."

Well, it was his story, Manning thought, and he could tell it any way he liked.

Manning could hardly deny his own weariness, though. He'd been pushing a broom since he arrived, along with vacuuming half a dozen rooms on the second floor of the Hanns Seidel, and clearing more bags of trash from the kitchen than he wished to count. Now and again, he'd encounter Magda Flaus, who would pretend to ignore him.

Manning swiped the key to a room door after knocking to ensure nobody occupied the suite. He stepped inside, flipped on the light switch and proceeded to go about dutifully cleaning the suite. He emptied the garbage cans and brought them back to his cart.

Magda Flaus stood near the cart, the look in her eyes a mixture of seduction and amusement.

"What the hell are you doing in here?" Manning asked. "In fact, how did you get inside?"

She held up a blue card, one like Manning's, which he immediately recognized as a master access key. "It would seem being a top-ranking member of the *Landeskriminalamt* comes with a few privileges. There is a much different level of respect for the police here in Germany than in other countries."

"You mean, like the U.S.," Manning said.

"I wasn't intending to imply that," Flaus replied quickly.

"It is what it is. Personally, I wish I could deny it, but I can't."

"Though it is probably much more bearable to that sense of Canadian pride."

"I serve the U.S. government without reservation or prejudice," Manning said. "Not much more I can say about it than that."

"It is all right, Gary," she replied. "You don't have to defend it."

"What do you need?"

"I just came to check on you," she said. "Make sure you were okay."

Manning sighed. "And they say the idea of female chivalry went out with the feminism of the 1970s. I'm touched."

Flaus's brow furrowed and she cocked her head. "Do you mock me now?"

"Not exactly. I'm jus—"

The phone on her belt rang and Flaus held up a finger as she whipped it from her belt. *"Magda Flaus heren. Ja?"*

Manning watched with interest as Flaus said *ja* several times. It was obviously news of some kind, but he couldn't deduce if it was good or bad based solely on Flaus's expressions.

She hung up the phone and looked him the eyes.

"What is it?" he asked.

"Your friends encountered some trouble," she said. "My people are now out in force, looking for them. They will need our help."

"We'd best get back to the hotel and wait for them."

Flaus nodded but said nothing.

HELMUT STUHL AND Howe von Ruden sat in their sedan across the street from the entrance to the Hanns Seidel Convention Center and watched the comings and goings with disinterest. So far, they hadn't seen anyone who even remotely resembled a member of Mukhtar Tarif's team. For a while now, von Ruden had been postulating that Tarif wouldn't be stupid enough to use his own people. Their ethnicity would draw too much attention, particularly at an organizational summit on Islamic terrorism, of all topics.

"There is nothing to indicate the scope of this summit is confined to the terrorist acts of the Muslims alone," Stuhl reminded von Ruden.

"Come now," von Ruden said.

While von Ruden used such phrasing a lot—much more in an attempt to sound aristocratic than for any other reason—Stuhl knew the truth about Howe von Ruden's background. He'd been born the child of a poor family in the Rhineland and raised in a compulsory system of education. He allegedly possessed three degrees of higher learning, and yet it was common knowledge he'd never attended a day of university classes in his life, either in Germany or any other country. And von Ruden hadn't done an honest day's work in his life.

"Do you actually think these Americans care?" von Ruden continued. "This is an American summit composed of politicians from half a dozen U.S. protectorates, not to mention Canada and England. Do you think they're here to talk about the starving children in Kenya being subjugated by evil terrorist factions running rampant through Africa?"

Stuhl was about to liberate his tongue and deliver a powerful lashing against his cohort, urging him in no uncertain terms to shut up, when his mobile phone buzzed for attention. Stuhl considered any interruption to the whole, ridiculous conversation nothing short of a divine gift.

"It's Otto," the voice said.

Well, this would probably be good news. They had assigned Hans Gewalt to gather as many resources as possible and check out the activity reported near the Isar River. There had been reports that Tarif might have been hiding the LAMPs there until he could make them operational and use them against the summit members.

"What do you have to report?"

"Our men have been murdered."

"What?"

"Slaughtered by the Americans. They're dead, so many dead. And we have heard that it may be the same men who killed Burke."

Well, there wasn't anything they could do about that now. Stuhl felt the loss. They had already suffered so many losses at the hand of Hezbollah, and now this American team had taken to cutting into their ranks when they hadn't done a thing to the Americans. They could not fight a war on two fronts. It just wouldn't work. Such a strategy had never worked for any fighting unit—Burke had taught him that much.

"This shall not stand," Stuhl said. "We must eliminate the threat posed by Tarif and his men. That is the only reason the Americans are coming after us. They cannot find Tarif's operations any better than we, and so they are destroying us little by little in the hope of drawing Tarif into the open."

"They are clever, these Americans."

"I don't care how clever you think they are," Stuhl said. "You need to gather the remainder of whatever men you can find and go to the Isar River. I want Tarif's fucking head on a pole. Maybe we still have time to stop this before the Americans have killed us to the last man. Do you hear me, Otto?"

"I hear you."

"Wait for us," he said. "We will meet you at the alternate rendezvous point within an hour."

Stuhl disconnected the call and threw his phone against the dash. He announced the news to von Ruden, then started the engine and pulled into the sparse traffic flow.

"We've been wasting time sitting here," Stuhl said. "The enemy is awaiting us on another field of battle."

Through clenched teeth, Howe von Ruden replied, "Then before this night is over, we shall turn it into a field of blood."

CHAPTER TWENTY-FIVE

As the sun dipped behind the cityscape of St. Louis, Missouri, Able Team went into action. Able Team met the first six of their enemy on the ground floor near the lobby of the main hospital wing. The Hezbollah gunmen—dressed in fatigues and masks—penetrated the facility by blasting their way through four armed security guards in the ambulance bay, then blowing a locked fire door off its hinges with some plastic explosive. Unfortunately for the terrorists, they found the opposition waiting on the other side of that door a bit more formidable than the security team.

Lyons took the first invader with a hip-level shotgun blast. At that proximity the force blew the terrorist off his feet and drove him into the remainder of his comrades who waited behind him. The gunners tried to scatter and find cover, but it proved a futile exercise considering the vast, open area of the empty bay. As a second terrorist retreated down the wheelchair ramp, Lyons raced through the door and brought him down with a double-tap to the back. The terrorist flew to the ground face-first, skidding his chin on the rough concrete.

Blancanales followed with a firestorm of rounds aimed at another pair of terrorists who had knelt with SMGs at the ready, prepared to ventilate Lyons while he was otherwise occupied. A flurry of .40-caliber S&W rounds punched through the two terrorists almost simultaneously. Holes erupted out of their backs in a spray of blood, severing the spinal column of one terrorist and blowing rather large holes in the other one's liver. The Hezbollah gunners dropped lifelessly to the pavement.

Schwarz started to acquire target on the last two with his own MP-5 when sudden movement in his peripheral vision demanded attention.

The Able Team warrior spun and snap-aimed his SMG in the direction of four more terrorists who had made their way through a side entrance at the far end of the hallway. Schwarz let out half a breath and squeezed the trigger. The first salvo got one of the terrorists across the legs, shattering both femurs and leaving a steaming trail of hot blood as the man continued forward in uncontrolled motion. He finally slid to the floor out of view. The second terrorist turned into Schwarz's second burst and caught four rounds to the stomach. The impact drove him into a plate-glass window with enough force to shatter it. The Hezbollah fighter continued over a knee-high frame and landed on the pavement just outside the lobby with a smack of his skull on concrete.

Schwarz got numbers three and four with a sustained, chest-level volley. The .40-caliber slugs did their work without hesitation or remorse. Bloody holes erupted in the sternum of one terrorist and slammed him into a nearby support pillar. The other spun completely under the impact, the muzzle of his weapon flying skyward. The terrorist's finger jerked reflexively on the trigger before he took two more rounds to the spine and teetered over to land face-first on the polished tiles.

Lyons and Blancanales handled the last two terrorists with little fanfare. Blancanales opened up with a sustained burst that drove the two terrorists directly into each other's path. They shared the single shotgun blast from Lyons, one taking the brunt of it in his shoulder, the other suffering a rash of hot pellets through his cheek and jaw. Lyons's second shotgun blast nearly decapitated one of the terrorists, and both fell to the greasy floor of the bay.

The area secured, the two men turned to join Schwarz, who was finishing his handiwork inside with a mercy round into the terrorist with bilateral leg wounds.

"Damn, Gadgets, what the hell did they pump into you?" Lyons asked.

Blancanales could only let out a low whistle as he inspected the carnage around them.

"Like I told Pol," Schwarz said. "If I'm going to die soon, I'm going to do it my way."

"Maybe we should give him a fatal disease more often," Lyons said to Blancanales, arching his eyebrows.

"That's not funny," Schwarz cut in.

Blancanales let out a wolfish laugh. "I thought it kinda was."

"Let's move out," Lyons said. "We've still got plenty of work to do."

DWIGHT MAEBROOK SAT in his unmarked squad two blocks down from the hospital in smug satisfaction.

The idea to create diversions had been his brain-child, and obviously it had pleased Fayed Sarout. Once they had accomplished their mission and eliminated Delmico, Maebrook could expect his money. Of course, he'd decided not to take everything the Arab had told him at face value. These fuckers, he thought, couldn't even be trusted to keep their word among themselves. Why the hell they thought someone outside of their ranks would trust them was beyond Maebrook's capacity to comprehend.

Well, what the hell did any of it really matter now? He'd made a deal, and he planned to keep his end of the bargain. Sarout had promised to make sure he killed the three cops, as well, but especially the blond one. Yeah, Irons, that self-righteous pig who thought nothing of hassling fellow members of law enforcement. The problem with guys like that was they couldn't see past their own egos. They thought they were the only ones who existed in the whole wide world, and nothing and no-body else really mattered to them. Maebrook had run into a hundred like them.

The police radio squawked for attention, then the dispatcher called out his unit number. Reports of gunshots fired. The Hezbollah circus had finally come to town.

Now all Maebrook had to do was wait for Sarout to contact him. They had already set up their meeting point for the airport; a most appropriate place if there was one.

Yes, very soon Dwight Maebrook would have his money and be gone.

FAYED SAROUT LISTENED with abject horror as the reports came through. More than half of his force had already been eliminated by the American resisters!

All the curses of God on Maebrook, Sarout thought.

Sarout put the American cop from his mind and considered his options. He would deal with Maebrook's incompetence later. In this case, he knew Tarif would understand the reason for Sarout's need to exact vengeance. This had become a matter of honor. Maebrook had betrayed them, sent them into an unstable situation. His plan to divert the attention of the Americans had been contrived by assumption and assembled with undue haste. Sarout knew he should not have trusted the imaginings of that Western lout.

After careful consideration, Sarout knew what he had to do. The only way they could hope to accomplish this mission now would be if he led his men on the final assault. There would be no redemption for him if he sent his men to an uncertain death. He would experience none of the rewards this Earth had to offer, and he would certainly be inconsolable in the afterlife of the deep abyss were he to back out of his commission now. This was the time for warriors to prove their mettle.

Sarout disembarked from the panel truck parked near

the rear entrance of the American medical facility. He moved to the rear and hammered his fist on the door. It rose upward suddenly, and men armed with assault rifles began to pour from the back. Sarout watched them with confidence and pride as a dozen of his fiercest, most skilled warriors prepared themselves for the jihad. This was what he had trained them for. The hours of prayer and meditation—they had finally come full circle. They would complete their mission, of this Sarout was assured, and today the Americans would once more feel the fist of God.

"TEAM 4 TO CONTROL," a voice blared over the security radio as Able Team stepped off the elevators on the fourth floor.

Lyons snatched the borrowed radio from his belt. "Go, Team 4."

A burst of static and then, "We're getting reports of at least a dozen armed men headed for the rear entrance."

"Can you stop them?"

"We've got no coverage there, sir."

Lyons looked helplessly at his comrades. "Damn it to hell! Where do you suppose Maebrook's people are? They should have been here by now!"

"You said it yourself, Ironman," Schwarz replied. "We can't trust Maebrook did anything about this. For all we know, the guy's skipped out altogether by now."

"I'll hunt him down if he has," Lyons vowed. "Come on, let's go."

Lyons led them to the stairwell and led the charge as

he descended three at a time. "We can't afford to let them get to the upper levels. No matter what."

Both Schwarz and Blancanales acknowledged their understanding. The men of Able Team reached ground zero in less than thirty seconds and spread out onto a mezzanine overlooking the lobby. The bodies of the terrorists they'd already battled lay still on the ground. Lyons gleaned a bit of satisfaction in considering how that would serve as a fairly intimidating sight for this fresh band of Hezbollah fighters. Even fanatics couldn't utterly evade the psychology of warfare, no matter what their level of dedication. There were some things no human could overcome easily.

"At least we'll be able to hold the advantage of high ground for a bit," Schwarz noted.

"Won't do us a whole lot of good if they manage to get even a couple of their men to the elevators," Lyons said.

"Yeah, but you're assuming they know which floor Delmico's on," Blancanales pointed out.

Lyons's pallor looked almost ghostly and something bordering on the maniacal danced in those sharp blue eyes. "Oh, don't kid yourself, Pol. They know."

The time for debate had passed as the first sounds of footfalls reached their ears, and a moment later the terrorists appeared directly below them. Lyons held up his hand, a signal they should wait until as many as possible were in sight before they opened up, and then when the time seemed right he dropped it.

The terrible trio opened up with a hailstorm of autofire and rained an almost unending swath of metal destruction on the terrorists grouped below them. The terrorists began to fall under the onslaught as dozens of rounds ripped through bone and flesh, punctured vital organs and blew apart skulls. Bodies fell one on top of another through two full clips from each MP-5 40 and a full, 10-round magazine of shotgun shells before the terrorists had composed themselves enough to escape the line of fire.

Lyons did a quick head count and came up with seven either dead or incapacitated. As the echoes of gunfire died away, the men of Able Team could hear the low hum of elevators start up from two different directions. The elevators were on either side of the mezzanine, and Lyons knew immediately that they wouldn't have any reason to stop on that floor.

"Move!" he told his friends.

Able Team reached the stairwell and bounded up the steps. Lyons had already arranged to have the majority of the patients evacuated from that area and into an unused ward on the fifth floor. As he alighted on the landing between the third and fourth stories, Lyons stopped to peer out the window. Fire trucks and ambulances were now arriving, and an army of cops including some members of SWAT.

Lyons whipped out the security radio and keyed it up. "Control to all teams, the police are here. Direct them to the fourth and fifth floors and advise them federal agents are on scene."

"Uh, Team 2 to Control, how can they identify you?"

Lyons looked deadpan at his teammates and Schwarz shrugged. "The question's not exactly out of line."

Lyons scowled, then barked into the radio, "Tell them we're the ones who aren't wearing the headdresses and carrying machine guns."

He got no reply.

The Able Team warriors continued their ascent and Lyons emerged on the fourth floor just seconds ahead of the terrorists riding in the elevators. Blancanales and Schwarz started through the doorway but the Able Team leader raised his hand. "No! You guys keep going and make sure Corvasce and the patients stay safe until the cops arrive."

"But they won't be going to the fifth floor, Cal!" Blancanales protested.

"Just do it!"

The two men looked at each other, then nodded and continued for the fifth floor. Lyons pushed through the doors of the surgical ward and dead-bolted the doors behind him. That wouldn't hold them long, but it might buy him enough time to get Delmico to a safer location. Lyons raced down the hallway to the far wing where they had set up the isolation ward. He ran through the double doors, locked them behind him, then considered his final destination.

Lyons stepped through the plastic sheeting, not bothering to even put on a mask. It wouldn't make a whole hell of a lot of difference at this point anyway if he didn't keep Delmico alive. Lyons sprinted across the small lab to the utility closet, inserted the key he used to lock it and yanked the door back. Delmico sat with his back to the rear wall of the closet, cross-legged. He looked up at Lyons with bloodshot eyes, and a strong odor of chemicals assailed Lyons's senses. Near Delmico's feet were two bottles of empty cleaning solutions, some of it spilled onto the floor of the supply closet.

"I'm sorry," he said. "I had to do it. I have no future left.... I *had* to do it. Do you understand?"

"No. I don't." Lyons cursed under his breath, then pressed his lips together and reached down to grab a handful of Delmico's lab coat. He hauled the scientist to his feet and considered his options. There was only one way out of that lab, as far as he knew, and now was the only chance he'd have of taking it.

Lyons effortlessly tossed the scientist over his shoulder and rushed to a window on the far side of the lab. He leveled his AS-3 at it and squeezed the trigger twice. It shattered under the blast, and Lyons swung the stock around to clear away the line of jagged glass that ran across the bottom of the recessed frame. He stepped up and through the window onto the roof that covered the third-floor cardiac wing. He had first studied the layout of the hospital from a map provided by the information desk, and noted it as an alternate escape route if problems occurred.

Lyons circled the roofline until he came to a fire escape leading to the fifth floor. He set down his burden, then extended the curved wire stock of the AS-3. He leaped up and used the stock as a hook to pull down the fire-escape stairs. That accomplished, he hauled Delmico onto his shoulder once more and began to climb. Lyons reached the fifth-floor fire-escape landing and pried his fingers into the gap from where he'd instructed

Corvasce to leave the door ajar once they'd evacuated everyone to the fifth floor.

"Why on earth would you want me to do that?" Corvasce had asked.

"Just trust me," Lyons had replied.

Lyons moved inside with his burden, found an empty room and rolled Delmico off his shoulder and into bed. He then rushed down the hallway and found Corvasce and a nurse congregated at a desk with an army of security personnel as well as Blancanales and Schwarz. The pair looked up at him and the surprise registered completely on their faces.

"Ah," Lyons said. "It's almost a Hallmark moment."

"What in the name of—" Schwarz began, but Lyons cut him off.

"Doc, I've got Delmico back there. He's ingested something, some kind of chemical. Probably trying to kill himself."

Corvasce shook his head and then began to issue orders to the staff. "All right, folks, let's get to it. I want you to start bilateral IV solutions, stat. We also need to administer activated charcoal by NG tube and…" The staff rushed away with him to carry out their orders.

"What about our Hezbollah friends?" Schwarz asked.

Lyons popped the magazine from his AS-3, inserted a fresh one and jacked the slide to chamber a shell. "This is where we'll make our stand. With any luck, I've delayed them enough we should have police backup right about the time they step off the elevators."

"You're going to try to take them alive?" Blancanales asked.

"That's up to them."

"They'll probably put up a fight, you know," Schwarz pointed out.

"I certainly hope so," Lyons said.

IT DIDN'T TAKE Fayed Sarout's men long to realize that somehow they'd been duped.

The entire fourth floor of the hospital had been abandoned and Simon Delmico was nowhere to be found. Once more, the American cop, Maebrook, had given them false information. Sarout ordered his men to abandon the search and get to the elevators. Somewhere he had heard the announcement over an abandoned security radio that police were arriving. They wouldn't be able to go back the way they'd come. Their only hope of escape would be to advance to the fifth floor and find access to the roof. Perhaps they could hold a fortified position there long enough to make escape by helicopter.

Sarout commanded half his men to take the elevator and the others to accompany him via the stairs. They ascended to the fifth floor and stepped into the main hallway. Closed double doors lined either end of the hallway. A group of frightened nurses stared at them through one set of the doors. Sarout considered heading in that direction but quickly dismissed the idea. To have to deal with the medical staff would only serve to hamper their escape. They needed to get away and regroup. Capture was not an acceptable alternative. If they had to, they would fight their way to the death.

Sarout's men emerged from the elevator, and he im-

mediately ordered them to the doors at the far end. They
reached them and a push of the button caused them to
open inwardly. Nobody appeared to challenge the men.
Immediately ahead was a nurses' station, totally abandoned, and one hallway running down either side of the
ward. The lights were off, the ward eerily illuminated
only by shafts of sunlight streaming through the windows of the rooms that lined that hallway.

Sarout's men proceeded down one hallway, surrounding their leader as they moved with trepidation.
Something oppressive seemed to cloud Sarout's senses.
He could almost sense that they had walked into some
type of trap, but still they met no enemy as they proceeded. It was almost as if they were proceeding deeper
into the lair of a lion or bear, but continued despite the
fact, partly out of a sense of self-preservation and partly
out of simple necessity.

And for the first time in his life, Fayed Sarout experienced fear.

ABLE TEAM WAITED until the terrorists had proceeded far
enough into the ward to make their play.

There wasn't any point in endangering bystanders
unnecessarily. They had reviewed the layout and knew
that if Hezbollah gunners got deep enough into the deserted ward they would trap themselves there, thus neu-
tralizing any chance of escape through the taking of
hostages. The only thing left for the enemy to face was
the choice of an insurmountable physical boundary—
a seventy-five-foot drop from the roof of the hospital or

a veritable army of police officers led by a hardened trio of urban antiterrorists.

The police SWAT crew launched tear gas into the ward and warned the terrorists to surrender. Instead, Hezbollah gunners took up staging positions in rooms at the back of the ward and fired blindly toward the cops through a choking haze of CS. Wearing masks and armed with fresh M-16 A-3 carbines, Able Team advanced down the unoccupied hallway of the ward and hit the terrorists in their flanks. The battle lasted less than thirty seconds. There were no enemy survivors.

CHAPTER TWENTY-SIX

Gary Manning breathed a sigh of relief when all four of his friends walked through the door of their hotel room.

After a round of handshakes and some personal jibes, the men of Phoenix Force got to business. First, they looked over the materials McCarter had taken from the GFR's subterranean base. Magda Flaus was able to translate the vast majority of the papers, and the data they revealed left little doubt the GFR had somehow managed to catch Tarif's scent. Perhaps hours remained until Burke's second in command, the man who was running the show, would sic the dogs of war on what remained of Tarif's force.

"This is a map," Flaus reported to the team as they huddled around the table where McCarter had spread out the papers. "These red circles indicate all the places the GFR's intelligence had pinpointed as potential Hezbollah safe houses."

"The GFR actually has an intelligence network," Rafael Encizo said. "Impressive. I didn't think they were that large of an organization."

"It does go against most of the information the Farm gave us," James said.

The other members all looked at their teammate, but it was Manning's intent gaze between James and Flaus that made him realize his slip of the tongue. If Flaus had actually picked up any tidbits from what he said, she didn't give any sign of it. Manning had to admire her for that. In all likelihood, she'd noticed James's indiscretion in his reference to "the Farm" but she elected not to say anything. Not that James's remark hadn't still been rather cryptic. Flaus had to know by now that Manning's friends were hardly a pack of choirboys. The uncomfortable silence passed soon enough and Flaus continued.

"Most of these locations are already known even to my own people," she said. "They wouldn't have been very successful in their pursuit of Tarif's men."

"What do you mean?" McCarter pried.

"Well, I mean, this information is at least six months old, possibly more. These locations *were* Hezbollah safe houses at one time, perhaps, but all of them have been abandoned. In addition to that fact, they wouldn't be able to hide the equipment they stole from the British government at any of these sites. There isn't enough room and they would have drawn way too much attention."

Warning alarms sounded in Manning's ears and he looked at McCarter, who had picked up on it, as well.

None of them had mentioned anything about the LAMPs to Flaus at any time. In fact, they hadn't discussed one minute detail of their mission parameters with her. As far as she knew, they were only searching for members of the GFR because they had been smuggling Hezbollah terrorists whom they believed were planning another major terrorist attack against the U.S. in and out of the country.

The sudden hush that fell on the room quickly drew Flaus's attention, and she noticed McCarter and Manning staring at her. There was no mistaking their accusatory expressions. Flaus looked Manning square in the eyes, and he could see she was trying to read what was behind them.

"Why do you look at me so?" she finally asked.

"You mentioned Hezbollah hiding equipment stolen from the British," Manning said.

"That's right," McCarter added. "And I don't recall any of *us* saying a thing about that."

"What, so now you think *I'm* in bed with these mercenary bandits?" Flaus asked. She laughed. "Do you really think that a British RAF cargo transport crossing along the borders of our airspace could actually go down and the *Bundespolizei* wouldn't know anything about it?"

Flaus now exchanged looks with each of them, in turn, and got to her feet when they just continued to stare expectantly at her. She smiled. "Who do you think it was that told your government about this, eh? Do you think you just happened to come by the information? It was the GSG-9 who first heard about it!"

"Then why didn't you do anything?" Hawkins asked.

"Because we didn't know where to look," she said. "And also because we couldn't be sure that Burke and his people were involved in it. We weren't even sure if the plane had crashed in German territory. It was only an educated guess."

"So they let on to the American and British intelligence services, knowing they'd send in people to look for the bloody thing," McCarter concluded. "That's just great."

"Do you know how many lives have been lost due to the inaction of your government, Magda?"

"We couldn't be sure," she protested. "And anyway, I am helping you now."

"Yeah, only because we asked," James said. "It's not like you came right out and offered assistance."

"Fine then," Flaus said, grabbing her coat off the back of a nearby settee. "Perhaps it is better that I go and not involve myself further."

McCarter stepped in front of the door and favored Flaus with a warning smile. "Not quite yet, missy."

"We need you to tell us where the GFR are most likely to hit Tarif's people," Manning said. "And then you're free to go."

"I'm free to go now," she said, but after looking at Manning a moment longer she shrugged into her coat and pointed to an area on the map bordering the Isar River. "Here. This is the most likely place for Tarif to hide until he's ready to launch his attack against the summit. And I'm fairly certain that the GFR knows it by now, too."

McCarter turned to his teammates. "Gear up, mates. Quickly."

"I'm going along," she said. "I have a stake in this, too. With Choldwig Burke dead, I'm certain Helmut Stuhl is in control. I've been hunting this man for many years. If we can take Stuhl out of power, that will end his hold over us. Over Germany. The GFR will be finished once and for all."

"No way," McCarter said. His eyes flicked in Manning's direction, then he added, "I'm afraid you proved you just aren't trustworthy where we're concerned. Your loyalties are divided, and I can't have that driving us to distraction. It's going to get ugly, and I like to be sure everyone who's playing on my team really *is* playing on my team. Maybe if you don't understand that, Gary here can explain it to you."

And with that, McCarter went to secure his own equipment, leaving just the two of them alone in the dining area of the hotel suite. For a moment, Manning thought about pointing out the fact to McCarter that it was Flaus's information that had paid off in a big way. But then he decided against it.

"I'm afraid he's right. Besides, we need you to stand by at the Hanns Seidel in case we're wrong about this. If you're away for too long, your people are going to get concerned and come looking for you. You need plausible deniability on your side for what we're about to potentially do. It won't do you any good to get caught consorting with special operatives conducting illegal operations inside German territory."

He could see Flaus wanted to argue with him, but

then whatever she had planned to say seemed to leave her. Once more, they were parting on rather awkward terms.

"It seems we just cannot catch a break with each other, Gary Manning," she whispered. Flaus stood on her toes to kiss his cheek, wiped away the lipstick smudge, then turned and opened the door. *"Auf wiedersehn, meine liebchen,"* she whispered, and then she was gone.

Manning took a deep breath and let it out slowly. He stood there for just a moment, watching the closed door. Part of him wanted to run after her, but it seemed as if someone had loaded his shoes with concrete. The moment moved past when he felt a slap on his shoulder and noticed Encizo standing there and holding out his gear bag to him.

"Come on, soldier," he said with a wink. "Let's go kill some bad guys."

WITH THE HEAT OF THE DAY long gone and a cessation of activities for the night, a biting cold settled in and nipped at the exposed skin of Mukhtar Tarif's fingers and face.

Tarif had trained in many different kinds of environments, but he'd never grown all that accustomed to the cold. The coldest times, he'd spent training in the mountains of Afghanistan, and he recalled how miserable every minute was there. The chill of the mountains remained like no other he'd ever experienced. It was a cold that rode on thin air and you either kept bundled up and moving, or you stood a chance of suffering exposure and even death. To have lit fires meant certain death, because the planes flying overhead would use infrared radar to detect the heat given off by the fires and direct bombs into those areas.

So it seemed with the cold here in Germany, Tarif had another reason to hate the country. He hadn't been happy since approving a twelve-hour delay in their plans. Sarout also hadn't reported back to them, which meant either the operation hadn't begun yet, was still under way or had failed entirely. Well, if their elimination of the American scientist didn't happen as planned, it wouldn't be Tarif who answered to his father for it. Sarout would have to account for his actions, as he was the one really in charge of their operations in America.

Or at least that's what Tarif understood he'd been telling all of his friends.

"You look troubled, Mukhtar," Harb noted. "Cold and tired. Why not come closer to the fire?"

"I shouldn't have waited," Tarif said. "It was a mistake to let Marwa Shazzad talk me into delaying our operations. The longer we wait here, the greater our chance of being discovered."

"Discovered by who?"

"The Americans. Burke's people. Anybody." Tarif let out a deep sigh. "Maybe we should leave. Right now."

Harb sat up against the thick tree trunk he'd been resting against and looked at Tarif with surprise. "That would be suicide. We have everything planned to the last detail. To change those plans now would introduce complications for which you had not accounted. It could result in disaster."

"You sound like Shazzad." Tarif spit. "Are you telling me you're a coward?"

Something went dark in Harb's complexion, much darker than Tarif had ever seen it. "Be careful, Mukhtar. It is my single service to you that I hold above all else, primarily because of the promise I made your father. But I will not hesitate to cut your tongue out of your head if you show me disrespect again. I'm sure your father would empathize with me on this point. I am deserving of your loyalty as I have shown you the same. Do we understand each other?"

Tarif studied his friend and servant a moment, and realized there was unadulterated truth behind what Harb had said. "I am sorry. You are correct, I have shown you disrespect. I am just very tired. Please don't pay any attention to my ranting."

Harb watched his master a moment longer, then sat back, apparently placated by Tarif's show of sincerity.

Tarif knew he'd come a little too close with that one. He could get away with many things being the son of Kadils Tarif bin Nurraji—his ill-treatment of true subordinates like Shazzad in particular—but there were limits to what even a Tarif might say with impunity. And if one man among them stood able to take Tarif's tongue from him, it was Harb.

"Try to get some rest," Harb urged. "Sleep. And when you awake it will be time to finish what we've begun."

"OUCH!" DAVID MCCARTER exclaimed in response to his head slamming against the roof of the LandCruiser. "Why not watch where you're going, Rafe?"

"Sorry," Encizo said from behind the wheel. "I'm just trying to get there before the GFR does."

"Well, killing me won't help that."

"Aw, quit your whining, boss," Hawkins drawled from the back seat. "It's not much fun for us back here, either."

McCarter noted they were drawing close to where the GFR had circled the map, so he ordered Encizo to pull off the trail they discovered, stop and kill the engine. They had been driving without headlights for the past ten minutes or so, which had made the going a bit rough. Even at the slower speeds, the trail was filled with ruts and uneven patches of hardened dirt, enough to ward off even the most dedicated of four-wheeling sportsters.

The five warriors bailed from the LandCruiser, stowed all but their essential gear and then set off along the bank of the Isar River with only weapons and night-vision goggles. They had managed to get a resupply from one of Stony Man's local gun runners. He'd equipped them with M-16 A-2s—a couple of which included M-203 grenade launchers—and 9 mm ammunition for their pistols.

Phoenix Force proceeded along the tall grasses aligning the riverbank in staggered formation, keeping far enough apart that they could see each other but not close enough that a grenade or eagle-eyed machine gunner could take all of them out at once. They had been down this path too many times not to take the same precautions they always took.

Their journey came to an abrupt halt with a shout of

voices followed seconds later by the staccato sound of automatic weapons.

"Damn!" James proclaimed. "It's on, guys."

The Phoenix Force warriors broke formation and raced through the brush. The grass ended abruptly and they stopped short of a steep hill that dropped into an expansive field. Against the nearby tree line they could see the muzzle-flashes of assault rifles and make out the dance of shadows running to and fro against the light of campfires.

Phoenix Force continued on across the open field but kept their heads down in the event the enemy spotted their profiles before they could get in close.

James spotted the first of his enemies and he went prone just outside the reach of the firelight. The ex-SEAL spotted a pair of GFR gunners pumping a maelstrom of hot lead into a tent that James guessed was most probably occupied by Hezbollah terrorists. James flipped out the leaf sight of his M-203, acquired his target at an estimated thirty meters and squeezed the trigger. The weapon kicked with the recoil of a 16-gauge against James's shoulder and a moment later the pair of GFR gunners along with the tent disappeared in the red-orange blast of a 40 mm HE grenade.

McCarter caught the next pair of GFR gunners as they turned to their right, distracted by the whoosh of flame and roar of the grenade's explosion. The Briton dropped to one knee, raised the M-16 A-2 shoulder-level and squeezed the trigger. The short burst took one of the mercenaries in the ribs and shoulder and drove him to the ground. His partner apparently didn't notice his man had gone down at first, but McCarter could actually see the look of shock on the merc's face when he turned to see his comrade screaming and writhing on the ground. The man looked straight in McCarter's direction as the Briton triggered his second volley. The 5.56 mm slugs punctured heart and lungs and lifted the man off his feet. He crashed to the cold earth and twitched twice before going still.

Encizo and Hawkins drew up close to the tree line before selecting their targets. The two had traveled the thirty or so yards from their initial engagement point to the woods in leapfrog fashion. A pair of Hezbollah terrorists spotted them just seconds before the Phoenix Force duo recognized the threat and opened up full-tilt with a machine gun. Encizo had the other grenade launcher. He sighted on the terrorists' fortified position and triggered the M-203. The 40 mm grenade executed a lazy arc and came down right on top of Hezbollah machine gunners. They disappeared in a violent blaze of fire as the high-explosive grenade did its intended job. Hawkins gave his teammate a thumbs-up as Encizo nodded an acknowledgment while slamming a fresh grenade home.

Manning had set in prone position well outside the tree line and engaged the night-vision scope attached to his M-16 A-2. The Canadian made a slight adjustment for windage, then panned the battlefield until he acquired his first target. The head appeared barely visible beneath the pile of fallen branches but showed up just the same. Manning leaned up to the scope, locked the stock to his shoulder. Experience had taught him that most snipers missed due to bad timing. They either waited too long or they rushed, and the ability to kill another human being at great distances through nothing more than a rifle scope was an acquired skill.

It was one at which Gary Manning had become proficient long ago.

Manning eased back on the trigger. The M-16 assault rifle barely recoiled against his shoulder and Manning's eye never left the scope. Like any good sniper, he knew a follow-up shot was an all-too-real eventuality for which he had to be prepared. In this case, it didn't matter. In the shimmering firelight he could see the geyser of blood that spurted up above the level of the makeshift cover of fallen tree limbs. He'd obviously hit an artery.

Manning swung onto his next target, the profile of which he recognized almost immediately. He'd seen the man somewhere before, but for just a heartbeat he couldn't place it. Either way, he'd identified his target as a GFR gunman and there was no moral decision that had to be made here. Bottom line: there could be no survivors this time around. Both the GFR and Hezbollah had to be stopped. And they had to be stopped right here, right now.

Manning took a breath, let out half and squeezed the trigger twice more. Both rounds struck the man in the side of the head. The first one spun him hard enough that Manning caught his full faced expression of shock just milliseconds before the second round flipped him backward and knocked him out of sight.

HAWKINS SAW the GFR gunner fall under the marksmanship of one of his colleagues, albeit he couldn't be certain which one. Not that it mattered, since the death of this man had obviously engendered a fear in his cohort. The guy stupidly leaped from the tree where he'd sought cover and tried to retreat.

The Phoenix Force commando had never been one to shoot someone fleeing, but he knew the importance of completing the mission. The parameters were simple. Completely and utterly eradicate the GFR and Hezbollah by whatever means necessary. It was that last order, the one that McCarter had passed right from Hal Brognola, that made Hawkins feel justified in what he did next. Without hesitating, he trained his sights on the retreating form and triggered a sustained burst. The high-velocity rounds punched through the man's back and sent him flying forward under the force of his escape sprint. The man struck the earth face-first.

The sounds of battle died away, leaving a silence much like the one experienced right after a Fourth of July fireworks finale.

EPILOGUE

There were less than a dozen places in the world where an ex-cop could go to escape justice.

This very thought went through the mind of Carl Lyons as he rode in a Kiowa Bell piloted by Jack Grimaldi over a back road of midstate Tennessee, not far from its eastern border with Arkansas. Corvasce hadn't managed to pull Delmico through his ordeal, but he'd gotten enough information from the scientist before his death that they had successfully synthesized the antibody needed to counteract the effects of Shangri-La Lady.

With his friend out of the woods and the sick college students now well on their way to full recoveries, Lyons had set out to pursue the worst kind of a fugitive: a dirty cop. Having served many years with distinction as a member of the LAPD, Lyons had no use for dirty cops, especially not the sniveling and cowardly kind. Dwight Maebrook had brokered a deal with terrorists, the enemy of not just his nation but the entire world. Such men couldn't be allowed to wear a badge and gun, much less breathe the air of free America. Maebrook had tried to subvert the very ideals of liberty and freedom in a country where he'd enjoyed the same. He'd betrayed the trust of those he policed as well as his government. And Carl Lyons knew only one kind of justice for a guy like that.

He'd learned of it from a man called Mack Bolan.

"It's too bad, Ace," Lyons told Grimaldi through the headset.

"What's that, Carl?" Grimaldi asked.

"Too bad Maebrook didn't remember all police vehicles are now marked with a secured GPS unit, and that we knew where he's been this whole time. Like he actually thought he was going to elude us. Just goes to show how stupid the poor schmuck is."

Grimaldi chuckled. "I don't suppose it would do much good to appeal to your sweeter side by asking you to give this guy a fighting chance."

"No dice," Lyons replied.

"But Hal said—"

"Yeah, I know what Hal said," Lyons countered. "But since when has that ever made any difference? This is one of those things that just has to be done, Jack."

They rode in silence for another minute and then Grimaldi said, "There he is. Silver, unmarked sedan. Two o'clock, range about three hundred yards."

"I got him," Lyons said, settling his binoculars on the speeding sedan.

The Able Team leader panned the surrounding area

for other vehicles and saw none. Good, that would make things a bit easier. The last thing they needed was a witness. With any luck, the pair could be back to St. Louis before anybody knew they were missing.

Lyons traded his binoculars for a large tube he'd procured from Stony Man's Gulfstream jet. There were definite advantages to having a unit stocked with all the finest weapons of war. The M-72 LAW might have been quantified as obsolete by modern military standards but it still remained a device of tremendous tactical value to the Stony Man units. And it was particularly useful on missions like this one.

"Bring me around, Jack," Lyons said.

The pilot obediently swung the chopper in a wide arc and closed the distance to achieve acquisition range. Lyons stepped onto the skid, braced his other foot inside a restraining strap just inside the side opening of the Kiowa and extended the LAW. The sighting plane flipped obediently into position and Lyons raised the weapon to his shoulder. Grimaldi completed his maneuver and Lyons had a perfect line of sight on the target. They were approaching from the front and Lyons imagined how Maebrook would be wondering just about now why the chopper was flying so low. He would have paid real money to see the expression on Maebrook's face, but somehow he didn't think he'd lose much sleep over it.

Lyons steadied the LAW, locked it against his shoulder and depressed the rubber firing trigger atop the tubed weapon. There was a whoosh, a puff of smoke and the sensation of heat on Lyons's neck seconds before the sedan disappeared in a brilliant ball of flame. The force was great enough to completely shear the roof from the vehicle and then gasoline ignited and sent up secondary explosions. Lyons didn't bother looking back at the carnage.

"Now the mission's accomplished," he said.

TAKE 'EM FREE

2 action-packed novels plus a mystery bonus

NO RISK
NO OBLIGATION TO BUY

Look for

THE SOUL STEALER
by AleX Archer

Annja Creed jumps at the chance to find a relic buried in the long undisturbed soil of Russia's frozen terrain. But the residents of the town claim they are being hunted by the ghost of a fallen goddess said to ingest souls. When Annja seeks to destroy the apparition, she discovers a horrifying truth—possibly leading her to a dead end....

Available May 2008 wherever you buy books.

ROOM 59

A nuclear bomb has gone missing. At the same time Room 59 intercepts a communiqué from U.S. Border Patrol agent Nathaniel Spencer. But as Room 59 operatives delve deeper into Mexico's criminal underworld, it soon becomes clear that someone is planning a massive attack against America...one that would render the entire nation completely defenceless!

Look for

aim AND fire

by

cliff RYDER

GOLD
EAGLE

*Available July 2008
wherever you buy books.*

GRM593